How to Make Friends
with
Demons

How to Make Friends with
with
Demons

Graham Joyce

Night Shade Books
San Francisco

S

First Edition

ISBN: 978-1-59780-142-3

Night Shade Books
http://www.nightshadebooks.com

All sorts of people contribute to a book but I particularly want to mention the assistance of Simon Spanton at Gollancz UK; Dan Byles for military fact-checking and advice; Matt Weiland and Peter Crowther and for publishing the short story out of which this novel grew in The Paris Review and Postscripts magazine respectively; Chris Fowler for his influential short story "At Home In The Pubs Of Old London"; Jeremy Lassen at Night Shade books; Gary K. Wolfe at Locus magazine; my wife Suzanne for outstanding editorial insight and proof reading; and finally to The Pixies for "This Monkey's Gone To Heaven".

"Down there everyone lives folded within himself and torn apart by his regrets."

A description of hell given by a possessed man to Father Gabriel Amorth, the Vatican's Chief Exorcist.

Chapter 1

There are one thousand five hundred and sixty-seven known demons. Precisely. Okay, I know that Fraser in his study claimed to have identified a further four, but it's plain that he's confusing demons with psychological conditions. I mean, a pathological tendency to insult strangers in the street is more likely caused by a nervous disorder than the presence of a demon. And chronic masturbation is what it is. I suspect that Fraser didn't even believe in his own case studies. I think he just "discovered" four new demons so that he could peddle his bloody awful book.

I should know: I did after all go to college with him. (One time he got me so mad I broke his nose, and I'm no fighter.) In any case, I prefer Goodridge's original study and his much stricter category of definitions. I like strict definitions. Right, I'm going to footnote it for you, but just this once: firstly because I hate the messy intellectuality of footnotes and secondly because, as you will know, it was Goodridge himself who brilliantly identified that the footnoting affliction is itself demonic[1] and is the cause of much of the madness and disorder you find amongst university academics. What's more, it's a particularly nasty species, attracting to itself the company of several other

---

1. Goodridge, R W, "*Categorical Evidence for the Prevalence of the 1567 Forms*": London and New York: Coleman-Ashcroft, 1973. pp 839-43

1

fourth- or fifth-level infestations; and as anyone with any knowledge of this area will tell you, once you let one in, the gate is wedged open for the rest.

I'd been clean for twenty years or so before I picked up my latest demon. I don't even know how it happened. All I know is that it first attached to me in a pub in central London, and that it was embedded long before I could cut it out with the scalpel and ammonia of disciplined thinking. Disciplined thinking: listen to that. It's me I'm talking about.

I shouldn't have been thinking about demons, but that morning before it happened I found myself in one of those meetings which is really a kind of slow and agonising descent into death. The meetings where your thoughts drift like whisps of cirrus over the Pennine hills on a lovely summer's day. Two hours of rapture led by a Home Office junior minister on the subject of Young People and Anti-Social Behaviour Orders. Half a dozen civil servants in designer suits with creases sharp as paper-cuts, their *key projects* and *outcome capability frameworks* exploded by the spectacular and eccentric interventions of representatives from the Scout Association, the Girl Guides, the Woodcraft Folk, the Youth Clubs and some foggy entity called the British Youth Council.

"A sense of decency," insisted the representative from the Scouts, prodding the table in front of him as if squashing an ant. "A sense of knowing what's right from what's wrong." His name always escaped me, because I was distracted by his peppery but neat moustache and the fabulous, burst-fruit condition of his puce face. He didn't actually work for the Scout Accociation any more. He'd been retired fifteen years, but they still trotted him along because he "liked to stay involved." Nothing wrong with what he was saying, either, it's just that it was *all* he said, and at *every* meeting. He prodded the table again. "Basic decency."

Collectively we are what is called a "think tank." I like that.

It makes us feel strong. It's just that the tank, having rumbled onto the beach of reason, has tumbled into a sand-trap and is lodged face-down in the wet mud, its clapped-out engine smoking and its gears grinding noisily but without any sense or hope of traction. *Oh God*, I thought, *this is going to run way past lunch.*

I mean, it's important enough, this think-tank work. We all get to feel vital, central, when guided through the high security of the glittering steel Home Office buildings in Victoria and escorted to a meeting room of blonde wood tables, every place primed with plastic bottles of sparkling mineral water and Glacier Mints in tiny ceramic dishes. But it's the usual agenda: youth is going to hell in a handcart, again, and oh dear what can we do to stop it?

"A greater sense of responsibility and recognition," professed the lady from the Youth Clubs. She was wearing a very smart lilac beret, even indoors. I've no idea why; it wasn't cold.

But the most astonishing thing was the sight of the junior minister taking notes and engraving his face with lines of earnest sincerity, as if the words "decency" and "responsibility" had just been minted fresh. Never ever ever been said before. The bugger even wrote the words down on embossed government notepaper! Not that any of us were fooled for a second. Just as with emails from Nigeria and certain ebullient young women, you can be sure it's a trap. When all the contributions had been made and noted, the junior minister's second assistant laid out the latest government initiative for which our support was invited. Note that it was our support that was invited, not our comments.

It was a community service plan designed to engage disaffected and unemployed youth in semi-voluntary activity. It was linked, we were being told, to a greater recruitment drive for the Territorial Army.

Oh no, I remember thinking, where are we going tomorrow?

Iran? Syria?

Its seems incredible to me that the government can recycle the same "initiatives" every seven years, even if they railed against those very ideas when in opposition. The junior minister's second assistant then took half an hour to roll it out, like a carpet in an Arab souk, smiling fanatically, trying to get you to take home something you neither want nor can fit in your luggage. He managed to weave the words "decency" and "responsibility" into his presentation three or four times, rewarding the old Scout and the slightly less old Youth Clubber with plenty of steely eye contact.

I personally have opposed this drivel more than once over the years, but I've learned my lesson. The eager young man from the Woodcraft Folk clearly hadn't.

"We don't want soft conscription. We want p'litical responsibility. Real decision-makin'. This is jus' patronising."

The junior minister glanced at his watch and started talking about new paradigms in politics and not waiting around for people stuck in the fossilized formations of the past. This was my cue.

"Well, minister, I think there's a lot of radical thinking on offer here, plus some complex issues which need to be sifted. I recommend we all go away and reflect very deeply on both the opportunities *and* the risks involved in this paper."

The junior minister beamed at me. Even though I don't have the power to open or close these meetings, he knew enough about committees to hear the final whistle being blown, and he was thankful. Papers were shuffled and we were on our feet, leaving the old Scout to look around as if he might have nodded off and missed something.

The truth of it is I found out a long time ago that if I spoke up against these briefings my influence with funding bodies was buggered and the people who I represented lost thousands of pounds in grants.

I tried to get out fast, but the old Scout hung me up to talk about decency. The young man from the Woodcraft Folk swept back a forelock, eyeing me as if he couldn't work out whether I'd just rallied to his cause or knifed him in the back. The bereted lady from the Youth Clubs was meanwhile bent on tipping Glacier Mints into her handbag.

Nodding ferociously, I disentangled myself, rode the lift down to the ground floor and skimmed my security badge back to the receptionist. Then I was out and hurrying to the banks of the Thames, filling my lungs with the odours of its tidal mud. You can only sell your soul once and mine had gone so long ago that on that day I didn't even hear the whisper of its ancient lament.

By the time I got to Bloomsbury I was late, but I found a minute to buy a copy of the *Big Issue* from a hoary street-vendor with a sleeping dog. Not because I'm a nice person but because it was November, pinching-cold out, and I have a phobia about homelessness. I folded the paper to fit into my coat pocket and stepped out of the crisp, chilly lunchtime air and into the street-corner Museum Tavern, a pub—rather unsurprisingly—located directly opposite the British Museum.

The place was bustling. I glanced around but didn't see the person I was looking for. There is a mirror in there reputed to have been vandalised by Karl Marx. It warms the cockles of my heart to think of the father of Communism trashing the joint after a few pints of Victorian wallop. In the mirror I saw someone rising from a seat and advancing towards me.

"Billy! What you having? La Belle Dame Sans Merci?" It was the poet Ellis, rising from a tiny scratched and polished round table in the corner near the entrance. I drew up a seat and lowered myself into it. No one calls me Billy, but I didn't say anything.

Ellis fell back into his own seat with a bit of a thump. "Get the poor sod a glass of house red, will you?" he said to his lovely companion, a slender woman in her twenties with whom I'd already made a point of avoiding eye contact.

"The Pinot Noir would be the thing," I qualified, shooting an over-the-shoulder glance at the girl while unwinding my silk scarf.

Ellis waited until she was engaged with the barman before asking me, in an underbreath, "Well? Have you bloody well got it?"

"Sadly, no," I returned, with an inflection of my voice designed to irritate him.

"So when will you be getting it?"

"Ah! That's kind of you." My wine had arrived chop-chop. The young woman handed the glass to me so delicately and theatrically that I detected the training of a ballerina or a mime artist. Our eyes met briefly. She had dark lashes and green irises grained with nut-brown. I felt a squeeze of disgust when I thought of Ellis enjoying her, he being only five years my junior; and then that sentiment was trailed by the usual stab of envy that in turn generated a species of regret followed by a chill of boredom at the way in which every pretty face I met could yank my chain and engender this domino-sequence of emotions. In response I did what I always do: I poured wine on it all.

"Is that okay for you?" she asked me.

Interesting accent. Modulated old London working-class, I'd call it, but buffed up a bit and been around the world. Not unlike me. "It's very okay. Thank you."

"I think it's bloody great," she said, taking a sip from her own glass of—I guessed—vodka and tonic. "This thing you do."

"Aw, shaddap," Ellis said to her.

"He's an old cynic," she said, nodding at Ellis before placing—with a delicate click—her glass on the scarred table. "But you change people's lives."

"For God's sake!" Ellis protested. "He's older than I am. And more bleeding cynical."

"He can't be," she said, looking at me, not Ellis. "He helps people out."

"Helps people out? I could tell you a thing or two about *Doctor Helps People Out* here."

She held out a tiny white hand across the table. "My name's Yasmin."

No it isn't, I wanted to say, because she didn't look or talk at all like a Yasmin. Demon of false naming, we know all about that one. But I held my tongue. "William Heaney."

"I know."

Well, there we had it. She knew my name before I'd revealed it; I didn't know hers even after she'd declared it to me. Another demon in there somewhere. Perhaps we held each other's gaze a splinter too long because Ellis said, "I think I'm going to vomit."

"How do you two people know each other?" I asked genially.

And as she told me, my demon, my real demon, who had been listening, crouched, always attentive, breathed its sweet and poison breath in my ear. *"Take her away from the lout. Take her home with you. Lift her skirt."*

She talked at length and I listened. Voices are sometimes like the grain in a strip of wood. You can hear the character of someone's experience in their voice. Hers was warm, and vital, but damaged. I followed the lovely tracks of her elegant hands as she spoke. I wondered how he'd found her. Ellis has a routine; I've seen it executed at his poetry readings. Anna, I thought would be a better name for her, Anna.

"And I dunno, we just… clicked," she said.

Yes, I bet you did is what I thought. When she'd finished talking, Yasmin—or Anna as I was already calling her—sat back, a little self-conscious that she'd enjoyed the stage for five minutes. Ellis tugged at his ear lobe and said nothing. "Well," I said, raising my glass across the table, "here's to clicking."

We all touched our glasses together.

I explained that I was on my way to GoPoint when Anna announced that she used to work there several years ago. I was surprised. She didn't seem the type. "So you know Antonia?"

"Course. She's a saint."

"She is. I'll mention your name to her."

"So when might you have it?" Ellis growled, strong-arming his way back into the conversation.

I dealt him the poker face. "I'll let you know. Of course." Then I drained my glass and stood up, rewinding my silk scarf around my throat against the November cold.

"Are you going there now?" Anna said. "I have to walk that way back to work. I'll walk with you."

Ellis looked miffed.

"That would be lovely," I said, shucking on my coat, "but I have one or two errands to run first and I don't want to hold you up."

I don't know why but I got a sense that she was disappointed, though if that were true she disguised it. I could see she didn't really want to be with Ellis, and I felt a wee bit sorry for him. What fools we make of ourselves over women. What naked prey. I promised Ellis to contact him when I had more news and I shook hands again with Anna/Yasmin/whoever. She said she hoped that we might meet again. As I turned I caught my slightly foxed reflection in the Karl Marx mirror. She was still looking at me; and he at her.

Then I was out of the Museum Tavern and striding across Bloomsbury towards Farringdon.

The window in the door to the GoPoint Centre had been kicked in since I was there last. Someone had made a hasty repair with a sheet of chipboard, which had offered a nice target for a graffiti artist with a tag like a Chinese ideogram. Below the tagged board, a woman with a head of unkempt, swept-back long curls, raven-black but grey at the temples, was sitting on the steps looking blissed out. Her sweater was a stained rag with pin-hole burns dotted on the chest and her jeans were filthy. She wore swollen Dr. Martens boots, the kind once favoured by elegant British skinheads.

"Gorra fag, 'ave you?"

"I don't smoke and neither should you."

"Got the price of a pint, then?"

I sat down on the step next to her. The concrete slab shot a piercing cold through my buttocks. She looked up at the sky between the tower blocks and said, "I was in a printing house in hell, and saw the method in which knowledge is transmitted from generation to generation."

Other people might have John Clare or William Burroughs or Thomas Aquinas quoted at them by this woman. For some reason it was only ever Billy Blake for me. "I'm really sorry, Antonia. It hasn't come through yet."

Without taking her eyes from the clouds overhead she reached out and put a hand on my knee. "No worries. I know if anyone can get it then it will be you, and even if you don't you will have tried your very best." Then she turned to face me with those cloudless blue eyes, and she smiled. "And you know how happy it makes me that you try for us? You know that, William? It's *so* important for me that you *know* that."

"How long before they come and close you down?" I asked.

"Don't fret, William. Lots of time."

"A month?"

"Slightly less."

GoPoint was a refuge for the homeless, the wayward, the desperate, the lost, the drowned-at-sea-but-don't-yet-know-it. It was an unregistered charity. It couldn't be registered with the Charity Commission because it kept no books. GoPoint stuffed to the gills maintained thirty-seven beds, and right now with November burrowing deeper and deeper into winter it would be working at capacity and beyond. The saintly Antonia Bowen, sitting on the steps quoting William Blake at me and looking exactly like one of the inmates, was the institution's manager, inspiration, apologist, advocate, fundraiser and janitor.

A fuckin' saint, I swear it.

Her clients came through her doors with nothing and sometimes left with Antonia's clothing. She dressed herself in whatever rotten garb was left behind; paying herself and her intermittent staff with the casual donations that came her way. One or two staff members were paid from eccentric contracts with this or that social welfare scheme. She was a deep thorn in the side of the social services and the government agencies because she made outrageous guerrilla raids on their offices. Because all help had been refused, on one occasion she and five of her inmates carried the corpse of a woman who'd died on the premises down to the offices of the Department of Health and Social Security and left it in the reception with a Queen's Silver Jubilee tin tea-caddy for donations.

Now Antonia's landlord, with an eye to property development, had hiked up the rent. GoPoint, well in arrears, was threatened with closure. I was working on something that might buy her a little time, but there had been a hitch and it was proving difficult.

"I'll come back next week, hopefully with better news," I told her.

"You're one of my heroes, William. I wish there were more like you."

"You don't know me, Antonia! I'm not worth bothering with."

"You're one of the kindest, warmest men I've ever met."

She linked her hands around my arm and when she looked at me with those cloudless eyes, I couldn't take it. She was one of the seraphim. I had to change the subject. "Hey, I met someone who worked here. Pretty thing. Said her name was Yasmin."

She blinked thoughtfully. "I don't think I'd be able to employ someone called Yasmin."

Ah, so we do have prejudices, I thought. A pin-prick in your sainthood. That's a relief.

She was still thinking. "Hey… unless it was the girl who started the library. Have you seen our library lately? Come inside."

The "library" was a dozen shelves of second-hand mostly paperback books. I had no intention of visiting it. Firstly, GoPoint was infested with demons for obvious reasons. The clients had to vacate the place between midday and four o'clock so that they didn't merely rot on their pallet beds all day long. The idea was to give them purpose. It was while they were out of the building seeking purpose that the demons became most active in their prowling, relentless search for a new host. Secondly, demons do tend to cluster around the yellowing pages and cracked spines of second-hand books. I've no idea why.

Not that I discussed demons with Antonia. She, who every single day walked with purity of heart in a place teeming with demons, said that although she'd seen them, she didn't want to discuss them.

I simply made my excuses. I got up off the steps, dusting the seat of my trousers. "Antonia, your conjunctivitis has come back. You should get it seen to."

"It's nothing."

I was about to argue with her when a young woman with a shocking set of teeth and wearing a dirty padded jacket—it looked like the insulation you might put round a hot-water cylinder—lumbered up to us. "Is it four o'clock?" she said in that Mancunian vibrato you get when loss of drugs wobbles the sternum. "Is it? Is it?" Her eyes were popping. Two huge dilated pupils had the words *intravenous hellhound* written on them in spiralling calligraphy.

"No," Antonia said to her. "It's about two thirty."

The Mancunian turned her beggar's gaze on me. I felt a tiny

bit scared, and sad for her at the same time. "Are you sure it's not four o'clock?"

I looked at my watch for her. "Not even close to four."

She spun her body away from us, but clearly without any idea of what to do with herself. She hung her head, stuffing her hands deeper into her water-cylinder lagging.

"I'll be on my way," I said. "I only dropped by to keep you updated."

"And I appreciate that, William. I really do." A blissed-out smile told me that she meant it. With Antonia it was never just rhetoric.

As I stepped around the lost Mancunian girl in the padded jacket I heard her ask Antonia, "Eh! Eh! So when will it be fuckin' four o'clock? Eh?"

Chapter 2

When I got home that evening the telephone was ringing. I didn't hurry. Sometimes I didn't bother answering at all, since it was usually only someone who wanted to talk about something or other. I hung up my keys, slipped off my coat and chose a Moulin-à-vent 1999 Beaujolais from the rack. I finally answered the phone, squeezing the receiver under my chin while I pulled the cork from the bottle and poured myself a very large glass of the rubicund relief & rescue.

It was Fay. "How are you?"

"I'm good, Fay. You?"

To have Fay enquire about my health and temper at all was new. Even if it was only a formality, it was progress. Normally she simply launched in. Anyway, once she'd got the hideous semblance of caring out of the way, she flew like an arrow to the clout. "The children have talked about it. Claire will see you, but Robbie doesn't want to have anything to do with you."

I took another sip of the rain from heaven. It splashed on my tongue like a soft shower in the arid desert; it swooped over my palate like an angel robed in red. I think the Grand Masters must have been looking at the wine in the glass when they clothed their models on the religious canvas. Come here my love: let me array your nakedness with the juice of the grape.

"Well, that's something."

"He might come round," Fay said. "I'm trying to stay out of

13

it, but I won't let him not see you." I heard a sucking noise. Fay always seemed to be eating something when she was on the phone. Ice cream, maybe. Or honey or chocolate sauce, from her fingers.

"I appreciate that, Fay." There was an uncomfortable pause, so I said, "How's the celebrity? Is he feeding you all well?" I knew if I turned the conversation to Lucien it would curtail the call.

"Busy with his new programme. There's some issue with the contract."

"There always is." Oh yes. Be advised of this: contracts demon is a spirit of martial force.

Fay had left me, three years ago—for a celebrity chef. He's on the telly. He's very good with pastry. Spinning it out with sugar and all that. I really can't be bothered with pastry myself. Anyway, he left his wife and his two kids for my wife and my three kids. I would have offered a straight swop but my God you should see his brute of an ex-wife. My eldest child, daughter Sarah, is studying at Warwick University; she has always been on "my side," so, two out of three ain't bad.

Fay came to the point of her call. "So Robbie wants to know if this applies to his tennis and his fencing as well as his school."

"How can he ask me that if he won't talk to me?" Really! The little shit!

I thought I heard her shift the phone from one hand to the other to suck the freed-up fingers. "Obviously he's asked me to ask."

"Obviously he has to ask me himself. And obviously you'll explain why that is necessary."

"That's your answer?"

"Obviously." ·

Fay sighed. She's good at sighs. She can invest the entire weight of disappointment over years of marriage into a single sigh. "All right. I'll let him know."

"Thanks for your call, Fay."

I replaced the receiver and topped up my glass. Yes, there is still pain. There is still hurt. I lash the suppurating sores with red wine.

I know what you're thinking. For the record, and since I don't expect you to be an expert in the identification or taxonomy of these things: alcohol is not a demon. It's merely one of a series of volatile hydroxyl compounds that are made from hydrocarbons by distillation. It's a scientific process involving the transformation of sugars. The fact that it is highly addictive or that it can drive men or women to extreme and destructive forms of behaviour does not make it a demon. When people say "his demon was alcohol" they don't know what they are talking about.

I myself am mildly addicted to the fermentation of the grape and it has on occasion caused me to behave recklessly. But there is no imp in the bottle. Grant you, a demon may take up residence and—spotting a weakness in its host—encourage a destructive habit. But that is a hell-horse of a different colour.

The reason why my fifteen-year-old son will no longer speak to me? Because I chose not to pay the fabulous fees required to propel him through the towering gates of the privileged Glastonhall any longer. I did not like what he was becoming behind the mullioned windows of that expensive institution. I took no pleasure in the mark of "excellence" stamped on his brow. More than that I didn't like the way he treated the waiter when I took him to lunch at Spiga in Dean Street.

I don't know if Robbie has developed his contempt for what used to be called the working classes from the shadowed cloisters and manicured lawns of Glastonhall, or whether it has been served to him, piping-hot, by Lucien the celebrity chef. But it soured my wine. I felt a deep stab of shame and, of course, of guilt that I hadn't been there to guide the habits of his early manhood. It doesn't take much for us to treat every other person in this world first with respect and then with kindness, if possible. All other virtues are only targets, whereas these two are imperatives. In the days that I'd been set apart from the upbringing of my son he'd turned into a posh, sneering little viper, unnecessarily abusing the waiter in Spiga. Of course, I crossly told Robbie about what George Orwell said regarding people who bring you your food. But I made sure the waiter heard the boy get that dressing-down before he fixed up our salad.

I also decided that a dose of a thousand days at the local comprehensive might help Robbie's true education before he followed Sarah on to university. Claire had to suffer the same fate. Though she was already doing A levels, and didn't mind in the least being switched from snooty St. Anne's. In fact she kept telling me her new school was "cool." Robbie's school was not cool. In fact, I think he found it a little hot down there in the trenches, studying Information Technology with the sons and daughters of plumbers, car salesmen and desk-jockeys like myself. Oh, and of non-celebrity chefs, it occurred to me. So now we weren't on speaking terms.

Lucien the pastry chef might have baled him out. Why not? He was more of a father to him these days in the sense that Robbie chose to live with him and Fay instead of me. But then my network of spies had told me that Lucien, for all his celebrity endorsements, voice-overs and book deals, had money problems of his own; something I would leave Fay to discover rather than inform her and risk her hating me still further.

A footnote on snobbery: Robbie's, Lucien's or anyone else's. No, not a demon either. Just a deeply unpleasant human trait magnified and cemented by a vigorous British class system; vicious, sadistic and thriving very well in the twenty-first century. If Robbie wanted to continue to knock tennis balls over the net with his conceited privately educated cronies he would have to find the humility to fucking well ask me for the cash.

There was some post to open. I tore one of the envelopes and my heart quickened to see that there was a development on dear old Jane Austen and one or two other things. By the time I'd finished perusing the letter and opened the rest of the post I was draining the last of the Beaujolais into my glass. Which, even for me, was some kind of a record.

Chapter 3

I deal in rare books and manuscripts. Not as a profession, but as a hobby. Second-hand and antiquarian books, as it states on my card. But not for profit, which it does not state.

Oh no, not for profit. Not any more. Originally, when I started the game back at college in the early 1980s, profit was exactly the motivation. Those were the days when Madam Thatcher set her nose to the wind and her commandments were clear: thou shalt trample the faces of the poor and rub thy hands with glee. How we rubbed. Rubbed and rubbed.

But all that rubbing produces smoke, and out from the smoke poured the djinn. That old story of the lamp is a mere externalization, for the simpler mind. The rubbing of hands is quite enough to do the trick. The avidity. The avarice. Out pour the demons, exulting in profit.

Luckily for me, I became ill, and recognized the dangers. Others of my ilk from that era were not so fortunate. They went on to make vast profits or to pursue fame.

It started for me when a slip-cased copy of *The Shanachie*, an Irish miscellany of short stories—featuring no less than Yeats, Shaw, Synge and Lord Dunsany—fell into my hands. I was a student at teacher-training college in Derby and while trying to sleep with a girl called Nicola I was roped into helping with a stupid jumble sale designed to raise money for the homeless. Despatched to a large house on the London Road, I collected some boxes of dusty books from a spindly old woman who stank of cat urine and who jawed incomprehensibly at me as I humped book-laden cardboard boxes to the student societies' minibus.

I remember feeling tricked. I had hoped to spend that Saturday morning with Nicola, and in doing so gain some advantage over her many other pursuers, and here I was, my sinuses wheezing with house-mite dust, fending off invitations to sip Darjeeling with a stinking cat-lady.

What else was in those boxes? I don't know but I've lain awake at night wondering. I recall rummaging through a fairly vile assortment of mildewed volumes for which the entire box might yield no more than a few pence at the jumble sale; and since I was already a fan of W. B. Yeats the copy of *The Shanachie*, neatly slip-cased, took my fancy.

It stayed on the shelf in my student bed-sit on the Uttoxeter New Road for some months, until a bookish, stoned, pot-dealing brother of a fellow student crashed on the floor in my room one night. At breakfast time he ran a nicotine-stained finger along my bookshelves and pulled *The Shanachie* from its resting place. He said he thought it might be "worth a few bob" and offered to trade me a quarter ounce of very fine Thai grass. It seemed like a good deal, but for some reason I declined, and after he'd gone I decided to check it out for myself.

I got two hundred quid for it—a handsome figure for a student in those days. Today it would fetch possibly ten times that amount. But the point is that it set me on a trail. If one of these things could turn up so casually, I decided, then there must be more out there. And I was of course correct.

Fast forward to some thirty years later and the letter that had just arrived indicated that there might be hope yet for the Jane Austen project to arrive in time to offer a reprieve for Anthonia's GoPoint. I no longer profit personally from my forays into the antiquarian book-dealing world. Without fail I turn over the margins—often huge—to some useful cause. I'm good like that. In this case, GoPoint would get the loot. Obviously I would like to enjoy the fruits of my labours for myself. But if I did, then I wouldn't be able to cheat the demon.

In the book-hawking game—just as in the worlds of art-dealing, arms-trading and drug-trafficking—securing the object of sale is only half of the business. Of equal or greater importance is the identification, cultivation and gulling of the buyer. The mark, if you will. In this case, the inveterate collector. The obsessive, the driven, the covetous customer who cannot breathe easily until he or she has secured yet another grain of sand for the hourglass of all eternity.

For this type of client is not a victim of an ordinary psychological condition. This is not like alcoholism, or snobbery, or other social afflictions. This is easy prey. For this one, for the mark in question, is settled under the wings of that most red-toothed of demons.

"Did you get it?" Otto asked me as I stepped into his gaily attractive toyshop in Ealing, even before the pretty bell over the shop door had stopped tinkling. He even stepped back from a transaction with a paying customer. Note the absence of a how-are-you, good-to-see-you, how-is-your-belly-for-spots and all of the rest of it from the normally genial Otto. Just this unpleasant leaping to the point to betray the presence of the leathery inner creature.

Otto Dickinson picked up his demon somewhere in southern Iraq near the Kuwait border during Operation Desert Storm in the first Gulf War of 1991. Strictly speaking his demon should be described as a djinn, and it took up residence while paratrooper Otto, having removed his helmet, was resting under the shade of a tree with three other members of his battalion. Otto was exhausted. In the heat of the afternoon he closed his eyes and slept for perhaps only a second. Or maybe he didn't sleep at all but drifted in the measureless space between waking and sleeping, whereupon the Arabic demon, seizing the opportunity, slipped down from the tree as softly as a speck of wind-borne sand falling through the air to land upon a single hair, and then found ingress through the cavity of Otto's sunburned ear.

Otto, recovering from his split-second of sleep, woke to hear his comrade paratrooper Wayne Bridges reading aloud from a scrap of paper:

A reed had not sprung forth, a tree had not been created,
A brick had not been laid, a brick mould had not been made,
A house had not been built, a city had not been formed.
All the lands were sea then Eridu was created: The holy city,
And with Eridu the first shadow, and within the first shadow
The seed, the egg, of the very first demon.

"What's all that about?" Otto asked sleepily

He didn't get an answer because Wayne Bridges took a bullet through the throat, fired from a Kalashnikov rifle poking out of the rubble of a house in an area previously declared clean of snipers. Otto, seeing the muzzle-flash from the rubble, was up and running and calling for backup.

About twenty minutes later, after several tons of ordnance had been dumped on the lone sniper, Otto returned to inspect the body of his dead comrade. Wayne Bridges still had wedged between his fingers the document from which he had been reading when he was shot. It was a very old pocket guidebook to the archaeological sites of Sumeria, Akkadia, Babylon and Assyria. Otto flicked through the pages, went to return it to his dead comrade's pocket, but the demon spoke gently in his ear: "*No. Keep it.*"

Otto told me all this himself. Except the part about the demon. He was unaware—and still is—of what happened to him in that moment. I never try to tell him, or anyone else for that matter. It's always counter-productive. But, even without the open-jaw hiss and wings-at-full-pinion sudden waking of a slumbering demon, it is immediately obvious to the trained eye.

"Well?"

"Please, Otto, finish serving your customer. I'm in no hurry."

Otto looked back at the customer—a stunning photo-model mum with a baby slung from a rope-like contraption at her breast, tanned legs, gold high-heels and done up for the opera—as if she had just materialised. He appeared irritated by her presence. Then he remembered his manners, assured the lady that the hand-carved tumbling gymnast was free of lead paint, and completed the sale quickly.

I waited until the tiny bell cleared the way for us to talk. But if Otto wanted to dispense with the pleasantries, I didn't. "How's the toy business."

"Up and down. It's hard to compete with the giants."

Otto was one of the very lucky few. With the British government refusing to recognise Gulf War Syndrome, Otto had returned from the Gulf to be diagnosed with degenerative arthritis at the age of thirty-two, accompanied by migraines, asthma, skin disorders and burning-semen syndrome. As I say, one of the lucky ones because he got a war pension and sunk what assets he had into his toyshop. Fifteen years or so after his combat duty had ended, it seemed like the toyshop was a fox-hole and he was still fighting for an escape out of his war experiences.

I liked Otto, and I hoped that instead of ripping him off I would have to disappoint him when he was outbid by the vile poet Ellis. Despite his "up-and-down" maunderings and his "little ol' me" routine, I knew that his toy business was doing very well and that he had a chain of almost a dozen of these neatly crafted toyshops. Otto had spotted that the 1990s had produced a sudden rush of baby-making amongst the well-heeled. The selfish eighties had given way to the caring nineties, we were told. Then the full horror of parenthood had caused a stampede back to work amongst the coiffured mums, frantic to shake themselves free of the clamping jabberwocky jaws of their infant charges; which in turn led to a tide of guilt, flowing more freely than mother's milk. And guilt, where it could, lavished money on finely crafted toys.

Otto saw that he should stock his shop not with the cheap plastic imported playthings that children actually wanted, but the expensive handcrafted toys that reflected so well on the parents who placed them decorously around the nursery. Otto coined it.

And so fed his collecting demon.

Otto was prepared to pay me over £90,000—an intermediate price—for a first edition *Pride and Prejudice*. Personally I can't abide Jane Austen. Can't read a line without hearing it offered up in the squeaky tones of a spiteful piglet. Emily Brontë I'd want to drag into my house and kiss her thin lips, but Austen, no. I don't think Otto was a great fan either. That's how it goes: you start by collecting the things you admire, then you go on to collect the stuff other people are collecting.

Otto had no wife, no kids, no addiction to drugs, cigarettes or alcohol. Where else might his money go? After the slew of prissy Hollywood costume dramas, Austen collectibles had generated more interest than ever, and here I was, offering an 1813 first edition printed for Egerton. "I'm told I'll have it next week, Otto."

"That's what you said last week." Otto had what you might call poached-egg eyes. He looked at me morosely.

I shrugged. "I think it's reliable. But I have to tell you, there's a third bidder."

"Oh? I suppose you won't tell me who it is."

"Come off it, Otto." I'd revealed to him Ellis's identity *on strictest understanding you don't use this information, Otto*, but only as part of the confidence. Of course there was no third bidder, but because I'd told him who the other guy was, he'd have to believe there was also a third.

Otto dug his thumbs in the elasticated waistband of his trousers and hoiked them up a little. "Oh well. I can't go much higher."

No businessman can. Unless he wants to. I pretended to be interested in a pair of joke spectacles in which eyes drop forward on springs. I tried on a pair. "These are terrific. You have terrific stuff. I'll take a pair for my nephew. The new bidder has put in ninety-one."

"Sorry. I'll have to chip out at that."

I took off the joke glasses and handed them to him along with a ten-pound note. He took both from me with hands in the grip of a terrible rash—from the chemicals or the depleted uranium, I guessed—and rang up a figure on his till. "Never mind, Otto. You want me to keep you informed of what comes in?"

He handed me the joke glasses in a plastic bag emblazoned with his toyshop-chain logo and was about to open his mouth when the bell above the door tinkled. We both turned.

The figure looming in the doorway looked like the Ancient Mariner. The man's face was red as if from exertion and his grey hair hung lank at either side, almost plastered to a grey beard. His teeth were stained with nicotine. He wore an army greatcoat and strong fell-walking boots, one of which was laced with string. He shuffled deeper into the shop, and barely seemed to notice me there.

"Seamus!" said Otto. "How are you, me old mucker?"

"Just came in to say hello." Seamus's voice was crazed in the way of an Old Master painting. "You don't mind?"

"I've told you before I don't mind. Don't mind a bit. William, this is Seamus, an old mucker from Desert Storm. Seamus, have a cup of tea."

"We don't mention Desert Storm," said Seamus. He glanced at me from under huge eyebrows composed of tangled steel wires.

Otto tipped me a salute. "Right. We don't mention Desert Storm."

Christ, I thought, if he was a combatant in the first Gulf War he couldn't be more than about forty or fifty years old: yet he looked like someone who had drowned at sea a hundred years ago and returned as a ghost. "Let's not, then," I said, winking affably at Seamus. I don't know if it was my wink that offended him, but I felt a flash of tension run through his body. A thunderous expression passed across his face. He turned away from me rather obviously.

"Shall I get that kettle on then, Seamus?"

"No. Not stopping. Only came by to say hello." He glanced around the shop as if trying to remember something. Then he darted another look at me, as if I were someone not to be trusted.

"There was a message for you," Otto said, opening his till.

I saw Otto pull out a few large-denomination notes and stuff them quickly in an envelope. Then he came from behind the till and handed the envelope to Seamus, who took it without a word. That was Otto for you: sparing the finer feelings of a tramp who wouldn't have wanted me to witness this handout.

Seamus folded the envelope and stuffed it in his army great-coat pocket. He stared at the floor, as if slightly confused.

"Sure you won't have that cup of tea, Seamus?"

"Ah, that was it!" Seamus was suddenly animated. "That was it! I come to tell you I'm onto something! A secret!"

"Oh, what's that?" said Otto.

Seamus waved his hands in the air as if limply fighting off an aerial attack. "No! No no! I'll tell you when I have it all bang to rights. A secret! But you'll be the first one I tell, you will be! Now I have to be on my way. I've an *himportant happointment*." He said these last two words as if mimicking the aristocracy. And he laughed. Still chuckling, he turned and shuffled out of the shop.

"Poor fucker," Otto spat angrily after he'd gone. "Far worse than me. Got nothing. Fucking outrage." Otto turned away from me but I could see him thumbing back a tear. Then he turned back to me. "Seen it, have you? The book? With your own eyes?"

"Not yet, Otto. I only know what I've been told. Which is: three volumes from a Victorian collector's library, half-titles supplied, occasional light foxing and offsetting, contemporary green half morocco, spines gilt, marbled sides, red sprinkled edges. Covers worn at spine and edges, joints starting. Modern slip case, of course. What you'd expect. An exceptional copy, they say."

If it wasn't a fake I'd be interested in it myself, I almost added.

"Hell's bells," Otto said. "All right, sod it: ninety-one-and-a-half."

Chapter 4

Yes, of course the *Pride and Prejudice* was a fake. We should have had it ready there and then but there had been a small technical problem with my printer's nose: he'd pushed too many drugs up it. Then he'd been chased across his workshop by—and I had to laugh when he told me—demons. Not real demons, of course, but drug-induced fancies, which I suppose may at times seem just as terrifying as the real thing.

The consequence of the fray was that a bottle of turpentine substitute got spilled across not the fake, but one of the volumes of a *real* first edition which we'd obtained—on the pretext of potential purchase—to study in the production of the copy. Whatever the drug-induced phantoms had done to my forger's mind, the turps had done real damage to the morocco leather cover of the original. It left us with a number of options. We could pay the seventy-eight-thousand asking price to the vendor; we could replace and age-simulate the damaged cover before returning it; or we could replicate two copies and keep the genuine but damaged item and retain it for sale in a couple of years' time.

We chose the latter option, even though it set back our trading plans: hence my milk-round visits to Ellis, Antonia and Otto. As a legitimate dealer it was easy enough for me to stall the vendor of the authentic copy; I just didn't want the extra time to allow my buyers to either go off the boil, or even to discover there was "another" copy on the market at the same time. As any salesman will tell you, the art of selling is the art of closing.

Forging rare books is not like forging Art. The original print run for the first edition of *Pride and Prejudice* is uncertain. Perhaps 1500 copies were produced. Where do all these copies go? Book lovers are notorious hoarders. Even assuming three-quarters of the copies were used for lighting fires and stuffing Victorian dolls, no one is surprised when a house-clearance turns up an extra couple of copies for auction. Unlike a singular painting by Turner, or a Constable.

Naturally, a book has to cross a certain price threshold before faking becomes lucrative. The *Pride and Prejudice* edition, like many books from that period, was published in three individual volumes: the materials alone required to replicate and age the paper and to season the binding, not to mention access to museum-effect print machinery, will set you back several thousand pounds. Plus the multiplicity of skills required dangerously expands the number of people who know what you're up to. So you need a genius who can do the lot.

"I'm a donkey. I'm so sorry, William." Ian Grimwood was a remarkable painter, sculptor and printer, and no hee-haw. Sadly no one, or at least no paying person, shared his artistic visions.

"Accidents happen," I said, clearing a space for myself to sit down in his chaotic studio in Farringdon.

He sat rubbing a large, scarred hand across the dome of his shaved head. I'm sure that he would never be the sort of man to apply kohl or eye-liner, but, exaggerated by the baldness of his head, it always seemed that way. His grey eyes had a glitter like a rime of frost on a winter pavement. "I wish you hadn't told me all about those boys and girls."

He meant GoPoint. The homeless. He'd negotiated me down when I told him what I was doing with my share of the loot. I'd tried to get him to stay with his fairly priced original pitch but he wouldn't. He'd been homeless himself once, he told me. I could believe it. He was the working-class hero that Ellis kept pretending to be. Unlike Ellis he carried the wounds, the way an old boxer carries every single punch he took in the ring, the way an old political campaigner carts an economy of hope.

"That's the trouble with this game, Stinx," I said. I held up my hands. I had some dye or paint on my fingers. "It gets you all moral. It's horrible."

He threw me an oily rag. "I hope you keep schtum about my good deeds. I've got my reputation to think about."

"Not back on the marching powder, are you, Stinx?"

"Who you been talking to? It wasn't coke, it was crystal meth. A moment of stupidity. A tiny indiscretion. Won't happen again, Your Honour. And I mean it."

"You serious?"

"Serious. I 'ad a dark night of the soul, William." He looked out of the big, dirt-smeared windows of his studio. It was a converted Gothic warehouse and we could see the roofs and chimneys of Clerkenwell sweeping away from us. "Lucy left me again."

That lacerated old heart of his. He was in love with a woman who left him on average once every three years. Seems she couldn't stand living with a genius. Last time she left him it was for a commodities broker. The time before that it was a wine importer. Before that I can't remember, but the pattern was clearly to swing from the bohemianism and chaotic brilliance of Stinx to the ultra-conservative; then after six months of life in the twin-set-and-pearls lane she would rediscover his virtues, returning to give him another spin like a favourite but chipped and scratched psychedelic album from the 60s.

We belonged to an unofficial club, Stinx and I. A society of abandoned men. We called ourselves the Candlelight Club, I can't remember why—something to do with W. B. Yeats. There was one other member, Diamond Jaz, who'd been dumped by his male lover. The circumstances of our meeting some three years ago was strange, not to say auspicious.

* * *

It was the sixth of June when Fay told me she would be leaving me. The date is burned in my brain because I'd returned early from work—no, the book thing is a hobby, not my principle employment—after an angry exchange with a government junior minister. Luckily for everyone involved I was only early enough to see a man whom I vaguely recognised leaving my house in Finchley to climb into a shiny blue soft-top BMW. Well, I did recognise him, didn't I? He was on the telly.

Confrontation, admissions, recriminations, tears. The full shopping-list. "It doesn't matter," I tried to tell Fay. "I've been inattentive. It doesn't matter."

Oh, but it did matter. Even my trying to take the blame was part of the problem, apparently. I was stunned to discover how *over* it was between us already.

I wanted to avoid facing the children so I left the house and walked. I walked blindly until I came to my senses in Kentish Town. Then I slithered inside the Pineapple, which was pretty quiet at that time of the day. I sat at the bar and ordered a glass of wine. I must have made short order of it, because I very quickly asked for another.

"That first one didn't touch the sides," said a gruff voice from two barstools away.

I didn't pay him much attention. The Pineapple attracts an odd mix of trade—that's where I later met Ellis—and this hunched, tattooed brute with a shaved head was like a scary species of genie behind his cloud of curling, blue cigarette smoke.

He tried again. "You look like how I feel," he said. He held his cigarette with the cone pointing in towards the palm of his hand, like a schoolboy smoking behind the bike-sheds. His knuckles were tattooed, old-style. I could see "LOVE" on one hand; I only guessed at "HATE" on the other.

I met his gaze from behind the wreathing smoke. I was sure

he wasn't about to grant me three wishes, but there was a sympathetic cast to his eye. I don't know why, but I blurted it out: "My wife's left me for another man."

He sat upright and wafted a hand through all this curling smoke, as if to look at me better. "My life!" he said. "My life!"

I thought it an odd remark. I mean, it must happen to lots of men somewhere every day. I took another nip of wine.

"Same here exactly!" he said. "When?"

"About an hour ago."

"Stone me!" He chuckled. "Well, stone me!" He rotated his stool away from me, checked out the bar and sucked hard on his ciggie, still shaking his head.

I wasn't feeling companionable, but I felt obliged to ask. "What about you, then?"

He turned back to me. Now, as he regarded me steadily, his eyes looked sad. Huge skin-folds hung from under them, each like a miser's pouch. "What I'm saying. About an hour ago."

I wasn't sure for a moment if he was taking the piss. Then I decided he couldn't be. We chatted a little bit, offering guarded information, and concluded that we'd been dumped by our respective spouses—spice?—within moments of each other.

He reached a leathery hand across the bar. "Ian. Though everyone calls me Stinx on account that I reek of some sort of chemical or other. I'm a painter."

To my discredit I assumed he meant the sort of painter who slaps a coat of magnolia on your hall-stairs-and-landing. I didn't realize my mistake until much later. We weren't about to spill our emotional guts, so in turn he asked me what I did.

"I'm director of a youth organization. Well, kind of a youth organisation."

"What's that, then?"

"I head up the National Organisation for Youth Advocacy. NOYA."

"What's that, then?"

"It's an umbrella outfit. I represent a number of organizations to government and official bodies, that sort of thing."

"How's that work, then?"

"We lobby for change, make representations, sit on funding committees. You know?"

"No, I don't get it."

I suddenly felt depressed about my job as well as my marriage. "No, no one ever does. I dread meeting anyone new because I feel worn out just trying to explain my job."

Stinx waved a nicotine-yellowed finger at the barmaid, a freckled redhead with button-eyes. "Haven't I told you before not to leave a man with an empty glass?"

"It's my first night on the job," she said, pouring me a fresh globe of wine. She was Australian, as are all bar staff now in London. Compulsory. "So that's kinda gotcha."

"You're too fast for me," he said. "Have one for yourself."

While we skirted around our respective matrimonial disasters I noticed another man sitting at the bar fiddling with the text on his mobile phone, though I had the impression he was eavesdropping on our conversation. He was Asian and extraordinarily handsome; the kind of groomed figure you see in moody men's magazines with full-page adverts and quarter-page articles. He tapped away at his text with growing impatience.

Meanwhile Stinx shuffled one stool along to sit next to me. "What's the wisdom, then?" he said seriously. "What is it?"

"About women? You must be joking if you think I know the answer to that."

"Date blokes instead," the Asian man said without looking up from his text.

We both turned our heads towards him at the same time. "Well, I suppose that's one answer," Stinx said gruffly.

"Except I've just been dumped." He held up his phone. "By text, would you believe it? The arrogance of it."

Stinx reached over and grabbed the phone from him, reading

the message. "My life!" He wagged his pollen-gold finger at the Aussie barmaid again. "Give this one another drink, too. We seem to be forming a club."

"Great. Can I join?" said the barmaid.

"No, you bloody cannot. But you can have another drink."

So the Candlelight Club was formed. It's a curious thing, but when Diamond Jaz joined the conversation we had a warm sense of our own ridiculousness. Camaraderie flushed through us like a good wine as we paraded our wounds. I'd seen it before on the hospital ward when I had my appendix removed. Men in hospital drop their competitiveness and become tender, solicitous, motherly, wanting each other to recover. And so were we. I surprised myself by talking at length about Fay and how much she had meant to me. Stinx waxed poetic about Lucy and actually cried at one point in the evening, though we were saturated with booze by that time, so it was allowed. And Diamond Jaz, the baby of the group who did indeed turn out to be a photographic model, explained that he was bisexual and could therefore speak with authority on the difference between being dumped by a man you loved and a woman you loved: he said there wasn't any.

It was like falling off the world, and falling for days, until you hit a shelf. There you lay for a while until, struggling to your feet in the dark, you found steps hewn in the stone. Though your heart felt too heavy to climb the steps, climb them you did, knowing they were without number.

I remember saying all this—or slurring something like it—while the Aussie barmaid tried to get us to drink up so that she could go home. Everyone else had already gone, and she'd locked the door while she cleaned up around us. Anyway, after I'd finished I looked up to see Stinx and Jaz regarding me with glittering, storm-holed eyes. I'd either impressed or bored them into silence.

Stinx, slobbering slightly, dug an eagle's claw into my shoulder and one into Jaz's shoulder and gripped both hard. "It's all right, boys," he snarled, mashing his words. "Because we're falling *togiver.*"

And fall together we had. Over the last two years or more, meeting up once a fortnight pretty much without fail. There's fidelity for you. We were what those eighties feminists kitted out in humorous dungarees used to term a *support group*, except we never used to call it that. It was a drinking club, an eating club, and some evenings it was a laugh-until-the snot-comes-down-your-nose club. Say what you like, we were a spiritual salve for each other.

When Lucy came back to Stinx, Diamond Jaz and I waited with trepidation and then with relief as we attended their "re-marriage" ceremony and knees-up. Meanwhile Stinx and I watched, with the kind of horrified fascination that you might have for someone juggling two or three buzzing chainsaws, as Jaz passed through one relationship after another. And they attended, like a pair of anxious parents, to my utter failure to recover from Fay; even setting up from time to time—God help me and the poor women involved—dates of a romantic nature.

But here he was, reduced or returned to the state in which I'd found him that first evening in The Pineapple. His resort to drugs—I don't even know what crystal meth is, but it doesn't sound like something anyone with a moderate interest in mental stability would want to grapple with—was desperate, because Stinx had a historical affiliation with pharmaceuticals. It was a serious threat to our forgery project. Though I was more concerned with Stinx's state of mind than the project, except of course where it might cause problems for Antonia and GoPoint.

"She left you? Lucy left you? When?"

"Night afore last. No, the one before that. I've sorta lost

one night."

"You could have called me."

"I tried. No answer. Tried to call Diamond, too, but he's in fucking New York modelling cashmere scarves with Ground Zero as a backdrop, I ask you."

"Get your coat." I said. "Come and stay at my place."

"No, mate, I've got this job to finish."

"It can wait."

"No, it can't. I've already put you behind. I can't let you down William. I can't. Nor can I let down those boys and girls."

"Is it going to work out? The two copies, I mean. Six vols in total, isn't it?"

"It's not like it's twice the work. I'll have to finesse a few differences between the two. Spine and edges. Joints and stuff. But I'll 'ave it for you. Work through the night. And the next night."

Stinx made it sound easy but I knew he proceeded sheet by sheet. He was a master forger. Originally an accomplished bookbinder, Stinx had been called to make restorative work on some old books that had suffered water damage after a cellar flood. He'd quickly grasped that between restoration and reproduction there are several grey areas. This work was child's play compared with some of the things he'd done in his colourful life.

"Want me to stay over? Do the coffee? Marmite on toast?"

"You sling your hook, mate. You got work in the morning."

He was already turning away from me, digging his hand under the back of his collar, surveying his workshop. I decided to leave him to it. But before I left I saw something skitter under a workshop bench. I thought I saw tiny black eyes watching me. I decided to say nothing to Stinx.

The door to his workshop faced one of those steel industrial cage elevators still working from the days when the building was a warehouse. He followed me out and opened the cage for me.

"Call me," I said, "if crystal meth comes knocking."

He pointed a gnarled, golden finger at me as the cage began to descend. "Be lucky, William."

Chapter 5

I'm not sure what it was that I saw under the table in Stinx's workshop. People are extremely ignorant about demons and their nature. It is possible to walk into almost any bookshop and find some kind of encyclopaedia or A-to-Z of demons. How disappointing these publications are, for they generally turn out to be nothing more than lists of the names of gods of various cultures. Beelzebub, for example, the god of the Philistine city of Ekron; or Asmodeus, the Persian god of wrath. These are only demonic in as much as the Judeo-Christian religions took them to be rivals.

These are not demons. These do not number in the one thousand five hundred and sixty-seven, as brilliantly catalogued by Goodridge. And anyway, if it's long lists of gods you want, you need go no further than the Hindu religion to stop you in your tracks. Diamond Jaz, who was at one time in his youth training for the Sikh priesthood, informed me that they are countless; and the last figure I was quoted was "in excess of three hundred and thirty million." Right. And of course, the person trying to count them is in the grip of that particular demon Goodridge characterized as the "demon of counting the ever-changing number."

I was thinking about this as I neared King's Cross. The light was already fading and a man in a long, filthy coat croaked at me from a doorway. I was thinking about the person working for some government agency whose job it was to count the homeless. I'd probably walked five or six yards past the shop doorway when I stopped and retraced my steps.

I looked hard at the wreck of a man in the doorway. His long hair was plastered to his face. Tear tracks—I'm sure that's what they were—ran down his grimy face and into his beard. He seemed to be all in.

He blinked at me. "Ain't it terrible, I'm trying to get a cup of tea."

"Seamus, isn't it?" I said. "We met at Otto's place the other day. You were with Otto in the Gulf."

He looked away, to the side. "Don't keep going on about it."

I wasn't sure he was talking to me. "How are you, Seamus? You look a bit rough, if you don't mind me saying."

"Cup of tea would be the thing."

I could have easily given him a couple of quid and carried on walking. But we all know what a cup of tea means, so instead I asked him if he knew about GoPoint. He said he'd heard of it. I found a business card and scribbled the GoPoint address on the reverse, plus a brief note for Antonia, and pushed it into his hand. Seamus looked disappointed. Then on second thoughts I hailed a black cab and steered Seamus into it.

"Thanks," said the driver. "I wanted him in my cab."

"Shaddup. Here's a twenty. Make sure he finds the door to the place, will you?"

Then I took the Tube to the offices of NOYA in Victoria.

It was about eleven when I rolled up to work. It makes no difference what time I go in. For one thing I'm often there until seven in the evening or travelling for the organisation, and for another I'm the boss. In any case, Val, my long-term secretary, holds the fort from nine to five. Val's a lovely girl. Old school. Immaculate filing cabinets and keeps a delicate tissue tucked inside her sleeve.

Very formal secretarial standards, too. Always opens the post for me and removes the envelopes unless marked "Personal and Confidential," which they never are. Except this morning, there it is on my desk with the other, opened mail: a white envelope.

"What's this?"

"You'll have to open it to find out, won't you?" Val often speaks to me as if I'm twelve years old. "Looks like an invitation to me."

Invitations come often enough—usually to some stiff formal reception or briefing hosted by a government agency and preceded by a pernicious glass of chardonnay or some filthy sherry. Inside the envelope was a stiff white card. A small publishing house called Winding Path was inviting me to the launch of a book by one Charles Fraser.

"Bloody Hell!" I said aloud. "There's a name I haven't heard in a while."

The publicist had added a little note, telling me that Charles Fraser had acknowledged my contribution to the book and that they hoped to see me there. *What contribution?* I thought.

Val laid a file on my desk and looked over my shoulder at the invite. "How exciting for you," she said, as if I'd been chosen to play for the junior school football team. "Is the author someone you know?"

It was at teacher-training college in Derby in the early 1980s, just after my interest in antiquarian books had hatched. I'd moved back into halls of residence for my final year and the college chaplain was interviewing all inmates of Friarsfield Lodge in turn. The Lodge, a shambling Edwardian white-walled mansion converted into single studies, accommodated twenty-two male students. Sometimes the place was a zoo, but mostly it was a dull, tranquil residence with bathrooms full of drying rugby shirts and drying rooms cluttered with football boots or potholing gear. It was approaching Christmas. Fraser I knew from my English class, but I hadn't spent much time with him. We were being interviewed in our own rooms, and I saw from the posted schedule that I was to follow Fraser.

We'd had plenty of notice to get rid of any pornography or pot-smoking paraphernalia before the chaplain's gentle knock on the door. He came in rubbing his hands, like a surgeon about to perform a routine appendectomy. He declined my offer of tea and sat himself in a chair by the gently hissing gas fire. I sat on my bed.

The college was originally established by the Church of England. Even though the government had stripped the church of its controlling powers, the church still took its ministry seriously, providing a chaplaincy and offering the usual ceremonies at the beginning and end of term. Dick Fellowes, a wiry and effusive character with sparkling eyes, was normally informal, but that day he was got up in his dog collar. For the record, he also sported a blonde goatee at a time when no-one else did, not even for a joke.

He was nobody's fool. He sat on the Students' Union committee, but because the students wanted him there. "So, have you seen it?"

"Yes."

"You've been up to see it?"

"Yes."

"Since this all broke out, or before?"

"I was with the porter when he opened it up."

"Oh yes. So you'd never seen it before the fuss?"

"You can't get in, normally. It's supposed to be locked."

All the time he was asking me these questions he was looking not at me but around my room. For clues. He keenly surveyed the posters on my wall. His eyes fell on an African carved-wood mask a girlfriend had given me because her mother found it spooky and didn't want it in the house. When he got out of his chair it was with the litheness of a jungle cat. He went over to my bookcase and started rubbing his hands again. He crouched down with his back to me. I know he checked out the spine of every single paperback on my shelf. There were certain things I'd removed along with the porn and the pot; now I wondered if there were dust marks that would tip him off to the fact that, like the British Library, I had a secret or withheld collection. After he'd done with my books he started leafing through all my tapes.

He turned and flashed me a huge smile over his shoulder. "I know I'm here to talk about that thing upstairs, but I find people's music collections *fascinating*, don't you?"

Sure.

He waved one my tapes at me. "I adore this! Does things for your head!"

"They've got another album just out," I said helpfully.

He stood up, evidently satisfied with my taste in Indie rock. He turned and twinkled his eyes at me. "Then I shall have to put it on my Christmas list. Shall we go up and take a look at the thing?"

He followed me out. I made sure the latch was down to lock the door and he expressed surprise. He wanted to know if I always locked my door. I pointed out that there had been one or two petty thefts recently. He said he wondered what the world was coming to when students couldn't trust each other any more.

Dick Fellowes led the way up the first two flights of stairs. I noticed that he wore very tight black trousers and black patent-leather shoes. There was something mincing and effeminate about the way he trailed his hand along the banister and swung round the post at the top of the stairs. I knew that he'd once nursed a student all night through a bad acid trip. Apparently he'd been good enough to sit with the ninny and reassure him until the effects had completely worn off. A rumour did the rounds that Fellowes had buggered the student before persuading him it was all part of his hallucinations. I fell on the minority side of believing this to be a malicious story.

I think that was when I first learned the glorious cost-free feeling of righteousness that comes with defending other people's reputations.

At the end of the corridor on the uppermost landing was a tiny set of steps curling up to an attic door. The attic was supposed to be available to us as storage space when we had to clear our rooms between terms so that the college could rent the premises for conferences. But the attic was permanently locked and to get access you had to go and see the head porter, a doleful, pipe-smoking, pint-sized sack of misery with a cubbyhole office reeking of tobacco and nastiness, and guarded by a vicious one-eyed Alsatian. The porter's office was half a mile away. Never disposed to loan out the key, he insisted on a scheduled appointment during which he would with great ceremony drag out his huge bunch of keys and exercise his dog all the way from his office to the attic. Everyone spared themselves this theatricality by just not bothering, which was of course the porter's intention. Instead the drying room and the laundry room served for any essential storage.

This time Fellowes had the keys to the attic. The door was a bit stiff: he had to put his shoulder to it. When the door opened, it released a kind of sigh. Fellowes stepped in, pirouetting neatly to hold open the door for me. When I was inside he gently closed it behind me. I don't know why but I would have preferred the door open.

He crossed the gnarled old varnished floorboards and with his hands on his hips stood looking down at the markings on the floor. A pool of December sunlight was beamed onto the floor by a porthole-type glass window at the far end of the attic room, making the markings look fainter than they actually were. It was a good few seconds before he asked me, "Do you know what it is?"

"Of course. It's a pentagram."

"Pentacle," he corrected.

"What's the difference?"

He answered just as if I were enjoying the benefit of one of his college tutorials. "The circle around the five-pointed star is what makes it a pentacle," and here he looked up at me, "and not a pentagram."

"Devil worship," I said.

"Is it?"

I must have coloured. "Well. That's what it looks like."

Inside the chalked circle was a five-pointed star, and surrounding the whole thing was a larger, concentric circle. At each of the five points was a candle stub and a small ceramic bowl containing maybe salt in one, some spice in another. Various symbols—possibly Hebrew—were chalked there, and between the concentric circles was a long Latin inscription.

"Someone seems to know their stuff," he said. "Or they are just pretending to."

"What does this Latin thing mean?"

"It's not important," he said. "Plus I'd rather not say it aloud. So, you didn't put it here?"

"Heck!"

"Is that a no?"

"Yes, it's a no."

I stooped to rub at the chalk on the floorboards. It wasn't the usual kind of stuff that dusts away easily.

"Chalk on the floor is just chalk on the floor," Fellowes said. "I'm a bit more disturbed by this fellow."

He turned to the wall. There was a goat's head: a real goat's head, with a very impressive set of horns. It had been pushed onto a nail at about eye-level. Some objects had been removed from around the goat's head but I didn't say anything. I didn't want to incriminate myself. Fellowes was watching me closely.

"You're a lad about campus," he said. "You get around. You see what comes and goes. Any ideas?"

"What, about who might have done it?"

He folded his arms, nodded. I looked down at the *pentacle* on the floor and shook my head slowly.

"None at all? You see, when the same question was put to other students they all had one or two ideas. Your name cropped up more than once."

"Well, we all have our enemies," I said.

"We do, Mister Heaney, we do."

"All right, it's a long shot, and I've got no real evidence to back it up," I said, "but if it's just ideas you're after, I can think of a couple of names."

"Let's close this place up again," said Fellowes. "You can tell me downstairs."

Chapter 6

I skimmed the book-launch invitation card across my desk and got on with my work. I had a number of papers to read from various committees and I had a report to prepare. The demon of acronyms was busy that morning: the DEFS were encouraging all INGYOS to prepare a response to the YOPA statement on EEC grants for voluntary CRY groups.

It wasn't easy to switch off. I was seriously worried about Stinx, and whether he was going to come through on the book. It was true that he'd never let us down on a project, though it always came in his own time. And time was what Antonia and her colleagues didn't have. If they defaulted, the bailiffs would be sent in with indecent haste and the GoPoint project would be all over.

I left off my report writing and went online to have a look at what was in my own private bank account. Not much at all, but I did at least have the money I'd saved from Robbie's Glastonhall fees. I wondered what the betting odds would be for a) Stinx coming through with the forgeries; b) my making a good sale; and c) this all happening before the GoPoint premises got turned into designer shag-pads for young stockbrokers.

I made an online enquiry about a loan.

All these concerns, not to mention the arrival of a book-launch invitation triggering memories of gravely misspent youth, made it difficult for me to concentrate on my work. Then, just as I was patently not about to commence the writing of my report, an email popped into my inbox. It was from an address I didn't recognize, with the header "Good To Meet You." I almost deleted it. It was the kind of header you expect from a Nigerian phisher who—quite reasonably—wants to share several million dollars with you in return for the use of your bank account for two minutes.

But I opened it, and found it to be from Yasmin. It took me a blink or two to remember who she was—so indelibly inscribed as Anna was she in my own head. She'd enjoyed meeting me that lunchtime in the Museum Tavern. She would have liked to have chatted for longer. She was sorry not to be able to spend a few more minutes together as she made her way back to work that afternoon. If I wanted to meet up one lunchtime on another occasion, she thought that might be fun.

My cheeks flamed.

Perhaps it was the thought of fun that made my face burn. What was all this gibberish about fun? Fun wasn't really something I went in for. Fun and I had parted company on the high road of life at about the time my hair started to thin and my knee joints lost all compression, quick handshake, no fuss, farewell.

Fun.

I'm not sure if I breathed the world out loud. I'm sure I did no such thing, and neither did I make any movement, but from across the room of that high-ceilinged old office with its moulded plaster tongue-and-dart cornices, Val looked up at me from her own work. How can that be?

"All right?" she asked, smiling pleasantly.

"Fine, Val, fine."

She put her nose back in her work. I pretended to re-engage with mine. Something was seriously wrong with that email. I read it again. It made no sense at all. Why would a hip, appealing and exciting young woman want to offer herself to a mothballed old stiff like me? I was no less suspicious than I would have been of the Nigerian phishing scam.

I deleted the email, put aside all thoughts of Yasmin, forgot about Stinx's nose and dismissed Charles Fraser's book-launch party. Instead I directed the full onslaught of my passions into the YOPA report to all INGYOS.

Chapter 7

It was dark by the time I got home that evening and I was surprised to find that I had left a light on. The tall standard lamp in my living room was burning softly. This bothered me. I don't leave lamps on. I wondered if Fay had been there. Or one of the children. For some reason I made sure Fay had a key to my house and now I hate the fact that I gave her a key. Some people do not know when a relationship has ended, and I'm one of them.

Nothing was otherwise disturbed and there was no indication that anyone had been there. I thought that I must have left the lamp switched on when I left that morning. I'd had a lot on my mind what with the upset with Stinx and his lack of progress on the book, and the threat to Antonia's project. I slipped off my coat, drew the curtains and went straight for a beaker of the rubicund relief & rescue.

I put on some music. I often feel as though a man my age sipping his wine alone in a dimly lit room should play Bach cello concertos, but it tends to be The Stranglers or The Jam. The Buzzcocks. I'm not actually going to get up and pogo round the room but it does stop me feeling quite so alone.

The telephone went. It was my son, Robbie.

"Hold on," I told him. "I'll turn this down."

"Lucien says—"

I interrupted him. "How are you?"

"I'm fine. Lucien says—"

"No, after you say, *I'm fine,* you say, *How are you, Dad?* It's a fussy little ritual, I know, but it's an important one."

There was a pause. "Lucien says—"

"Okay, so you don't want to observe the ritual. What does Lucien say?"

"He says he'll pay for my tennis and my fencing if you'll pay for Glastonhall."

"So if I go the starter, the main course and the dessert, he'll stretch to the after-dinner mint?"

"What?"

"Here's a little life-lesson, Robbie. When asking people for money, observe the pleasantries, respect the rituals and always, always clench the buttocks."

"What?"

I hung up on him. Sometimes it's great being a bastard. Then I turned up the Buzzcocks. Loud.

Five minutes later the phone went again. This time it was Fay, wanting to know what happened.

"He's raging," she said. "He's slammed his bedroom door so hard one of the hinges has come off."

"Find a screwdriver. Take off the other hinges. Tell him he can only have his door back when he's learned how to use it properly."

"Be serious. He wants to talk about Glastonhall."

"What's that? Can barely hear with this dammed music so loud."

"Then turn it down!"

"I can't, I've got people here. You know what these young folk are like."

"What young folk?"

"Sorry, can't hear. Tell him to call me when he's stopped sulking. Bye!"

I poured myself another glass of red-robed oblivion and

switched on my home PC in an angry mood. Do I hate my boy? Of course not. I just want to comb the fireball nits out of his hair and get him to remember that I spent the most important years of his life gently training him not to be a shit.

Anger makes you drink faster. Sometimes when you're furious the drink doesn't touch the sides. Or even the shadow of the sides. If you're really incensed, drinking is just like driving a petrol tanker one hundred miles per hour into a fiery pit.

I had email. I deleted the spam with rapid keystrokes and stopped at one called "Second Attempt." It was from her again. Anna. Yasmin. Whatever.

She apologised if she was repeating her last message. Her email account had been playing up, she said, and some of her emails had strayed. She asked about GoPoint and Antonia. She made no mention of Ellis. She was, she said, "available for coffee or a glass of wine" at any time.

Available for coffee or wine? *Here we go again*, I thought. Whatever for? What on Earth could she want? I doubted she was after antiquarian books. Perhaps she was looking for a job or a reference or contacts or something. It was all a bit baffling. Then I wondered if Ellis had put her up to it. The pesky poet didn't trust me an inch over the bidding for *Pride and Prejudice* and he was right not to: his over-developed proboscis was just sniffing out the wrong rat. I guessed that was it. Maybe he thought she could sound me out over a jeroboam of wine, lead me into an indiscretion or two.

The very idea! I think my heart has become a wineskin over the years. Authentic, tanned goat-hide, triple-stitched, proofed with pitch, fashioned for an airtight nozzle. Nothing gets in or out. No matter how much I have to drink I don't spill, unless I want to. I hit the delete button: get ye hence, saucy maid.

But then the screen prompt asked me: Are you sure you want to delete. And I thought: *Am I sure?* I got up and lowered the volume on the sound system. And I composed a reply: light,

jocular but maintaining a suitable distance. And just as I hit
send I heard a knocking on the door.

It was Stinx. "Bloody Nora! I've been 'ammering away on this
door for fifteen minutes. I went for a walk round the block, came
back and banged again. I could hear the music but I couldn't
bloody raise you!"

He had a huge artist's portfolio under his arm. He marched
into the kitchen, unzipped it and began to lay out his work on
the table.

"Is it finished?" I asked hopefully.

He beamed me a smile triumphant and radiant. "Almost."

He'd come to report progress, not completion. My heart
sank. Well, not quite sank, but took on water, gurgled, listed to
one side, tried to recover steam. I hid my disappointment and
poured him a glass of vino while he shucked off his coat and
laid out the samples.

"You should see the vellum I'm making for it, too," he said
proudly. "Best yet."

I'd rather he'd got on with the forgery than its wrappings,
however magnificent the latter. "Excellent."

"Well, it's something I can do while I'm waiting for fixing and
processes and all that."

I hadn't a clue what he was referring to. I picked up one of
the paper samples he'd laid out on the table. It was mottled and
fluffed and it seemed to smell exactly right. There were also the
boards in green half morocco and with gilt spines, ready to be
roughed up. I had no objection to what was actually there, which
all looked very good. Masterful even, but it was nowhere near
complete. What's more, we needed two copies. Clearly there was
a long way to go. I laid down the samples. "Congratulations,
Stinx, you've done it again."

His way of accepting my compliment was to blink at me.

"How do you get the wonderful smell?"

He flicked his head and looked away. I didn't want him to tell me. It was a rhetorical question. "Do we celebrate, William?"

"We certainly will. When it's done, we will."

"Never mind that," he said, reloading his folder with the samples. "It's as good as done. Get your coat."

"Isn't that a bit premature? I mean when exactly will the thing be ready?"

"Fullness o' time, William, fullness o' time."

"I've got our guy on the hook: we don't want him jumping off."

"Get your coat, I sez. Jaz is already on his way. Lamb and Flag."

Covent Garden, then. Stinx left his samples at my place to be collected later. We took a cab. I kept congratulating Stinx on his workmanship, thinking that lavish praise might encourage him to complete the job, but all he would say is, "Giz a break, William."

The Lamb and Flag is a bit of a surprise to find in Covent Garden. It has the appearance of an old coaching inn. The clientele is mixed and the pub is replete with demons loitering amongst the old fittings of knotted wood, but for some reason they tend to leave you alone. Jaz was already there at the bar, with champagne in an ice bucket and three glasses waiting.

"I would have preferred the non-fizzy stuff," I grumbled.

"Oh, stop being a grouch," said Jaz. "Tell him to celebrate, Stinx."

"Celebrate."

Jaz grabbed the bucket and I took the glasses and we found a table in the corner. We poured the fizz, clinked the glasses and pretended everything was a done deal. I was thoroughly aware that all this "celebration" nonsense was designed to put my worrying mind at rest. It didn't.

The way it worked was that Jaz and I fronted the money for all the materials for Stinx, and later we deducted that amount from his truly modest fee. Jaz, who seemed to operate at the interface of the Art and Fashion worlds, was very good at identifying buyers. Jaz and I similarly deducted any expenses and the considerable profit all went to our agreed benefactor, which in this case was GoPoint.

We fell silent. Then Stinx said, "How was New York then, Jaz?"

"Fabulous. Love it. Shot of caffeine, hit of helium, you can speak like a native."

I've been to New York. I once fell in love there, in Central Park. But it was a trick, and she turned out to be a demon. I spoke nothing of that and said instead, "Meet anyone?"

Jaz was always meeting people. Men and women seemed to line up and lay down for him. Sometimes he would tell us about his exploits, funny, daring, bizarre. But his brow creased this time and he swirled his drink around in his glass.

"Yeh. A former soldier."

"Not another Guardsman!" said Stinx. Jaz already had a boyfriend in the Coldstream Guards

"They don't have Guardsmen in America," I said.

"I know that," said Stinx.

"They do, but they're like reserves," said Jaz. "No, he was a high-ranking officer in the 101st Airborne. Lovely guy. But he's a mess, body and soul. Depleted uranium, it just trashes the DNA. But he saw something there. In combat."

Jaz looked up at the two of us, and for a moment I thought that whatever his officer-lover had seen in the Gulf, it had carried over to Jaz. We must have been staring pretty hard because he almost shouted, "Hey, drink up! We're celebrating!"

So we drank up, and turned the talk to more cheerful things. Or pretended to.

I'm not a great one for clubbing but, having drunk too much on an empty stomach I was persuaded on to some candle-lit cave with scarlet Parisian brothel velour upholstery. Jaz was a member. It was the sort of place where undistinguished celebrities hang out with foreign footballers. Jaz called over a couple of magnificent and statuesque girls with whom he'd been on photo shoots. They were good company. Stinx and I were in high spirits and we were making the girls cackle. I could see the footballers checking us out, wondering what it was that we had to offer. Red-rot and vellum, I wanted to tell them: you should try putting it up your nose instead of Bolivian marching powder.

Then we were joined by a member of the minor aristocracy. (That's how the girls described him, anyway.) He endured half an hour of toff-baiting, mainly by Stinx, before taking quite a shine to me, much to Jaz's amusement. I found a private moment to communicate my misgivings to Jaz. When I told him that Lucy had deserted our friend all over again he agreed we might have problems seeing the project through. We both agreed that there was nothing we could do but sit tight and hope that Stinx delivered.

I was drunk and wanted to leave. One of the girls came to my rescue—I think her name was Tara. She lived in my neighbourhood so we agreed to share a cab. She took my arm on the way out and our movements were tracked ravenously by the two Chelsea footballers. I was so drunk I mimed for them a back-heel flip and header. One jutted his chin at me, while his friend's hungry midfielder's eyes said: Cunt.

In the back of the cab Tara told me, with an excited squeak to her voice, that the aristocrat was fourteenth in line to the throne. I'd quite liked Tara until that moment. "Just here will do fine," I said to the cabbie.

Tara squeezed my thigh before I got out of the cab. "Do you want to do something?" she said.

I leaned over and gave her a peck on the cheek. "I've never paid for it in my life," I said, "and I'm not going to start now. Goodnight."

She shrugged and opened the cab door for me. It doesn't matter how much I've had to drink, you start paying for sexual comfort and you invite flocks of them into your life. Throngs of them. Swarms.

I was so drunk that when I got to my front door I could barely get my key in the lock. Once inside I drank a pint of water in one gulp, kicked off my shoes and collapsed into my chair, where I instantly fell into a fitful sleep, dreaming of my days back in Derby, at the teacher-training college.

Chapter 8

I saw Charlie Fraser collecting his mail from the pigeon holes near the Students' Union. No one was around so I darted up behind him and whispered, "Watch out, he's on to you," and then kept on moving.

I found something in my own pigeon hole a few yards along the rack, and pretended to be absorbed in the minutes of the staff-student English Programme Committee. Even without looking up I could feel his brown, spaniel eyes boring into me.

"What are you talking about?"

I still didn't look up from my essential reading. "I'm just tipping you off, that's all."

"Who is on to me?"

I turned and smiled at him. "Okay. Please yourself." I walked away. *Sweat, you fucker*, I thought.

I thought it might be a day or two before he felt compelled to speak to me. In fact he broke cover sooner than that. Early that evening there was a short rap on my door.

He stood with his hands in the pockets of his black jeans. His capped black t-shirt revealed one of the Chinese ideograms sported on the bicep by just about every middle-class student at that time, and if he wore underarm deodorant it had let him down. I couldn't stop myself from wrinkling my nose.

"Yeh?" I asked, like he might have been selling insurance.

He didn't answer. I saw the toe of his boot tap once, but other than that he just stared at me.

"You want to tell me what it's all about?" I stared back at him for a while. Then I stepped back and let him come in. "Sit down," I said.

"No. I'd rather stand."

"Okay, don't fucking sit down. What's cracking off?"

He sniffed. "I've no idea what you're talking about."

"Really? Well, fuck off out of my room then, because you stink. And what about those fucking photos?"

He blinked. That was all I needed. He blinked. I'd been right all along and it was him. And I hadn't been able to stop thinking about the photographs since I'd discovered them pinned around the goat's head in the attic.

I'd needed somewhere to stow my antiquarian books for a while. I'd entered into a house-clearing partnership with a bad lot called Johnno, a guy who'd found his way onto List 99—the teacher-exclusion register—and been expelled from the college for supplying cannabis, more or less by the bale. Johnno had a house-clearance operation. Well, a van.

Johnno's technique was to go in to bereaved families or incompetent pensioners and offer them good money for some piece of tat. Having won their confidence, he'd then pick up anything valuable they had for a song. I got all and any books in return for furniture humping. It was unsavoury and I was already thinking of packing it in before somebody's aggrieved and psychotic son came after Johnno with a crow-bar. I became convinced that he would be after me, too, and I wanted to hide some books I'd collected.

The attic seemed the obvious place. I didn't want the college porter to know I was stashing stuff away in there so I went up to see if there was some way I could force the lock, or maybe take off the hinges of the door, I don't know. But when I got up there I saw a bit of debris on the floor and noticed that the wall enclosing one side of the landing by the door was no more than a flimsy plyboard panel painted over. What's more, the panel was floating loose at the skirting board. When I pressed my hand flat to the plyboard, all the panel pins popped out on one side. It wasn't difficult to squeeze through the flapping panel and into the attic.

That's how I discovered it all. The pentagram—pentacle—chalked on the floor; the curious symbols; the Latin and Hebrew slogans; the candles. And the goat's head impaled on the wall.

And the thing that made my stomach lurch.

Pinned on the wall around the head of the goat, and arranged strategically as if to mimic the shape of the star in the pentacle, were photographs of five girls. All the girls were students at the college, and all five were personally known to me. Their faces had been cut around and very crudely superimposed over the faces of nude models from glossy titty magazines.

They were all girls that I had been out with at one time or another during my college years, and one of them, Mandy Rogers, was my current girlfriend.

I felt suffocated. I wanted to get out of the room. The goat seemed to look at me, its beady eyes swimming, as if it were still alive. But my intimate connection with all five of those girls made it impossible for me to leave. I was panicking, wondering if and what it all had to do with me. I remember my skin flushing unpleasantly; it was as if something else had stepped into the room with me and brought with it a freezing breath on my neck.

I wanted to take down the photographs, but I was terrified of the goat. I stepped from one side of the pentacle to the other, and its eyes followed me. I was almost certain that if I reached out my fingers it would bite. Overwhelmed with repulsion and nausea I decided to get out. I opened the Yale lock on the door but before leaving I had a sudden, defensive thought: I popped the flapping panel back into place from the inside.

I let the Yale lock spring back into place behind me and hurried down to my room before anyone saw me. My first thought was to find Mandy and tell her that her picture had found its way onto the wall. But it seemed such a distasteful thing to show her. And secondly, I would have to explain my connection with one of the other girls, whom Mandy hated. I sat in my room gnawing my knuckles and wondering what kind of a freak would do all this, and what I should do about it.

At six o'clock all the inmates regularly abandoned the Lodge for dinner at the student refectory. Genuinely having no appetite, I made my excuses and waited for the last student to leave. When the place was empty, I retraced my steps back up to the attic and scrambled in, once again via the loose panel. This time I pressed the panel pins back into place immediately, hurriedly ripped down the photos of the girls and let myself out a second time.

Outside in the car park to the Lodge I burned the photos in a sand bucket. Then I washed my hands.

I barely slept that night. My thoughts twisted and turned, and my bedsheets with them. At first I managed to convince myself that I wasn't a target after all, and that the fact that I'd dated all five girls was pure coincidence. After all, I assured myself, it was a rampant egocentricity to assume that everything was connected to oneself. But then I tried to think of any other student in the college who had dated the same five girls, and of course I couldn't. At best I could think of only *one* guy who had been out with *two* of the set. I couldn't know for certain, since there are many kinds of liaisons, some as brief as a match-flare, but at college you get a pretty shrewd idea of who hooks up with whom.

Neither did the set of photographs represent a complete set of my "significant" playmates. Ruling out the one-night stands and the egregious follies, there were two more girls whom I would have described as major figures: young women who were important to me. So if someone was tracking my sexual and emotional history they hadn't made a comprehensive job of it.

All this ran through my fevered brain as I lay in bed. About two o'clock in the morning, I got up and made sure my door was locked. I checked the windows were securely bolted, too.

I tried to think what the five girls might have in common quite apart from me. It was hopeless: they were from different regions of the country and they studied a range of subjects. This one's father was a Harley Street doctor while this one's was a coal miner. This one didn't like sex much at all while another one had an alarming enthusiasm for being tied to the bed and vigorously spanked. I couldn't see any shared ground at all.

That's how the night was spent: It was a coincidence. It wasn't a coincidence. It was a coincidence. It wasn't.

I was fairly certain one of my fellow students in the Lodge was behind it all, though I didn't immediately suspect Fraser. Door security was pretty tight after one or two thefts, so whoever was using the attic had to have access to the Lodge, and would also have to have spent some considerable time there to discover the panel by the attic door.

There were twenty-two students in residence.

It was easy to eliminate a few cheerful friendly guys who didn't seem to want much from life besides beer, burgers and Saturday mornings spent swinging a leg at a leather football. Then there were the hard-line politicos on the ground floor, a little group of nervy Marxists who cloned themselves in dungarees and soup-kitchen haircuts: their only menu was dialectical materialism and a proposed ban on all forms of humour. It just wasn't their style to bugger about with a goat.

There was a deeply Christian cohort of four well-scrubbed lads; though I didn't discount them entirely because Christians are weird and so easily slip to their opposite master. I looked at them all closely but I couldn't see it. A few others in the Lodge were just too plain thick and unscholarly to immerse themselves in Hebrew sigils, so I ruled them out, too.

All this left me with three possibles—and out of these, one probable—but from there I couldn't make progress short of confronting each of the three directly. So in order to help me flush out the would-be diabolic magician I sought the help of the poison dwarf in his cave of gloom.

"Hi," I said genially. "I have to store some equipment in the attic at Friarsfield. Could I get it open?"

The porter's polluted cubbyhole was located under the stairs leading down from the college administrative corridors. I stood at the open door. The Alsatian lying under the porter's desk had his head between his paws, but its ears were pricked up and it looked at me nastily with its one good eye.

The porter didn't even look up at me from his red-top newspaper. Sucking passionately on his billowing pipe he said, "Can't you leave it in the drying room?"

"Not really. One or two things have gone missing lately."

"What is it?"

"Just a box of stuff."

"I'll come tomorrow afternoon. Leave it outside the attic door for me."

"I won't be around tomorrow afternoon."

"Thursday then."

"Won't be around Thursday either, I'm afraid. And I don't want to leave it in the corridor. Sorry."

His yellow teeth clacked in irritation on his pipe stem. He put down his paper and surveyed me for the first time, blinking at me, but without offering a solution.

"Tell you what," I said. "I don't want to disturb you. Give me the key and I'll bring it right back to you."

"Ha!" he said, rising to his feet. The dog raised its head, hopeful, looking at its master. "Not on your nelly, son! Come on, dog could do with a walk."

I shrugged. The excitable dog was up and ready, its leather leash already in its drooling mouth like a postman's finger.

The tiny porter took an age to slip on his coat. He munched on his briar stem again, whipped the pipe out of his mouth and said to me once more, rather unnecessarily, "Not on your very very nelly."

I'm still not sure what a *nelly* is, but having accomplished my purpose I didn't say anything. Together we marched along to the Lodge. I felt slightly ridiculous, striding ahead of a porter roughly half my size and a one-eyed dog. The porter, trailing blue pipe smoke, held the dog's leash in one hand and his horde of a hundred keys in the other. When we reached the Lodge, rather than tether the Alsatian outside, he dragged the animal in with us.

I had a box of junk at the ready in my room—I no longer wanted to stow my antiquarian books in the attic—and quickly caught up with the porter as he swept upstairs. I balanced the box on my knee as he performed the time-consuming ritual of identifying the key. When he got the attic door open, he let the dog go ahead of him and then stepped inside.

"Stone the crows!" he said.

"God," I said, coming up behind him. "I don't like that."

The porter's jaw dropped and he snatched the pipe from his mouth. I could see a row of metal fillings in his nicotine-stained teeth. He was looking at the goat's head.

"That's not nice."

"No," I agreed. "Not nice at all." I was waiting for him to declare that he would have to report this to the college authorities, but something happened.

The dog, which had stopped in its tracks in the middle of the room just like its master, cocked its head as if listening intently. Then it cocked its head to the other side. Suddenly it snapped its jaws at the thin air.

Next the dog gave a yelp, rolled violently on its side, scrambled up again and without warning ran full pelt at the small porthole window at the far end of the attic. The dog's nose hit the glass with full force, like a punch. The glass cracked but held as the dog rocked back, dizzy from the impact. Then it leapt at the glass a second time, whimpered, turned and ran out of the room trailing piss.

"Luther! Come 'ere!" The porter tried to call back his dog, way too late. The creature had bolted.

In another context I might have found it funny. But I didn't like what I'd just witnessed one little bit.

"This is bad." The porter looked at me. All his slothful confidence had vanished. "Bad."

"I want to go," I said.

I left first. The porter had a last look round the attic room and slammed the door behind him, as if to lock something inside.

Nothing else happened that evening. By mid-morning of the next day a letter appeared, pinned up on the notice board by the stairs, informing us that "a serious occurrence" had taken place and that we were all to be interviewed in turn and in our rooms by the college chaplain, Dick Fellowes.

My simple plan had been to toss my "*he's on to you*" squib at each of my prime suspects in descending order. But I'd rung the bell at my first attempt. And here he was, Charlie Fraser, in my room, armpits reeking, as good as declaring his culpability.

He hadn't admitted it yet, but turning up at my door was as good as a confession. I was angry enough to want to have a pop at him, but I also wanted to find out what in hell he was up to. I made a feeble effort at being indirect. "I don't know what it is you've done up there, but you should have seen the porter's dog."

He nodded. "No, that figures."

"Why does it figure."

"He's not too keen on dogs. In fact he hates dogs."

"Who does?

He shook his head. He obviously wasn't going to tell me.

"Who doesn't like dogs?"

Charlie Fraser looked down at the floor, then lifted up his head and stuck his chin out at me. He had this infuriating smirk on his face. It was superiority, confidence in some knowledge that I didn't have. Then he shook his head again, as if to say, no, there are some things you're not smart enough to grasp.

I'm not a violent person. I'd had one big fight in my life and that was when I was six years old. But that provocative smirk released in my brain a photo-flash of white heat and I stepped forward and hit him twice, once on his nose and once on his chin. He fell back hard against the door, but didn't go down.

His hand went to his nose, which was already streaming with blood. Nipping it between finger and thumb, he took a step forward. "You've broken my nose, you ape," he said. "Get me a tissue."

Chapter 9

Frankly, I didn't want to take Otto's money. I would much rather have closed the sale with the loathsome poet, Ellis. I once attended one of his awful poetry readings, in a bookshop on Charring Cross Road, where Jaz introduced us. I hadn't gone there to hear Ellis's whining verse; I'd gone for his custom.

I'm obviously out of touch in so many ways. My idea of a poet is of some rough diamond in a threadbare flying jacket, slouching, in need of a shave, his breath stinking of garlic and black beer: the kind of charming brat who thinks his rancid breath alone is a challenge for any woman. But my stereotypes were all unpicked with this glimpse of Ellis, who turned out to be one who appreciated the sharper weave and the finer thread.

I could tell you that his three-quarter-length coat fluttered with Armani's moniker, that the hidden lifts in the heels of his gleaming shoes obscured a Prada tag, or that the lovely Daniel Hanson scarf that he so carefully unwound from his soft white throat was handcrafted in China from the finest silk. I mean, what use to anyone is a well-dressed poet? I remember thinking it would be a pleasure to take his money for a forged book.

I also recall noticing something very odd about the poet's beak as he flicked off his scarf and eyed the thin assembly that had turned out for him on that damp night. It was as if the moment of wrinkling his nose one time too many at some nasty smell had been trapped on his face. Below the thatch of his scruffy hair it hung like an icicle from a barn roof; dripping, too, because he had a tic, a nervous habit of running his index finger under his snout as he glanced about him.

Oh hell, I thought, *have I really got to sit here and listen to this dog's spittle-flecked, yammering verse? Yes*, was the answer. We needed the sale, needed the money.

Jaz had told me that Ellis had been in the running for the laureateship. I had to check what that meant. Someone who composes poems about the Queen and is paid with a butt of sack, or a sack of butt, I can't remember. Anyway, Ellis didn't get it; he got a kick in the butt instead. But in my research on our target I'd studied a slim volume of his work.

Oh, give me the tongue of angels to describe his poetry. Well, it's very modern. It's clearly about *something;* but I have from it the feeling that I'm being told a joke which I don't get. Though I do get the sense that this doesn't matter, isn't a problem: that having the reader or the audience feel thick is part of the intention, that incomprehensibility is part of what makes his poems great.

Anyway, to my surprise he stepped forward and said, in what's called an Estuary accent round here and in a voice loud enough not only for the present audience of six, but for everyone on the lower floors, "Gawd! Bit parky for poetry, innit?"

My life! I remember thinking. *Stroll on!* Here's one who can jump easily from the Oxford High to my own dark origins on the Old Kent Road and back again without missing a single beat. And I thought: *You be careful, sunshine, you're on my manor now, and we are not mocked without payment.*

It was perhaps a week after our visit to the nightclub—a week in which I'd failed to hear a single report from Stinx—when I used my lunch hour to pay a visit to Antonia at GoPoint. As usual, GoPoint had been emptied of its inmates for the day, with the exception of a therapy group in the small meeting room. The door to the meeting room had a vertical glass panel and I looked in on them. The group sat in a circle on hard plastic chairs and Antonia was leading the group in discussion. I'm not sure what they do in these sessions exactly: lay out their life stories, lament where it all went wrong, resolve to do better. I expect that's the drill. Celebrity addicts pay thousands for the same drill at The Priory and I don't think GoPoint, for all its scuffed paintwork and patches of damp, is any more or less effective.

I watched through the window, rather uncomfortably, as Antonia, with her arms spread wide, explained her four-step routine. There were half a dozen men and women in the group, and also in a circle, behind their chairs, stood their respective demons.

Each member of the group had at least one demon; though one woman had three, clustered behind her chair. The demons were listening intently to what Antonia was saying.

A word on demons, as I don't expect everyone to know exactly what I'm talking about here. Demons do not have leathery wings. Neither do they have horns, cloven hooves, monkey heads or any of the usual representations from religious mythology. They can easily slip into or retreat from the human form of their hosts. But when they have externalized themselves—as they all had in this instance—they become passive, muted, even slothful, though this can disguise the danger they represent. They only have use for us to quicken their own intentions.

They are all squat, somewhat shorter than human beings, and are always slow-moving. Their substance is elusive to describe, being comprised of something akin to loose soot. People who are sensitive to demons will often refer to them as a kind of shadow, but unlike a shadow they are three-dimensional, detached and assert full integrity. Goodridge in his *Categorical Evidence* refers to their substance as *solid black vapour*. Fraser, right from the beginning, called it *swart-cast*.

Believe me, it is no joke. The first time you encounter this substance in the form of these beings, you feel like your skin is being flayed. The terror is such that the fluid of your eyes seems to freeze at the sight of them.

One of the demons became sensitive to my presence behind the door. It turned slowly, cast a disinterested gaze over me and returned its attention to Antonia. Their faces are somewhat indistinct: it's as if a lesser god had made a prototype being, without the full detail of Creation. But although their faces are blurred, they are individualised, unique, and their facial expressions readable. Right at that moment they all looked as though they were listening for a flaw in her argument, a fault in her position, a moment of psychic exhaustion, a chink. They fear Antonia. They cannot approach her. For them, an indomitable light burns around her, and for that reason she fascinates them.

Perhaps the most mystifying thing about demons when externalised is their passivity. They always seem to be *waiting* for something. Waiting for something to happen.

In the same way that the demon sensed my presence at the door, Antonia did, too. She looked over her shoulder, smiled at me and held up three fingers to indicate she just needed a few minutes to wrap up the proceedings. She returned to her summing up, and then the entire group got up from their chairs to embrace each other in turn. I believe they call it giving support. But as one did so I noticed her chair threaten to topple backwards, until one of the demons attending behind reached out a hand—a limb, a paw, a hoof, I don't know what—to steady it. Though the demons each took a step back away from Antonia as she approached to hug their respective hosts.

It was remarkable to watch.

Antonia came out of the room, beaming at me, letting the door close on the group, who were in no hurry to abandon the warm interior for the cold streets outside. Antonia kissed me on the cheek and grabbed my hand, leading me into her office—a tiny cupboard with a phone and a computer workstation. She put an electrical kettle on to boil and dropped teabags into a pair of mugs.

"I know," she said, still beaming.

"How could you possibly know?"

"It's all over your face, William!"

"No it's not," I protested. "I've got my poker face on."

"He whose face gives no light shall never become a star."

"Why are you always throwing William Blake at me?"

Antonia leaned over and pinched my knee between finger and a powerful thumb. "You clever bugger! You clever, clever bugger!"

"Hey! Hey! Stop messing! I haven't showed you the cheque yet."

"You don't need to. Here, I'm going to kiss you." She swung her lithe frame across me and sat in my lap. With her hands locked behind my head she planted an impassioned kiss on my lips. I mean a lover's kiss. A power kiss. She was still kissing me when one of her colleagues opened the door.

Antonia broke this kiss. "William has brought us a reprieve, Karen! He's saved us again. As a reward I'm going to fuck him until his dick is blue. Then you can do the same, Karen."

I tried to laugh it off but I was embarrassed. "That won't be necessary."

Karen was a slightly overweight redhead with pale blue eyes and a figure by Rubens. "You won't be able to stop her if she wants to. Or me. Kettle's boiling."

Karen told Antonia something about essential repairs to the heating system. At last Antonia climbed off me, giving me the chance after Karen had retreated to present her with the cheque.

Without even looking at the figure written on the cheque, she fanned it through the air, as if drying the ink. "I've learned not to ask you where this comes from."

"No, don't. Or I would have to lie."

I certainly would. There was no way that I was going to tell her that the cheque she had in her hand came from the money I'd saved on Robbie's school fees plus a sizeable loan I'd taken on my own account. If I had told her she wouldn't have accepted it. I tried hard not to think about what would happen if Stinx didn't come through with the work, or if we didn't make the sale. If either of those things happened I was going to be in a big hole.

"I don't care if it comes from the devil himself." She regarded me steadily. "What's wrong, William?"

"Nothing's wrong."

"You're not happy."

"Of course I am. I've brought you the money I promised. I'm ecstatic."

"Is it that wife of yours? Is that it? You have to let her go."

"She's already long gone, I'm afraid."

"Non-attachment, William. You can't be attached to people any more than you can be attached to things in this world."

Something always happened when she burned her eyes into you, as she was doing at that moment. Her eyes were like flint-stones. I felt like a little pile of dry kindling which she was trying to get to burst into life. It was always deeply unnerving. I got up and made the tea myself, since it was clearly going to be a long time coming otherwise.

"Send him a woman," Antonia said. "Oh please send him a woman. Someone to root out the invisible worm that flies in the night."

"I don't know who you're talking to, Antonia, but I wish you'd stop."

"You know perfectly well who I'm talking to."

I desperately needed to change the subject. "Antonia, you have to be careful. I go to these government offices, you know. Meetings with bigwigs. I hear things. Your name comes up occasionally. You make fools of them. They want to see you fall."

"They've always wanted that."

"They're scared of you. They're out to get you."

She brandished the cheque I'd given her. "But I have the protection of angels."

I wanted to tell her she also had the predatory attention of demons, but I let it pass. Instead I said I had to go. In fact I had to get back to work at the office. But before I went she insisted on hugging me.

The hug went on for way too long. But I let it, because I wanted her warmth and her golden light and her indomitable goodness to sweep through my bones; because her proximity was clean air in a dirty city; her peerless position was a vibrant colour amongst the multitude of rotting grey souls that was all of us in London; because her breath in my ear as she hugged me tight was the whispered promise of salvation.

Chapter 10

I don't know why I answered that young woman's email. I don't know if it was Antonia's excessive hugging, or her appeal to the heavens to send me a woman. But answer it I did, if only to say that, no, I wouldn't be able to meet with her.

Hear that? That's an interesting sound. It's the sound of me lying to myself. In fact what I said in my email was that I, too, enjoyed meeting her in the Museum Tavern that day. I said I was pleased we had a mutual connection through Antonia at GoPoint and that I was glad she thought it a cause worth supporting. I suppose I then went on a bit about the plight of the homeless, as if that was really what the correspondence was about. Then I thanked her for the invitation for wine or coffee but pointed out that I was terribly, terribly busy these days and couldn't think when I might possibly find the time.

There's the truth of it. I didn't say yes and I didn't say no. I merely complained that I couldn't think where or when. Then I told myself that was an end to it. But in fact, and without knowing it, I'd merely set her a little problem to solve. And through these tiny, tiny openings do demons fly.

The following day she responded to my email. In it she recalled that I'd mentioned to her that my place of work is in Victoria (I'm sure I hadn't); that she was working at a temporary job over there that very week (what a coincidence); and that she even knew a nice pub that served a very fine range of La Belle Dame

Sans Merci (had she nailed me so quickly?). I assumed that last touch was to let me know she'd been all ears that day I met her in the Museum Tavern.

What the bloody hell does she want? I thought.

I let another day go by before replying. Somehow I ended up arranging to meet her one lunchtime.

Meanwhile I was worried about Antonia. Though her warmth and light still flowed, I thought she looked tired. I mean, she was always completely knackered by the way she lived, and she wouldn't allow herself a moment's respite from the battlefield. I wondered what it did to her, when her inmates drew goodness from her every day like that; or even when I lingered over a farewell embrace, sucking the virtue from her, sucking, always taking.

It made me remember the Bible story of Jesus and the woman who can't stop her period. She reached out to touch the hem of his garment and Jesus said he felt the power flow out of him. I never understood whether that meant the unfortunate woman's menstrual blood was so bad that it acted on Jesus like green Kryptonite does on Superman; or whether it meant that the good stuff had jumped from him to her; or whether he was at first reprimanding her because he didn't want to be touched by an impure woman. And it's no good asking someone who claims to know about these things, because they don't. The Bible itself is an amorphous creature remade by every new reader into images of themselves. The point with Antonia and people just like her is: Do we steal their goodness?

Before I left GoPoint she said something odd. "Hey, you threw me a strange one the other night."

"Huh?"

"Seamus. The old soldier. Gulf veteran."

"Oh yes. You didn't mind?"

"Of course not. But he's in a bad way."

"Yes."

"Wakes up screaming the house down every night. Pisses himself with fright. Keeps calling someone a liar."

"Oh. That sounds bad."

"Worse than bad, actually."

"Fuckin' awful."

"Yeh, but we in the West have our oil from the Gulf, so it's okay that he has nightmares. When will it end, William?"

"It won't end. We'll continue to do evil and to tell ourselves we're doing good. It's called being rational."

She stared at me with the eyes of William Blake looking at a seven-year-old chimney-sweep. She is on fire with love. Sometimes I can't even stand to look at her. I waved farewell and walked back to work.

On my return to the office, Val handed me my telephone messages. "Are you all right?" she asked. "You look exhausted."

"I've been up to GoPoint. Always makes me feel drained." The truth was I was worried sick about the risk I'd taken with my bank loan.

"There was an article about Antonia in one of the tabloids on Sunday. Said she has a criminal record. And was in a psychiatric ward for three years."

"Did it say she was a former girlfriend of the current Home Secretary?"

"Really?"

"Oh yes. They'd leave that out. Until it suits them."

I retreated to my desk. There was a message from the junior minister's office, wanting to confirm my support for the government youth initiative. Bollocks, that could wait. There was also that crazy book-launch invitation card. I had no intention of going along. Charles Fraser was nowhere near the top of my list of college chums with whom I might have enjoyed being reunited.

In fact, there was always something unpleasant about Charlie Fraser. Right from the off I saw the words *suicide nominee* scribbled on his forehead in worry-lines. The thing about associating with Fraser was that the condition could become contagious. Back in my college days, I had no interest in spending any more time with him than it took to find out what the hell he was up to.

I fetched him a tissue for his bleeding nose, just as he asked. Though he hadn't commanded me with any confidence, he was a shrewd judge of psychology, and he'd correctly assessed that no further blows would follow the first. He'd spotted that I instantly regretted punching his face. He sat down and held his head back, stemming the flow of blood with the paper tissue I'd just handed him.

"I don't care what that shit is up there," I said, "but I want to know what it's got to do with me."

He shook his head slightly. His voice was distorted. Blood was trickling back from his nose into his throat, so he now had to lean forward. "You wouldn't begin to understand," he said. Or something like that. "It won't come back on you."

"What won't? What won't come back on me?"

He waved a hand through the air. "You're going to have to drive me to hospital. I need to get this looked at."

I stepped across the room and squinted at his nose. There was a lot of blood, most of it down the front of his shirt, but his nose looked pretty straight. I touched it with my forefinger.

He screamed the house down. It was obvious he was faking it now. There was nothing wrong with his nose, and I told him so. I grabbed it and gave it a waggle.

This scream, much louder than the first, left me in no doubt that he was just playing for sympathy.

"I'm going to faint. Call me a cab, then. It's the least you can do."

"Fuck off, Fraser! I don't punch people on the nose only to phone them a cab five minutes later."

He got up, wavered to one side and then staggered out of the room, still nursing his nose with the sodden, bloody tissue. It was easy to see this was all theatre. If I'd had an ounce of vindictiveness in me I would have clouted him again, harder. I followed him out into the corridor.

I thought he was headed back to his own room, and I intended to pursue him. Instead he went to the back door of the Lodge and out into the car park. "Where are you going?" I shouted.

Again he waved me away. He had a Fiesta with multiple dents and a holed exhaust pipe and he climbed in and started the engine. Working the gear stick with his free hand and steering with the crook of his elbow, he roared the throaty vehicle out of the car park.

I returned to my room. Blood had squirted up the wall in a precise diagonal. There was also blood on the carpet. I spent the next forty-five minutes cleaning it all up with an almost forensic care. I do wonder, in retrospect, if I had intuitively felt that Fraser's blood was contaminating.

I tried to put it all out of my mind by going down to the Students' Union bar and drinking six pints of bitter. "What's that on your neck?" said the girl behind the bar. It was Lindi, a half-Chinese student, one of the girls in the photographs.

"What?"

"On your neck. Looks like blood."

"It isn't blood."

"What is it then?"

"Blood."

I turned away from Lindi and within five minutes got into a senseless and aggressive argument with another student about whether Bob Dylan was fundamentally any good.

When I got back to the Lodge, I saw light leaking under the door to Fraser's room, which incidentally was located directly beneath mine. My dander was still up, and fuelled by the beer I decided to go and have it out with him again. I went to hammer on his door, but something made me tap very gently, almost furtively.

There was the sound of a brief scuffle from inside the room, and then silence. I listened at the door. I could hear things being packed away. I tapped again.

"Just a minute."

Soon enough, Fraser opened the door. He beckoned me in and closed the door behind me.

Something about the room took me by surprise. All sorts of crap was pinned to the walls: yellowing pages torn from books; newspaper articles; photocopies with lines illuminated by a highlighter pen. But distracting me from it all was the fact that his nose was up like a prize-winning tomato from the horticultural tent. Perhaps it was the beer but I had to suppress a snigger. He saw it.

"Glad you think it's funny. And the hospital confirmed that it is definitely broken, so I'd be glad if you wouldn't touch it again. They said it will heal on its own but it's still very painful."

"Sorry," I said.

"Apology accepted."

"I'm not apologizing!" I said.

"You just did."

"No, I said "sorry," but I'm not apologizing. That is, I'm sorry I'm not sorry I broke it. The waggle yes, the break no."

"You're pissed."

I sighed. He was right, I was: I'd drunk six pints of wallop on an empty stomach. I looked round for a chair and let myself collapse into it. "Talk," I said.

He put his hands on his hips and looked hard at me. "I will talk. I'll tell you everything. In fact I desperately want to tell someone, so I'm glad it's come out. But I'm not telling you while you're drunk."

"Glad what's come out?"

"The thing I will tell you about when you're sober."

"Tell me now."

"When you're sober."

"Tell me now or I'll break your other nose."

"See, you are pissed. Forget it. In the morning I'll tell you everything. But right now I'm going to bed. You can stay there or you can go."

With that Fraser kicked off his shoes, peeled off his socks and jumped into bed. That he was otherwise fully dressed didn't surprise me. He always did look and smell like he slept in his clothes, and this confirmed it. He'd turned his back on me, and had either closed his eyes or was staring at the wall. I was faced with the choice of rousting him out of his bed or leaving.

I surveyed the room again. The newsprint and the pages ripped from books and the photocopies spoke of a mind out of control. I wondered what Dick Fellowes had made of it. Though when I stepped across to look at the untidy collage more closely, some of it was just football league tables, but pinned up next to scraps torn from a Bible; or lecture notes adjacent to full-colour magazine adverts for lawnmowers.

Fraser was snoring—or pretending to. Maybe it was the effect of the swollen nose. I thought about punching him again, hard, maybe on the leg. Instead I left him to snore.

Chapter 11

On her return from lunch, Val told me that someone had chained himself to the railings at Buckingham Palace. Just the kind of everyday lunch time report you look forward to while working in one of London's many offices. Meanwhile I had to telephone the junior minister's office about the wretched government youth initiative. A chirpy female switchboard operator put me through to a decidedly non-chirpy staffer—the one who puts-the-powder-on-the-noses-of-the-assistants-to-the-junior-minister—who told me he was unavailable.

"Not chained himself to the railings, has he?"

"Pardon?"

"A joke. A small *jeu*."

"Who is this?"

I'd already told the dolt who I was, but I repeated my name, rank and number.

"Ah," said the staffer. "I think we just needed to know whether we had your support, that's all."

"I'm calling to discuss that very matter with the junior minister."

"So is that a yes or a no?"

"Oh, for God's sake," I almost shouted. "Tell him I returned his call." Then I put the phone down.

Some days are like that: you can't get hold of anyone and a sense of enfeeblement proceeds slowly down the spine and sets hard somewhere in the kneecaps, thereby stopping you from being able to stand up. But on such days you can return calls safe in the knowledge that the people you don't want to speak to won't be available. Then they have to return your return-call, and on it goes. I stacked up seven of these. Though it's a bit like gambling: you have to keep pressing your luck just for the fun of it, and it ran out on the eighth when I had to call the Scouts who were trying to downplay some unpleasantness involving a member of their executive board caught accessing paedophilic images from the Internet. They wanted to know if it might threaten their funding. I wanted to tell them: *I'd say it will.*

It was while I was trying to advise them on a press statement that my mobile phone went. It was Antonia. She very rarely called me, and almost never on my mobile.

"Hi, Antonia. I'm busy on the other line. Can I call you back?"

"It's pretty serious, my love."

Something about that *my love* made me get rid of the Scouts rather quickly from the other line. "Okay, Antonia. What is it?"

"Remember Seamus? The old soldier you sent me?"

"Yes. What about him?"

"Does he have anyone at all? Any family anywhere? I mean, anyone?"

"Heck, I don't think so. He's on the streets when he's not with you. I don't think there's any family."

"Anyone who might know a little about him? I mean anything at this stage."

"What's happened?"

"He's chained himself to the railings at Buck Pal."

"Oh, it's *him!* I'd heard something of that!"

"It's worse than that. They went to cut him free and he says he's got a bomb under his coat."

I felt my scalp flush. Then I remembered Otto. "Antonia, there is a guy. Served with him in the Gulf. Maybe he can help."

"I'm up here at Buckingham Palace now. Well, I'm with the police. Seamus told them he'd come from GoPoint and they drove me up here. It's a stand-off. They don't know if he's bluffing or not. But if Otto would talk to him it might help."

"I'll call him. Are you there now? I'll get to you as soon as I can."

Antonia gave me a number for the officer in charge, so that I could let him know we'd be coming. I called Otto in his toyshop. I got a silly laughing-policeman message from his answering machine. I left an urgent message and luckily he called me back instantly. I explained the situation and arranged to meet him so that we could go there together.

I knew it would take Otto at least forty-five minutes to get into town, so I finished up at the office, advising the Scouts to distance themselves from the paedophile and recommending that they move away from short trousers altogether. Just as I was pulling on my coat the phone went again. Val took the call and whispered that it was the junior minister's powder-boy. Or words to that effect. I waved her away and as I left I heard her lie sweetly that I'd already left the building.

I met Otto at Victoria and we hotfooted it up to the palace. The police had cordoned off Birdcage Walk and Constitution Hill, and a quite sizeable crowd had been pushed back way behind the Queen Victoria Memorial. A police officer in a flak jacket put his hand out to stop us getting any nearer, but I gave him the name and number of his commanding officer and after radioing ahead he let us pass. We were then escorted up to the command point.

I could see Antonia in a borrowed police coat, talking to an officer of rank. They were standing next to a police Land Rover, surrounded by a lot of armed officers in flak jackets. They all seemed to have earpieces and mouth-mikes. Up by the railings lay propped the lonely figure of Seamus. I could only see his head, because the area immediately in front of him, and the palace forecourt behind the railings, had been sandbagged.

* * *

Antonia introduced me to the commander, a tall, grey-haired figure with a long jaw and a jovial expression. "We've just worked out we were at school together," Antonia said.

"Who, you and Seamus?"

"No," the commander said, rubbing his large white hands together, "me and Antonia here."

That was Antonia. Give her two minutes and she'd establish the common ground. Five minutes and she'd have the commander on her committee. They both looked at me as if they expected me to join in the chat about schooldays, then the commander pulled himself up. "Are you the fellow who knows him?"

I said I wasn't, and introduced Otto. "We were in the Gulf together," Otto said. He sounded apologetic.

"He says he's wired. Was he trained in explosives?" the commander asked Otto.

"Yes. He was a colour sergeant. Knew a bit of everything. But he's not wired. You can take it from me."

"I'm going to need a lot more than that," said the policeman.

"He's not a bomber. Let me talk to him. I'm all he's got. I'll talk him down."

The commander glanced up at the heavens, which were filled with plump dark clouds. He seemed to bring the threat of rain down from the sky when he fixed Otto with his gaze. You could feel clouds moving overhead.

"He's just a dosser," Otto tried again.

"All right. We'll stand back."

"You've got to treat him well," Otto said. "He's been to hell, that man."

"Go and have a word," said the policeman.

"I'll come with you," Antonia said.

Otto looked at her. "No." Then he turned to me. "You come."

I looked at the commander and he nodded assent. For the first time the implications actually dawned on me of what might happen if Seamus *had* strapped himself up with explosives. But like Otto I knew that he had neither the means nor the resources, and together we walked across to the railings where the old soldier had chained himself, watched by TV cameras and a thousand eyes.

We stopped just in front of the sandbags. A long way behind Seamus, in the palace forecourt, the royal guards in their bearskin hats stood to unflinching attention, just as they did for the tourists every single day of the year. The commotion hadn't even scratched their routine. *How very English,* I thought. *How very fucking stupid.* Come the hour, I had no doubt they would change the watch with all pomp, utterly regardless of what was happening outside the railings.

"Seamus," Otto shouted, "what the fuck you doing?"

"Who's that?" croaked a voice from the other side of the sandbags.

"It's Otto, mate. Otto."

"Otto? What you doing here?"

"More to the point is what you are doing here, Seamus. Can I come and have a word?"

"Who's that with you?"

"A mate of mine. You know him. Can we come and have a little conflab? Talk tactics. Eh Seamus? Eh?"

"I don't mind."

Otto turned and signalled the thumbs up to the police clustered around the Land Rover. We stepped inside the sand-bagged perimeter.

Seamus looked very different. He'd shaved his head. Something very large was bulking out his coat. I didn't like being there one bit. I wondered why Otto had asked me to be with him.

Otto said, "Well, this is a right bloody caper."

Seamus turned his gaze on me. A fleck of hoar frost glittered in his eye. I thought again of the Ancient Mariner, and I wondered if I'd ever see another wedding. "Who's he?"

"We met before, Seamus," I said. "I sent you to GoPoint."

He wrinkled a leathery nostril. "I don't know you."

"You want a ciggie?" said Otto. "Go on, have a smoke. Go on."

"I'll have a smoke off you. Yeh, I'll have a smoke."

Otto lit a cigarette and passed it to Seamus. Then he lit one for himself. I don't smoke, but I asked for one, too. Otto said, "What's this all about, then."

Seamus tapped the side of his nose. "Special ops."

"There is no ops, Seamus. We don't do ops any more, you and me. We're in civvies. Better off, too."

"Not on about that."

"What you on about, then?"

"All a fuck, isn't it? It's all about a fuck."

Otto looked at me and wiped a finger under his nose. "What's all this about bombs? What you got strapped under that coat? You've got nothing there. Tell me there's nothing there. What do you expect to get out of this, eh?"

"I want an audience with the Queen. I want to tell her what I know."

"Eh? The Queen? Queen don't give a fuck about the likes of you and me, Seamus."

"I've been a fucking loyal soldier to the fucking Queen. I want to tell her what I know. And if she won't come down here, she can ride raggy-arsed to Birmingham." Whatever this phrase meant, Seamus found its utterance very funny. He tipped back his head. "Ha ha ha ha ha!"

Otto looked to me again. "Tell him the Queen won't come. Tell him she's eating pie in the palace, and too busy."

"He's right, Seamus," I said. "The Queen won't come here."

The old soldier looked around at the gritty pavement on either side of him. "Yeh," he said seriously, "it's a bit mucky, innit? Maybe we should sweep up a bit."

He looked at me. His idea for tidying up the street was in earnest. "Killed that girl, you know," he said to me. "Bumped her off, they did. It's known. Everybody knows."

"Which girl, Seamus?"

"Diana. Princess Di. Didn't want her marrying an Arab, did they? Lovely girl. Met her. Land mines thing. Got a thing about land mines, me."

"Right," I said, nodding. I didn't know which way this thing was going. "Right."

"You tell the Queen I need her down here. She needs to talk to me. Then if she winks at me, I'll know."

"Know what, Seamus?"

"That will be between me and the Queen. Queen don't wink, do she? So if she comes here and winks at me, I'll know all I need to know."

It was gibberish. It didn't give us a handle. I was trying to think of something to say when Seamus twisted his features at me. There was a fierce glint in his eye. Hoar frost. He said, "Terrible isn't it? I'm trying to get a cup of tea."

I was shocked. His words were an exact echo of what he said to me from the darkened doorway that time, the day I put him in a cab and sent him up to GoPoint. It was like I was suddenly back there for a moment, as if there had been a wrinkle in time.

I heard Otto say, "No problem, mate, I'll fetch you a cup of tea."

Otto winked at me. I don't think Seamus was supposed to have spotted the wink, but he did, and I saw him stiffen. Something passed across his face. He glanced between Otto and me as if we might be part of some conspiracy. I know it's a small thing, but I wished Otto hadn't winked at me like that.

"No," said Seamus, "Let 'im fetch it. You stay here with me."

I didn't mind being errand boy and I said so. "How do you like it, Seamus? Milk? Sugar?"

"Milk and three sugars. Get a cup for Otto, will ya? He's been good to me, he has. Deserves a cup of tea. My old mucker. Here, take this. I don't want it any more."

He handed me something that had been rolled into a cylinder. It was wrapped in a dirty red-and-white-chequered scarf: a traditional, tasselled Arab *shemagh*.

"Don't look at it now," he said. "It's what I know. Put it in your pocket for later."

I wasn't about to argue with him so I did as he instructed and made my way—slowly—out of the sandbagged area and back to the command point, where a huddle of police officers and Antonia watched my approach. I now saw they had marksmen in the shadows with high-velocity rifles trained on Seamus. It all seemed completely over the top. But I supposed there was the Queen to think about.

The commander, Antonia and all the others looked at me without saying a word as I drew up beside the police Land Rover. I said, "He wants a cup of tea."

Someone released a jet of air from between his teeth.

"He wants three sugars," I said apologetically.

"We can do that," said the police commander. He looked towards his junior ranks and someone went off to fix it. "We're here for days sometimes. So tea we have. Do you think he's wired?"

"I couldn't tell," I confessed. "Otto doesn't think so. There's something under his coat but I've no idea what it is."

I could hear an audio loop playing from behind the Land Rover. Seamus and Otto were talking. They had a video link, too. I realised they'd monitored every movement and every word when I'd been with Seamus. The tea arrived. Two plastic cups.

"Keep him talking." The commander said. "That's all I want you to do."

The tea was so hot it was burning my fingers through the thin plastic cups. I nodded and turned back towards the railings, trying not to spill the tea. Then I saw a white flash of light and was almost knocked backwards off my feet, spilling the tea every which way. A deafening bang sucked all subsequent sound out of the square and a twist of braided, black smoke funnelled up into the air.

Electronic car alarms, triggered by the blast, squealed everywhere. From somewhere an old-fashioned hammer-bell was clanging and policemen were running in all directions. My knees had buckled under me. The air reeked of something like ammonia. I tried to get up but my knees seemed to turn to slush and I went sprawling.

Antonia ran over to me, to help me up. We both looked back at the spot where Seamus and Otto had been. The railings where Seamus had chained himself were twisted horribly. A black ball-cloud hung over the spot, hardly seeming to move: it was like the air had been shocked into stillness. Antonia looked at me hard, searching, searching. Her own eyes were grey storms.

Alarms were still warning, uselessly; police were still running to and fro; and people in the crowd behind the Victoria statue were screaming. For some reason I looked at the palace guard beyond the sandbags in his grey coat and bearskin hat.

He'd moved. They're not supposed to move. But he'd moved.

Chapter 12

The police officers at the scene told us to stay exactly where we were, but it was Antonia who said to hell with that, and we slipped away in all the confusion. "If we don't go now," she'd said to me, "we'll be kept here and interviewed for hours."

I admire that. I admire someone who can make a decision in a moment of universal panic.

Antonia came home with me. She was anxious to see that I was all right. We walked back towards Pimlico where we managed to pick up a cab. When we got to my house, Antonia put the kettle on. But I said I'd had enough of tea for one evening and I opened a superior Pfeifer Vineyard Pinot Noir, guzzling it, which was ridiculous. I invited Antonia to have a glass before I drank it all myself, it being rather special.

"I wouldn't know the difference," she said.

"Of course you would," I said crossly. "People are always pretending not to know the difference between muck and brass."

She smiled faintly and accepted a glass.

"Why on Earth would he kill Otto, too?" I said.

"You sure the thing wasn't detonated accidentally?"

I looked hard at her. Antonia had moving crinkles, what people call laughter lines—rivulets made by tear-tracks more like—around her eyes. She also looked like she needed a good bath. I mean a real good soaking in hot, soapy water. She'd aggregated to herself the ingrained filth of the long-term homeless.

That's what I wanted to do for Antonia: take off her clothes and soak her in my bath, and sponge her very gently and slowly until she would stand up and the water would run from her body and this crust, this carapace of dirt and twisted care and worn-out compassion would crack open and fall from her pink, naked body and I could put a towel around her and keep her with me, here, where we could turn our backs on all of it and she could join me in my retreat from life.

Antonia got up and started inspecting my lounge, studying the prints hanging on the wall, sipping from her wine glass, touching objects around the room. "You live very well here, don't you?"

Was this my big chance to ask her to come down off her cross and live with me? Antonia was not conventionally beautiful, but she was the light of the world. What a project, if I could steal her from the world, and keep her all to myself.

"It's my hideaway."

"What are you hiding from?"

"Demons."

"Ahh, yes. Those."

"Don't mock. Seamus was crawling with them. They were like lice in his scalp. He detonated that bomb deliberately."

"Let me tell you what he did. He deloused himself before he died. He shaved his head. He was a victim, William, not of demons, but of evil people who sent him to a hell of their making and told him he was doing good. He couldn't stand it when he found out they'd deceived him. That's why he killed himself."

"But Otto was his best friend on Earth. He said as much himself. Why kill Otto?"

"He was protecting Otto," she said, "from the world."

"You're mad."

"Many people think so."

"Do you want to stay here? Stay the night? I have a spare room."

"You want a madwoman in your house? I would stay, William, but not in your spare room. I'd want to fuck you, and I'd like that, but it would mean too much to you."

I almost dropped my glass. "What?"

"You're the sort of person who takes sex too seriously. It has a religious significance for people like you. You get too attached. So, no, I won't stay. I'm going to save you from yourself. Someone will come for you but it's not me."

Antonia said she needed to get back to GoPoint. There would be all kinds of confusion and questions. She put down her glass, kissed me lightly and left. I went to the door and shouted after her to see if I could get her a cab, but she just waved and disappeared into the night. I was left standing there wondering who the heck had brought up the subject of sex, and who between us had just turned down whom.

Women. You've got more chance of figuring out Minkowski's mathematical theorem of four-dimensional space.

I went back indoors and flicked through the TV channels. Soon enough I found a live report from the scene of the explosion. Without being named, two men were pronounced dead at the scene. The cameras were at some distance and the police had taped off the blast area. Whatever remained of Otto and Seamus, there was nothing to see. I was slightly taken aback to see a tiny bit of footage of me when I was talking with Seamus. On the sequence shown I turned my body towards him in a way that fully shielded the moment when he handed something to me. In the commotion, I'd completely forgotten about whatever Seamus had passed on to me, but the footage reminded me with a start.

I switched off the TV and went to my coat. There it was in my pocket: the cylindrical shape wrapped in the red-and-white Arab scarf. The scarf had been tied in a tight knot, but eventually I managed to tease it undone.

It was an exercise book, like a child might use in school, rolled up tight. I flicked it open. On the first page was a sharply drawn pencil illustration of a kind of military coat of arms. It was stylized, like a tattooist's art. Three feathers inside a knot of rope, all crowned. Fancy scrollwork underneath the design simply read: *Ich dien*. I knew that to be German for *I serve*. It was a well-executed drawing. Underneath it was a drawing of a butterfly. Even though that too was executed in neat pencil strokes, I could see that it was meant to be a Red Admiral butterfly.

But the rest of the exercise book was filled with tiny, cramped writing. Every line had been filled and on many pages the spaces between the lines had been filled, too. The writing was so small that it was almost impenetrable.

I tried to read some of it, and though I could make it out it occurred to me that studying it would be a serious job, and that I might even need a magnifying glass of some sort to read it comfortably.

It hadn't escaped me that the police would at some point want to talk to me. I had no idea whether they had seen the exercise book pass from Seamus to me, but as they had recorded every detail, they would surely study the footage and realize what had happened. Unless, of course, my body had shielded the transaction from the police cameras in the same way that it had from the news cameras.

I did pause to ask myself why it mattered. After all, I could simply pick up the phone and tell the police that the man had passed me an exercise book filled with scrawl, and did they want to inspect it? But I didn't want to. For some reason that wasn't entirely plain even to me, I didn't want them to have it.

When Seamus sent me away to fetch him a cup of tea he was making safe the contents of his exercise book. He didn't want a cup of tea at all. He knew exactly what he was doing and he knew exactly who I was: the city geezer who had sent him to GoPoint.

He fully intended to take Otto with him when he detonated the explosives, but he did want to pass on his document. And he'd chosen at that moment, just before his death, to entrust the notebook to me.

And I wanted to inspect the writings before I let anyone else see them.

I'd converted the spare room of the house into a small home-working office years ago. I went there and spent almost two hours photocopying Seamus's journal. It wasn't easy. With the writing being so small, the quality of the print had to be very good and sometimes the definition wasn't up to muster. But finally I had it all. I filed away the photocopies in a drawer full of bank statements and prepared myself to have a good look at Seamus's journal.

Before returning to the lounge I unearthed a high-spec magnifying glass I kept on hand for the book forgeries. I opened a second bottle of Pinot Noir, inserted a Kraftwerk CD into the player, switched on a reading lamp and settled into my armchair.

The phone rang.

It was the police. A woman from SO13, the Met's Anti-Terrorist Branch. Which meant of course that Seamus was being regarded as a terrorist, rather than the mentally ill old soldier that he really was. The woman on the line told me they had been trying to track me down since the incident. I pointed out that I'd been home for some hours, so they couldn't have been trying very hard. She ignored my remark. Someone would be along to speak with me, she said.

"Can't it wait until the morning?" I asked.

"I'm afraid it can't," she said. "We'd like you to remain where you are until we've debriefed you."

Debriefed. That was her word. At least that suggested they didn't suspect me of any entanglement with Seamus.

I hid the exercise book behind a row of paperbacks on my

bookcase. Then I switched the TV on again to look for some more news while I awaited the knock on the door. The incident was still headlining. Though I knew it would only be hours before Seamus would become a casualty of the larger war of indifference.

While waiting up I had a disgraceful thought: one of the buyers for my forgery was now dead. This made it imperative that we close the sale with Ellis. If he dropped out we would have to start looking for a buyer all over again—a process that might take months.

I waited until one o'clock in the morning before going to bed. The knock on the door never came.

Chapter 13

I couldn't really go out the next day. I'd been instructed by the Police Terrorist Special Whatever Unit to wait for someone to come and interview me. It felt like house arrest. I had an attack of impatience in the middle of a bowl of Special Krunch cereal (having been rewarded for achieving middle age by occasional bouts of constipation, I was always impressed and heartened by Special Krunch) and put down my bowl to dial 1471. But of course, semi-secret agencies tend not to leave a call-back number.

I'd wanted to find out when I might be visited. I could instead just go about my daily business but, preposterously, I felt that might somehow incriminate me. I reached down the telephone directory and found the standard number for the Met.

"Hello," I said to the officer who answered, "can I speak to someone from the SO13 Anti-Terrorist Unit or whatever it's called. Please?"

"Who is calling?"

I had to give my name and my address and my telephone number all before being invited to explain what my call was about. I was then informed that my message would be passed on and that someone would call me back. No sooner had I finished my Special Krunch than the phone ring. A woman from SO13 told me that I would be visited before noon.

"Noon?" I said. "I haven't heard anyone use the word 'noon'

94

in quite a while. Normally people say 'mid-day.'"

"Goodbye," she said.

In the moment I put the receiver down my doorbell rang. When I went to the door, it was indeed a gentleman displaying an ID card and announcing that he was from SO13.

"Hell, that was quick."

"What?"

"I was joking." Perhaps it was the crunchy cereal that was making me light and humorous in what were, after all, very serious circumstances. In any case the gentleman gave me a look which said, *we don't do jokes in the Special Terror Whatever.* "You'd better come in."

He was a ginger, or more precisely a copperhead, with a trimmed beard and refreshing, unblinking blue eyes. He was very short, with a long raincoat that he refused to take off, even though I warned him that I had my central heating thermostat turned up high. He took out an old-style spiral-bound notepad and pen. We went through it all, how I knew Seamus, how I'd come to be there with Antonia, how I knew Otto. He particularly wanted to know what Seamus had said to me when Otto and I had been talking to him at the railings. I told him everything I could recall, all of it, right down to the Queen eating pie in the palace.

"He said he had a secret he wanted to tell the Queen."

"What secret? What was the secret?"

I coughed. "I've no idea. There probably was no secret, unless it was something about you boys bumping off Princess Di. You didn't do that, did you? Are you sure you don't want to take your coat off? You look pretty hot sitting there."

"How do you know there was no secret?"

"Look, Seamus was a homeless dosser. Mentally disturbed."

"Did he give you anything?"

"No. Why would he give me anything?"

"You are absolutely certain he didn't give you anything before you came back for the tea?"

"Certain of it, why?"

"We have a witness who says he saw something pass between Seamus and yourself."

"Witness? What witness?"

"It was the guardsman in his box outside the palace. He was about a hundred and fifty yards away but he says he saw something pass."

Of course. The guardsman. I slapped my brow with my hand, suddenly "remembering." "But yes!" I jumped to my feet, and he did, too. "The explosion drove it clean out of my mind. He gave me a rolled-up scarf. It should still be in my coat pocket."

I walked out into the hall, quite relieved that I'd returned Seamus's Arab headscarf to my coat pocket, and without the exercise book. The detective was very quick to follow me out into the hall. I went for the left pocket of my coat first, then "found" it in my right pocket. "Here it is." I made as if to unwrap the scarf. "What on Earth can it be?"

He reached for it but I was too quick for him and I stepped back.

"You're going to have to give that to me, Mr. Heaney."

"Can't I even look to see what it is? He did give it to me, after all."

"It's evidence. I'm sorry. We might be able to return it to you later."

For one foolish moment I thought about holding it high in the air like the school bully with a satchel, to make the short-arse jump for it. I yielded it up to him.

"Thank you," he said. With that, he returned to the lounge and collected his notebook and pen. It seemed he was done with me.

"Can I go out now?" I asked him.

What was making me fret to go out was my lunch appointment.

Somehow I'd made that arrangement with Yasmin, the lovely and intriguing woman from the Museum Tavern, and I still didn't know how or why I'd agreed to it. I wasn't certain what the point of our meeting was. I had a nagging feeling that it was what people tend to call a date.

Whatever, something made me rather nervous when I walked into The Plumber's Arms on Lower Belgrave Street. It's a slightly scruffy little waterhole, but a welcome relief from the wilderness that is Victoria. Half of the regulars in there were probably present the night in 1974 when a bloodstained and terrified Lady Lucan ran in after Lord Lucan had murdered the maid and high-tailed it. Our splendid aristocrats, they don't mess about, do they? The pub is all right but I keep seeing Lady Lucan's ghastly eyes peeping at me.

Anyway, she was there, having arrived early to save a table for us in the busy pub. Yasmin, I mean, not Lady Lucan.

She smiled. She had a glass of red wine on the table waiting for me and it was exactly the same colour as her lipstick. I don't know if this was deliberate. A trick. The light from behind the bar reflected in the wine, and her eyes, too, ran with warm catch-light. Her hair looked different from the time I'd met her in the Museum Tavern: a darker, richer mahogany contrasting with her pale skin. Her pretty dress left her arms bare. One of her exposed arms rested on the copper-topped table. A thin but expensive-looking bracelet glimmered at her wrist, drawing attention to her pale skin and the tiny blue veins at the crook of her elbow.

I sat down and unwound my silk scarf. She looked at me without blinking. Denied the ritual of ordering a drink, I felt it necessary to look away, at the bar, at the pictures on the wall, anywhere. Then I looked back at her and her eyebrow moved, I swear, microscopically.

"Well," I said.

"Well."

"You look lovely," I managed.

"Thank you." She hitched the slender strap of her dress a little higher on her shoulder.

"Have you looked at the menu?" I asked her. Two large cards lay on the table next to her white-skinned and beautifully veined arm. I grabbed one, grateful that it was the folding variety behind which I could hide my face for a moment. When I emerged to express a preference for a baguette, her hand was cupping her chin and she was still smiling at me. She summoned a waiter and ordered a baguette for each of us.

"I'm sorry," I said, "but I can't remember what our meeting is about."

She affected a stifled scream. "Haha!" she went. "Haha!"

I'm not sure why, because my question had been serious. I think. "What I mean is, I can't remember whether it was me who asked you here, or you who asked me."

"I think we asked each other."

"We did?"

"Yes, we did."

She flared her eyes slightly at me, and the gesture reminded me of someone, but I couldn't place who it was. I put the thought out of my mind. She had very mobile eyes: by which I mean that whereas some people's eyes are muddy and flat, hers seemed to be in a kind of constant flickering motion. It made me think of the invisible machine code behind a computer monitor. At least, I preferred to think it betokened a lively intelligence rather than an automaton.

Most of the lunchtime customers around us wore business suits. I asked her where she worked and she told me a little about it. When I asked her how long she'd worked there, she said too long. She obviously found it a boring subject because she kept trying to turn the conversation back onto me. I recognised the trick, and so I kept trying to do the same to her. Every so often while she was talking she would—completely unconsciously—

delicately hitch the strap of her dress a little higher onto her shoulder. I don't think for a second that this was deliberate, but this reflex kept drawing my attention to her shoulders and to her neck.

The baguettes arrived. Before taking a bite, I said, "Are you certain you didn't ask me first? To come here, I mean."

"Well, yes, but I was responding to you."

I chewed on that for a moment. "You responded to me?"

"Yes. To the way you looked at me. When we were in the Museum Tavern."

"Excuse me," I said lightly, "but I don't think I looked at you in any particular way. In the Museum Tavern."

"Really?" She was able to match my levity perfectly. "Must have been my mistake."

I cast my mind back to that day. I'm pretty good at disguising my thoughts and feelings, and I'm certain I gave nothing away. Not that there was anything to give away. Except that I do remember finding her attractive, and feeling a stab of envy that Ellis was probably intimate with her, though she couldn't possibly have seen that. Then a nasty thought resurfaced. Perhaps Ellis had asked Yasmin to spy on me. Perhaps she'd been sent to check out the book deal. That would at least explain her unnatural interest in me.

"How's Brother Ellis?" I asked mildly.

"Brother Ellis? I wouldn't know. Haven't seen much of him."

"Really? You don't see him any more?"

"I never was *seeing* him, actually. He was just a friend."

"A friend."

"You don't like him, do you?"

"I'd rather have my ears cut off than have to listen to his poetry."

"As I say: he's in the past."

"And what's in the future?"

She blinked at me. The long, steady blink. "Do you believe

people can speak to you without saying anything? That day, in the Museum Tavern. You looked at me and you spoke to me. Without even opening your mouth."

"I did? What did I say? Without opening my mouth."

"Oh, I can't tell you today. I will tell you. But not today."

I laughed. Not a social laugh or a polite laugh, or a let's-oil-the-conversation sort of laugh. It was unforced, a real chuckle, of the type that hadn't been triggered in a woman's presence in years. "Yasmin, you're a strange one!" I said.

"I am. Your glass is empty. Shall we have another?"

Chapter 14

The next morning, after Fraser had slept off his bloody nose and I'd snored off my half-dozen pints of beer, I went back to his room. He was up and about. He invited me to inspect the damage I'd done to his proboscis. It had turned a peppery-burgundy hue, but I wasn't in a sympathetic mood. I wanted answers.

"I need breakfast," he said. "Let's talk on the way to the refectory."

The refectory was located in one of the much larger redbrick lodges a few hundred yards further up the Uttoxeter New Road. We had to walk past a Victorian cemetery populated with stone angels and divided from the pavement by black iron railings. Then we had to climb a short hill to get into the all-female building housing the refectory. Fraser walked very fast.

"What was all that about the dog? About someone not liking dogs?" I said.

"Some*thing*," he corrected. "Not someone."

"What *something*? What exactly?"

He coughed into his hand. "I seem to have called something into being."

I glanced over my shoulder. One of the stone angels in the graveyard, wings at half-pinion, hovered behind me. For some reason my voice lowered to a whisper. "Look, you're not making any sense."

He suddenly became angry, but he didn't break his walking pace. "What the fuck do you want me to say? I don't know myself what I've done! What can I tell you when I don't know!"

Some of the other students heading towards the refectory noticed him shouting at me as we turned off the main road and approached the gates of the female lodge. "These rituals," I said calmly, "this chalk on the floor."

"Yes," he said. "I don't know what it is I've done. But the thing I called up. It's still there."

I stopped dead in my tracks, and he did the same. "What?"

"What I said."

I looked hard into his eyes and saw real fear. His irritating bravado was all gone. He looked like what he was: a frightened kid way out of his depth.

A hundred questions swarmed into my mind, all competing to get to the front of the queue. The road to the gates of the lodge suddenly felt like a narrowing gauntlet. In the jostling and the chaos I remained dumbfounded; I couldn't think straight. A few tobacco-coloured leaves caught in a breeze swarmed around my heels. Fraser started to walk on again.

I quickly caught up with him, but we paced the next hundred yards in silence. Finally I heard myself saying, "This thing you called up. What is it?"

"I don't know."

"What does it look like?"

"Shadow. But you sense it more than see it. And a strange scent; there's always a strange smell that comes with it."

We walked through the swing doors into the refectory and took our places in the queue for the canteen. There were other students immediately in front of us as we picked up our plastic trays, and more students filed in line behind us. It was impossible to discuss this further.

I took my plate of greasy bacon and eggs and toast, and filled a mug with steaming grey coffee. There was a tremor in my stomach. Perhaps Fraser had little appetite, too, because he opted for cornflakes. We found a place in the corner but no sooner had we laid our trays on the table than were we joined by another student.

"Mornin', stranger!"

It was Mandy, my girlfriend, a cheery, leggy, hard-as-nails Yorkshire lass. Mandy had a slightly witchy look: long, jet-black hair and swimming-pool-blue eyes, and a stack of silver rings pierced through one ear. She was one of the five girls in the constellation of photographs. Fraser stiffened.

The "stranger" routine was slightly barbed because I hadn't seen her for a couple of nights. "Mandy, this is Charles."

"I've seen you around," Mandy said genially. "What did you do to your nose?"

"Tripped on the stairs."

Mandy quickly lost interest in him and turned back to me. "Where you been hiding?"

Fraser was staring at me. Maybe he was nervous about how much I might tell Mandy. I made an elaborate performance of buttering my toast. "Hiding. Now let me see. Where have I been hiding?" There was a pause. I looked at Fraser, and he looked at me.

"Have you two been smoking, this early in the day?" Mandy said with disgust.

"No," I said truthfully.

She cuffed me playfully on the back of my head: that was her way. "Liar." She was onto something; she just didn't know what. "You're giving each other some pretty far-out spaces if you haven't."

I hid myself behind my breakfast again. After a moment I felt her tanned arm and her silver bracelet laid across my own arm. I looked up and she was smiling at me. At that moment someone dropped a tray of dishes near the canteen serving hatch; an action which for reasons utterly mysterious to me was always rewarded with a loud communal cheer. While Fraser's attention was distracted, Mandy made eyes at me as if to ask me why I was hanging out with him.

But I was unable to respond, and Mandy soon had to leave to make her sociology lecture. As she gathered up her things to leave, she said, "You heard about Sandie English?"

I looked up. So did Fraser. Sandie was one of those girls who was a pillar of the Christian Union student society, but who had dark sexual appetites she kept pretty much secret. "What about Sandie English?"

"You know she had a peanut allergy?"

"I knew that."

"She went to a wedding. Ate a sandwich from the buffet with peanut traces and it killed her."

"What?"

Mandy looked at Fraser. "She was one of William's ex-girlfriends," she said. Then she added, rather unnecessarily, "One of William's *many* ex-girlfriends."

What Mandy couldn't know was that Sandie was one of the girls in Fraser's photo-gallery.

Fraser swallowed. "Happens all the time," he said.

"What?" I challenged. "Being killed by a peanut?" I was shocked. We hadn't gone out together for long but I had met Sandie's parents. They were lovely folk. In fact, I'd liked Sandie's parents more than I liked her. I was trying to think how they would feel. They would be destroyed.

"Sure," said Fraser.

I shook my head. Mandy had to leave so I made arrangements to see her later. Fraser held out his hand to her looking for a handshake, a gesture thoroughly unfashionable amongst students at the time. "Bye. Nice to meet you."

Mandy shook his hand before leaving, but in a way that clearly left her with the challenge of having to decide whether to find a washbasin before attending her lecture.

"Phew!" Fraser said after she'd gone.

"What do you mean, *phew!*" I said sharply. I knew perfectly well what he meant by *phew.* Just about every male in the college, student or staff, felt *phew!* when they stood next to Mandy. It was like standing next to the open door of a furnace. But it enraged me that he'd just heard about the death of one of the five girls in the photographs and his only response was this oily flirting with my girlfriend.

"I'm just saying you're a lucky guy," Fraser said.

"Yeh? Well, don't say anything, right? Say nothing."

"Keep your hair on!"

I had a nine thirty lecture to think about. Alexander Pope. I made a quick decision that I was going to have to miss it. I told Fraser he was going to have to miss his lecture, too. Ignoring his protests, I collected up our respective trays and returned them to the serving hatch, and then I marched him back to Friarsfield Lodge.

I'd decided he was going to show me exactly what he'd done.

"What, you want me to repeat the ritual?"

"No, you moron, I just want you to describe exactly what you did and how you did it."

"It's not connected, you know. This thing we just heard about Sandie."

"I know that, you fucking freak. Do you think I'm simple? I just want to know what you did."

Fraser let me back into his room, which I'd now decided had an odour of mushrooms and toadstools. He showed me a few trinkets—candle holders, salt vats, various incense sticks like sandalwood and myrrh and patchouli. Then he started to describe how he'd drawn the markings on the floor of the attic and repeated a set of incantations.

I interrupted him. "But how did you know what to do? What to draw on the floor? Which words to use? All that?"

He blinked at me. "I got it from a book."

"What book, for fuck's sake?"

"Well, I'd been collecting books on the subject for a while. Then I found one by accident."

"So you just followed the instructions? Doesn't it tell you how to… get rid of… whatever."

"No, it wasn't complete."

"Complete?" I had a sudden bad feeling about this.

"It wasn't all there. It was a book and a manuscript I found in the attic."

The room swam. "You found a manuscript in the attic?"

"It was just lying around up there. Almost like it was waiting for me to find it."

"Show it me! Show me the book!" I felt dizzy. I wanted to throw up.

"Okay, calm down. It's here."

He had a hiding place for it, obviously to keep it well away from the attention of Dick Fellowes. He pulled a drawer all the way out of a cupboard and turned it over on his bed, emptying its contents of socks and underwear and t-shirts onto the scruffy duvet. Taped to the underside of the drawer was a brown padded envelope. He opened the envelope and withdrew the book he'd been referring to. Or to be technically correct, it was part of a yellowing book. The cover had gone astray, the spine had been torn off and perhaps the entire back half of the book was missing. Interleaved with some of the remaining pages were several sheets of onion-skin paper, on which were etched in black India ink and in fine, elegant handwriting a series of diagrams and descriptions of rituals.

I felt faint as I took the thing from Fraser's hands. You see, it was quite familiar to me. The book belonged to me. What's more, I was the author of the supplementary manuscript.

Chapter 15

We drank five or six glasses of wine each in the Plumber's Arms that afternoon, and we talked about I know not what. After the second glass I'd said I had work to get back to; and Yasmin said so had she. But I said oh heck let's have another and she said heck why not. After that third glass she dialled her employer on her mobile phone and said she'd eaten something at lunchtime that had disagreed with her and that she wouldn't be in. She looked me in the eye as she made the call.

That's youth for you. The cavalier lie. The irresponsible fib. The offhand disrespect for consequences. The casual dishonesty that conjures the excitement of an open narrative for their lives. I took out my own mobile and dialled Val, and told her I was feeling a little under the weather and that I probably wouldn't return to the office that afternoon.

Neither of us commented on what we'd just done, or the significance of the fact that we'd just cleared the next few hours simply to be together. But we'd changed into a smoother, less grinding gear, and we both felt the pleasure of the open highway ahead. We celebrated by ordering a fourth glass of wine.

Is it possible to fall for someone because of the way they hitch the strap of their dress? Why would that bundle of contingencies we call love fasten and feed on such a small thing? But as we talked I kept waiting, almost impatiently, greedily, for her to do it again. And there was another thing: this feeling that she reminded me of someone. Yet I didn't take that too seriously because it had happened when I'd got mixed up with Fay. It's a conjuring trick of nature, a phantom and a deception. You somehow feel that you must have known this person in another life; that you were waiting for them to slot into your world, like a missing jigsaw piece, or a lost chord. It's in the eye: there in the compression of the pupil or the glitter around the iris. You recognize that person and yet you don't, so therefore it can't be the hideous randomness of biology; it has to be destiny, it has to be a spiritual reunion of some kind, a rediscovery, a planetary alignment, a coming home.

This is the fraudulent demon of falling in love. It is categorised by Goodridge as demon number five hundred and sixty-seven. Almost everyone is prey to this demon at some time in their lives; for some fools, several times over. (And do not be tempted to attribute any special significance to its number, because if you do so you will fall victim to the numerologist's demon, which weaves its vicious web out of mere coincidence.)

I don't believe in this notion of "falling in love." I think we fall in sex, and after sex we have to either stand up for love or scarper. By which I mean love won't take things lying down. By which I mean the four glasses of wine were affecting me more than they would normally, and the things I was thinking were alarming me.

Most of all I was thinking: please don't let this turn into a love story at my time of life. Anything but that, because noone has any sympathy for that any more. And anyway I'd been banned from being in love. I'd inoculated myself.

"How old are you?" I asked her.

"Twenty-nine. But inside I'm older. Wiser."

"How did you come by your wisdom?"

Ah, then she did that thing: lightly hitched the strap on her shoulder, and looked round at the slowly emptying pub. Lunchtime was over, and most of the customers were not stuck there, like I was, like a fly in a spoon of honey. She said, "Do you think it's possible that some people could live a full life, let's say live through wars, fall in love many times, see regimes change around them and go on to die without being any the wiser?'

"I'm sure it happens."

The thing is, we were saying all these things but it wasn't like a real conversation. We were just making noises. Singing to each other, almost. Finding points of harmony. Exchanging old jokes. It didn't have to mean anything. After the sixth glass of wine—or was it the fifth or the seventh?—we were the only people left in the bar besides the staff. Tucked in a little corner. Her graceful, pale hand still lay flat upon the table. Mine too, fingertips a few centimetres from hers. Yet the gap between those fingertips was a canyon, a rocky desert. I knew that like a superhero I could leap that chasm in a single bound. I also knew that I must not. Would not.

I stumbled out to the toilets at the back of the pub. There I washed my hands and threw some cold water on my face. I stood there for a minute or two regarding myself in the mirror. For some reason I thought of how it would sound to Stinx and Diamond Jaz; or to my secretary Val; or to Fay and the children for goodness sake.

"What? What?"—and here's the mad thing: I actually said this to myself in the mirror, as if I was having a real argument with the man reflected there—"We had a few glasses of wine together, that's all!"

This robust defence with self was interrupted by a barman who swung into the Gents. He'd clearly heard me barking because he looked at me oddly before disappearing into one of the stalls. I pretended I'd been singing some death metal rock lyrics of the kind my son used to play in his bedroom at maximum volume. I don't think I convinced the barman in the stalls.

And of course it *was* nothing. Just a few drinks with a strange and pert young woman, about whom I knew nothing. I pulled myself together and returned to find her in the bar.

"Thought you'd abandoned me," she said lightly.

"I wouldn't do that."

Because it wasn't nothing. It was too much of something. I could feel myself going into a crash, so I had to pull out. I sat back in my chair. I looked at my watch.

She sensed the line go slack, so started talking about the television. She said she might have been mistaken but she thought she'd seen my face picked up by the news cameras the night before, outside Buckingham Palace.

"Bloody awful business," was all I could think of saying about it.

There was an uncomfortable pause and then, "Shall we go for a stroll along the Embankment? It's what I like doing best in all the world."

I was relieved, and eager to leave the Plumber's Arms, but the question of where to next was more than I could resolve. I was so way out of practice with women—and certainly with women of her generation—that I feared the obvious. If she'd said, *Your place or mine?* I would have needed to turn her down without knowing how. Then again, I was thrilled by her proximity: I'd spent the last few hours wanting to trace the blue veins on her pale white arms; plus something about her scent was maddening me; plus I wanted to taste on her mouth the wine we'd been drinking. But I wasn't ready or willing for any of this. The curve of descent was too steep.

But neither did I want to stop the conversation, whatever it was about. So we walked along the Embankment, from Lambeth Bridge, past the Houses of Parliament and on. It was cold, but dry cold. She linked her arm in mine, quite naturally, and though I stiffened at first I quickly relaxed. There was a diffuse sun, spinning a hint of lime on the Thames. London hurtled along at its breakneck business on either side of the river, but not where we were. We strolled all the way up to Blackfriars Bridge and it seemed but a few steps. I've walked there a hundred times, but on this occasion it was all new-minted. The chill wind from the water only made me more sensitive to the warmth of her body beside me; the winter light flaking the air seemed like a bright stage radiance; the engine of the city diminished to a purr, far away, harmless to our inviolable space.

At Blackfriars we stood for a while, trying to say goodbye, not knowing what to do next. I saw the flapping ghost of the Vatican banker hanged by his enemies under the arch of the bridge at low tide just a few years ago: it was just a phantom, mere history, fading.

"Shall we see each other again?" she said.

"You want to?"

"I just said so, didn't I?"

"When?"

I wanted to say, *In five minutes. Now.* I wondered if the next night would be too soon. Then I remembered it was the Candlelight Club the next night. I felt a stab of irritation that I had to see Stinx and Jaz when I wanted to be with Yasmin. I hadn't even left her company and already I was prepared to ditch my good friends to be with her again. Where is the sense in that? "Thursday? Can you do Thursday?"

"Where?"

"Do we have to decide now? I'll call you."

"Okay."

She stood with her arms at her sides, looking at me without blinking. I leaned over to offer a farewell peck on her cheek, but in my clumsiness, or maybe *our* clumsiness, our lips grazed each other's. A dry-lipped kiss, a kiss on lips made cold by the chilly air. But I felt something pass between her lips and mine, a fine thing, like smoke but sweeter, like a promise but less precise.

And yet it wasn't even a kiss. If she was Ellis's spy, she was taking the game all the way.

A tugboat on the river hooted its pleasure or derision at us,

I didn't know which. The light was fading fast as I watched her hail a passing taxi and climb in. I already envied the cab driver her company.

Chapter 16

Naturally I didn't say anything about all this to Stinx and Diamond Jaz when I met up with them in the Viaduct Tavern the following evening. I say "naturally," when in fact the Candlelight Club was formed, and ostensibly still met, as a talk-shop; a tool for charting the contours of our respective romantic lives. That is to say, Jaz persisted with his chronic treks through green valleys and glittering mountain peaks of a Shangri-La that always turned overnight into some wind-blasted icy crevasse of doom; Stinx adhered to the rolling hills and dark forests of his affair with Lucy; and I stalked the flat, arid planes, reporting on nothing but my intermittent communication with Fay and the children. I didn't want to tell them about Yasmin. Not yet anyway. I wanted to protect her, us, from the gallows laughter that characterized an evening with the Candlelight Club.

Stinx looked at me, wiping creamy Guinness foam from his upper lip. "Somethin' different about him," Stinx said to Jaz.

Jaz took a light swig from his bottle of designer lager and squinted at me. "You're right. There is."

I glanced around the pub in a futile effort to dodge their attention. Wrong move. It only confirmed for them that they were onto something.

"Come on, my son. Out with it."

The Viaduct Tavern is definitely one of my personal favourites, not so busy in the evenings, and an original gin-palace. Dark

113

mahogany carved wood made airy by gilt, silver mirrors and engraved glass. On the marble wall are huge paintings of three busty maidens representing Agriculture, Banking and the Arts. The Arts is wounded, bayoneted in the buttock by a drunken solider during the First World War. The pub is built on the site of the old Newark hanging prison and the cellars are former prison cells for the cut-throats and scum of Victorian London.

And it has ghosts, of course. Loads of 'em. What with the vile prison conditions and the hangings and so on. Builders and cellarmen and plumbers are always complaining of someone unseen tapping them on the shoulder. Do I need to point out to you that ghosts and demons are not the same thing? Ghosts are the spirits of the dead, I guess. Not that I believe in them. Demons, on the other hand, are the spirits of the living.

"There was a kind of spring in his step when he came in tonight," Jaz says.

"Just what I thought," says Stinx. "Springy. Bouncy. *Boing!*"

Stinx was already flying when I got there, and Jaz was just winding him up higher and higher. I kept waiting for an opportunity, a lull in the conversation when I might ask about progress on the forgery. The fact that Stinx hadn't mentioned it himself wasn't a good sign. I found myself looking hard at the colour of his nose, to see if I could detect any extra burst capillaries or softened cartilage.

"*Boing!*" went Jaz.

They did a decent claret in the Viaduct. I drained my glass. "My round," I said, and I got up to go to the bar.

When I returned with a tray of drinks, Stinx and Jaz were regarding me steadily, but had fallen into silence. They both blinked. I blinked back. A few more minutes went by in complete, blinking silence. I think it was the longest silence I could remember since we'd first met.

"Right," I said, "if that's how you're going to play it, I *will* tell you. But not until the big hand is on the ten, by which time I will have drunk at least a full bottle."

"He's back with Fay," said Stinx. "That's it!"

Jaz shook his head. He was the more perceptive of the two. "No, it's something else. I think he's got a new squeeze."

Despite my poker face, some microscopic tic, or a tremor from a tiny nerve in my jaw, or the stiffening of a single hair in my eyebrow betrayed me. Jaz leapt to his feet and clapped his hands in delight, kicking his stool over in the process.

"Nonsense," I barked, too quickly, giving myself away again. Jaz was dancing now: an infuriating little exhibition of a dance that used to be called *the Twist*, with his arms held tight at his sides. Stinx was staring hard at me, a man both amazed and deeply impressed.

Jaz righted his stool and fell back into it. "Come on, William: the evening is yours."

"It's nothing," I said. "Nothing." I told them about my lunch with Yasmin, and our walk along the Embankment.

I was tossing them the bare bones to chew on, but they weren't satisfied. "Where did you say you had lunch?" Stinx objected. "Plumbers?" Then how comes, how comes you're going down the Embankment. After lunch you should be going the other way. Right?"

"I had the afternoon off."

"You had the afternoon off?" said Jaz. "And she had the afternoon off? What time did you part company?"

"Christ, this is like a police interrogation!"

"Guilty!" Stinx roared. The pair of them were hooting at me, nearly falling off their stools. I didn't see what was quite so funny, but they were riffing on my discomfort. Then Stinx got serious. "Why you being so cagey?"

I darted a glance over my shoulder. No one was listening to us, but I lowered my voice anyway. "It's going nowhere."

"Nah nah nah," said Stinx, wagging a nicotine-stained finger at me. "Don't fall for it. He's just trying to deflect attention."

So I went back and told them the whole thing, which remarkably wasn't much more than what I'd already disclosed. I mentioned the parting kiss. They listened like it was all hard news. Then they started to offer advice, as if they were suddenly and passionately dedicated to getting me laid.

Naturally the idea had crossed my mind—of course it had. It had been over three years since I'd had sex with anyone other than myself, and images of Yasmin naked had been rippling across the back of my retina with disconcerting variety. What I failed to tell them was that I didn't think that I needed any strategy or guile or cool or programme to make it happen. I hadn't admitted it to myself until that moment, but I felt that there was a shocking inevitability about it. I might make two jumps to the side or one on the diagonal, but it made no difference: if I wanted it to happen, it was going to happen.

But it couldn't be allowed.

Jaz was on his feet again. The prospect of me breaking my three years of celibacy called for champagne, he said.

"Oh lord," Stinx protested, "we'll probably end up in that sticky club with the footballers and the tarts. Speaking of which, Jaz has another mark."

A "mark" was Stinx's word for a prospective buyer of one of our fake books.

"Oh?"

"Only I want to tell you this: someone was asking round the other day. Did I know William Heaney? Did I know Jaz Singh?"

"Really?" I wondered if this was also something to do with Ellis. And possibly Yasmin.

"Look, William, I might be being paranoid, but it didn't smell right. I can't say more than that."

I took a deep sip of the noble and beneficial juice. We'd never had the police sniffing around before, but we'd all agreed it would come one day. It had to. I could explain it through the law of demonology, but for the time being think of it as the police protecting you night and day. "What does Jaz say about it?"

"He says you decide."

I'd never thought of myself as the "leader" of our little enterprise, but I suppose I was. I coordinated the buyer and the product; I advanced the money for materials to Stinx; I negotiated the price and ultimately delivered the product. I guess I was the *capo*.

When Jaz returned with the fizz, I let him fill three glasses before I asked him, "When did you identify the customer?"

He twigged instantly what we'd been talking about. "A week ago. That is, I told him I'd put him in touch with you."

"And when did this enquiry come, Stinx?"

"Three days ago. Stranger."

I didn't like it. "It's too close. What do you know about the customer?"

"Not much," Jaz said. "He's another one of these public schoolboy types. Ex-military. Gay. That's all."

"Does he have books?"

"No idea."

"You'll need to get inside his house, Jaz. Look at his bookshelves to see if he's for real."

"How will he do that?" Stinx wanted to know.

Jaz raised his glass. "Anyway, here's to the abolition of celibacy."

Well, guess what: we ended up in that bloody club again. I can never remember the name of the place because we always drink too much and my store of brain cells for the hour preceding entry therein and much of the two hours thereafter is washed away like writing in the sand. I worry about this. I worry about how much of my life is not available to me. I want total recall. I want the full set of records. I don't want to think that some sinister organization has stolen half of the files on my life like they did with the enquiry into the death of Princess Diana. I'm not expecting to present these records at the Pearly Gates, you understand: it's just that if I don't have all the evidence how can I judge myself?

Oh, bugger it, let's just call it the Red Club. I didn't mind. Jaz always insisted on covering the bill when we went there, and my funds had become seriously depleted after taking out the loan and making repayments at bank rates that would embarrass a vampire. I needed to have a word before Stinx got too smashed.

"Has Lucy come back?" I asked him.

He wiped his nose, and shook his head.

"Stinx, listen. I need to know if there's any progress on *Pride and Prejudice*."

His answer was to down his glass of fizzing champagne in one go and wave a large hand through the air. "It's coming. It's coming." He looked round the club for more interesting company.

"Come on, mate. I want an answer."

He patted my shoulder. "Relax, it's nearly there." Then he waddled off to find himself another drink.

I didn't like this club any more than I had the last time I was there. Tara my neighbourhood good-time girl was on show, but the footballers were different. Tara cheerfully introduced me to one of them. He was a nice lad, but I thought he looked a bit too young to be out so late.

"Do you make a living from it?" I asked him.

"Of course he does," Tara giggled. "He plays football for England!"

"Marvellous," I said. "This is what we want. More young men playing for England." I tipped back my glass and looked round for a way out of the conversation.

Tara waved at some more people entering the club and

the footballer touched my elbow. "I've done something a bit stupid."

"What?"

He stepped round to my other side. The music was quite loud. He had to stand on tiptoe to speak in my ear. "I've got journos on my back. Paps. All that."

I had no idea what he was talking about. I put down my glass, left him standing and made my way downstairs to the Gents, where an elegant Nigerian was working for tips. I was splashing the enamel, as it were, when the footballer came in, seemingly having followed me. He slipped a banknote to the toilet attendant and jerked a thumb over his shoulder. The attendant cleared off quickly. I turned and washed my hands, and what with the toilet attendant out of commission, I had the indignity of reaching for my own paper towel.

"I've got to get 'em off my back,' the footballer said. "Tara reckons you're well connected. There's a wedge in it for you."

"I can't help you," I said.

"I understand. I know all that. This is unofficial. Just between me and you. You're in government, right?"

"Government? What on Earth did she tell you? Haven't you got people at Chelsea to help you? Whatever it is you've done?"

"I don't play for Chelsea."

"No. Look, whatever Tara has told you, she's mistaken."

The young footballer grabbed my arm angrily. I looked at his hand on my arm and it was enough to make him back off. Then, to my astonishment, he turned to the washbasin and began to cry. He was just a boy. I'm not made of stone: I reached out a hand to try to console him but what I saw in the mirror made me leap back.

There was a demon hanging from him. And the demon looked desperately sad. I knew exactly what that meant.

My stomach lurched. I had to duck into one of the stalls and I retched, emptying the contents of my stomach, mostly red wine, into the ceramic bowl. The footballer hadn't even noticed. As I came out of the stall, the demon tried to make eye contact with me, but the sadness and the grief and the sudden stench of its presence made me race from the Gents. The attendant was lounging outside.

"Go in and help him," I said.

Back upstairs I got myself another glass of salvation and cadged a cigarette from Jaz.

"You all right?" he said. "You look a bit pale."

"Where's that bloody Tara?"

"She's under the table with a faded rock star. What's she done?"

"Oh, for God's sake!"

"William, chill out! Come on, sit down. We need to have a chat." Jaz led me to a corner sofa upholstered in ghastly red velour. The Red Club always made me feel as if we were inside a giant throat, rubbing up against a set of tonsils. He called for a waiter.

"Just water for me," I said. "I feel dizzy."

"Look, you've got to write me some more poems. These idiots want me to go on tour now."

"Tour? Where on tour?"

"Bloody South Africa."

"Christ, where will it all end?"

This was not encouraging news. A couple of years ago, Jaz and I had arranged a kind of hoax. The Regional Arts Council had a reputation for doling out grants—cash grants—to ethnic writers. For a laugh we'd cobbled up an application where I scribbled some truly god-awful poems and Jaz submitted them. The Arts Council in question salivated and bit his hand off. He was a godsend: Asian, gay, he filled in their minority categories, so they immediately rewarded Jaz with a five-thousand-pound *bursary*, I think was the word they used for it. When we'd stopped laughing, we invested the money in our book-counterfeiting enterprise with Stinx.

But the thing started to get a little out of hand. The broadsheet papers loved his face so much they couldn't stop featuring Jaz in their Arts pages. Well, he's a good-looking boy and what with my shit poetry they thought they were onto something. He was sought out to give public readings and tours and all the rest of it. I warned him to pretend to be a recluse or shy or whatever, but he insisted he could carry it off. And he could.

In fact, he lapped up the attention. The readings and the performances always seemed to draw an audience of people who wanted to do more than admire his poetry. Next thing I knew he was reciting my doggerel at the South Bank and at the Institute of Contemporary Arts. Now the bloody British Council was sponsoring him on international tours! Worse than that, I hadn't got the heart to stop it all because Jaz was donating every single penny he made from this poetry hoax to GoPoint.

"You've got to give me some new material," Jaz said. "I can't keep reading the same old stuff."

"What do you want," I said dryly, "Asian-Gay or Gay-Asian?"

"Something rather lighter, I feel. My recent stuff has been getting a bit… miserablist."

I gave him an old-fashioned look. The problem with this game was that the bigger his reputation became on the poetry circuit, the more difficult it was to kill him off. Jaz knew everyone in poetry. He was the one who had introduced me to Ellis, after the near-laureate had written a splendid and scintillating review of Jaz's poetry in some literary rag. Ellis was even supposed to be providing me—sorry, Jaz—with a cover blurb when my/his/our anthology was published by Cold Chisel Press later in the year. Ellis said he was a fan and had invited Jaz to dinner one night; that was how Jaz had discovered his interest in antiquarian books, and that's how I'd originally met Ellis.

Sitting in the Red Club and thinking about Ellis made me think of Yasmin, of course. How I wanted to be with her. Just talking. I felt I could tell her everything. About the fake books and the forged poetry; about my paranoia that we would inevitably get caught for these scams; about the haunted footballer; about Fay and the children; about demons and how it all started.

Jaz was talking but his voice was like a radio station struggling for bandwidth, drifting in and out. I looked around me at the swollen red walls. They seemed to be veined and twisted and pulsating slightly, like a giant larynx. I had a horrible insight of myself and all the other people in the club as individuated fragments in the gagging throat of a drunken demon.

"You've gone ashen," Jaz said. "You're not going to throw up are you? Look out!"

Chapter 17

I don't know if she has spies, but somehow everything seems to get back to Fay eventually. I mean everything. The evening after my embarrassing but record-breaking projectile vomiting in the Red Club she called me.

Ostensibly she wanted to talk about the children. Sarah had come home from Warwick University for the Christmas break with a boyfriend who, according to Fay, looked like Nosferatu but not so handsome. Was he on drugs, did I think? Claire meanwhile had had a brush with the police after shoplifting a Cadbury's Chocolate Flake.

"A what?"

"A Cadbury's Flake. Stop pretending you don't know what a Cadbury's Flake is."

Robbie, meanwhile, was having a miserable time at the local comprehensive. Some girls had pulled him into the female toilets and dragged his trousers down.

I was still thinking about why I was never lucky enough to have this horror befall me when Fay said, "I hear you've been drinking a lot."

"What? Who told you that?"

"You were also seen on the Embankment, strolling arm-in-arm with a young woman."

"Seen? What do you mean *seen*? I don't remember trying to make myself invisible."

"William, I hope you're not having a mid-life crisis."

I thought about that for a few seconds. The usual indicators were not available: I wasn't married so couldn't have a mistress; and the thought of purchasing and owning a sports car is in my mind tantamount to walking the streets with one's penis exposed. Anyway what was this about "mid-life"? As far as I'm concerned, the crisis started when as an infant I was removed from the maternal breast and the situation will continue to remain critical until I am comforted by the black teat of death. There is no "mid" about it. Life *is* a crisis from the cradle to the grave.

"If I am having a crisis," I told Fay, "I intend to do so quietly. Now, what are you calling about?"

"Nothing," she bridled. "That is, I just wanted to see if you're okay."

"I'm okay. Okay?"

"I also wanted to tell you your maintenance payment didn't come through this month."

"Oh, I changed my bank account. I'll sort it. Make a double payment next month or whatever."

"Not like you to miss a payment. You're not going to leave us, are you?"

"Leave you?" I reminded Fay that she was the one who was in the spiriting-away business, and for celebrity pastry chefs.

"I mean, you're not going to shoot off into space so that we'd never see you again. Are you?"

"No," I assured her, "I'm not going to shoot off into space."

The one time that I nearly did shoot off into space was when I discovered Fraser had been basing his conjuring of demons on my book. In fact I *freaked out*, to use the parlance of the day. I remember staring down at the rotting book and my own manuscript pages as if it were a pit of snakes into which I was about to be tossed.

"It won't bite you," Fraser said.

I was paralysed. I couldn't speak. I wanted to destroy the book and strangle Fraser at the same time. But I also needed to disguise my reaction to the manuscript. There was no way that I was going to confess to him that I was the author of the fraudulent scribblings on the onion-leaves.

I was also trying to calculate the insane implications of it all. Fraser had scared himself half out of his wits with whatever it was he'd managed to summon. Of course, he might simply have created that psychological condition for himself; but independently of that I had most certainly sensed some presence in the attic. So had the porter. So had the porter's dog. I tried to think back over what I'd done with the manuscript.

The original book, the rotting publication, had fallen into my hands along with several other mildewed volumes buried deep in a cardboard box I'd collected from a doctor's widow during one of my house-clearance jaunts. Most of what was in the box was rubbish, but I had been intrigued by the occult content of the book. As I say, half of it was missing and the cover and all the frontispieces were gone. It had no resale value. It was impossible to tell who had published it, or when, or who had authored it.

The main body of the text was offered in long-winded style, but involved lengthy preparation for magical rituals. There were diagrams and formulae in the book, but frustratingly no instructions for the performance of the actual rituals. I'd assumed these were in the missing section of the book.

At the time there had been a heightened interest in occult publications. Bookshop shelves groaned with imbecilic titles like *Finding Your Egyptian Spirit Guide* or *Casting Runes for Your Cat* and the like. It occurred to me to use the book as a basis for a manuscript purporting to offer the secrets of magic rituals. I purchased the onion-skin paper and the India ink, and with a bit of research set about composing the rituals myself. My hair-brained plan had been to offer the manuscript to a publisher as a "sensational find."

I spent hours on the elegant almost copperplate script and the painstaking draughtsman-like illustrations, only to abandon the project well before completion. It was all too much like hard work. I figured it would take me a year to get the manuscript anything like ready for a publisher. So I packed the book and my unfinished occult manuscript, along with all my other old books, in the attic at Friarsfield Lodge, to gather dust.

And that's how Fraser had stumbled across it.

"I'm going to take these papers away," I told Fraser that morning.

"Not bloody likely. I need those."

"What for?"

"They might help me figure a way to... put it all back in the box."

I could have simply asserted ownership. But then I would have felt more deeply implicated. And though I hesitate to say it, more deeply threatened by what Fraser had done. It's barely rational—but then none of this was rational—but I thought that if Fraser knew my part in all of this then the thing that was contaminating him might make a virus-like leap to me.

"I just want to study them. I know a bit about this shit."

"You do?" Fraser said, disbelieving.

I mentioned a few things like the Key of Solomon and other fragments of magical jargon. Enough to impress him, anyway. He surrendered the papers to me. "I need to know exactly what you did."

"I just followed it as it's laid out there. It's clear as a bell."

A cracked, doom-laden bell, I wanted to add. "What about the pictures? The girls?"

He shuffled. "They were the object of the ritual."

"To do what?"

He flared his eyes open at me.

"You did this," I asked him, "just in the vague hope that you would get to fuck them?"

He blinked. I wanted to mend his broken nose just to break it again.

"Fraser, you're such a shit. Why all *my* girlfriends?"

"Because it was easy to get personal effects when they were here. From the bathroom, I mean. Hairbrushes. Bath water."

"Bathwater? You stole their bathwater?"

"Stole? They didn't exactly want it! In one or two cases it was easy to nip in while the water was draining. I mean, if their hygiene had been better, if they'd rinsed the bath—"

"Shut it or else. You're not one to talk about hygiene."

"I'm just saying."

"Well don't. What about the photos?"

"It's easy, William. You just pretend to be snapping something behind them."

"I take it that it hasn't worked."

"Not exactly."

"Not exactly? What's that supposed to mean? Has it or fucking well hasn't it?"

"Well, no, not yet."

I thought about his creepy handshake when he was saying goodbye to Mandy that morning. "I'm going," I said. "I'll take these with me."

"What will you do?" he shouted after me.

I ignored him. I felt like taking a bath myself.

I went to my room and sat at my desk, spreading out the onion-skin papers before me, trying to recall the sources for my fabricated rituals. I remember I had a pounding headache as I flicked through the nicotine-coloured pages of the torn book trying to re-create the inspiration for my pentagrams and pentacles and bits of Latin.

It occurred to me that Fraser hadn't given me the whole

story. His pentacle or pentagram or whatever the damn thing was that he'd chalked on the attic floor certainly wasn't one of my careful drawings, or I would have remembered it. True, it bore a superficial resemblance to mine—one pentacle looks like another, doesn't it?—but the infill, the text, the symbols, these were all new to me and couldn't have come from the drawings I'd constructed so carefully with compass and protractor.

With my head throbbing I pored over the onion-skin papers. A scholar of this material would probably be able to piece together the fragments I'd culled from so many sources: Egyptian charms found on papyrus; major and minor Keys of Solomon; Latin curses; hell, there was even stuff I'd invented myself. I recalled one evening sitting smoking a strong joint and talking in tongues for fun, just writing down the gobbledygook coming out of my mouth. It didn't seem possible that all of this could aggregate into an effective ritual invoking things I didn't even believe in.

It just didn't seem possible.

On one leaf I'd drawn a classical five-pointed star surrounded by a double-circle. I'd inscribed in the wheel of the double-circle the words ShBThAI, TzDQ, MADIM, ShMSh, NVGH, KVKB and LBNH. Underneath this I'd plundered from somewhere:

Know that the hours of the day and of the night together, are twenty-four in number, and that each hour is governed by one of the seven planets in regular order, commencing at the highest and descending to the lowest. The order of the planets is as follows: ShBThAI, Shabbathai, Saturn; beneath Saturn TzDQ, Tzedeq, Jupiter; beneath Jupiter MADIM, Madim, Mars; beneath Mars ShMSh, Shemesh, the Sun; beneath the Sun NVGH, Nogah, Venus; beneath Venus KVKB, Kokav, Mercury; and beneath Mercury is LBNH, Levanah, the Moon, which is the lowest of all the planets. Know that the hour of your invocation must correspond with its governing planet.

Baloney, all of it. I'd mixed that with other stuff I'd unearthed:

In the days and hours of Saturn you can perform experiments to summon souls from Hades.

Which is of course Greek, so I was confounding my Greek with my Latin and Hebrew, and my Egyptian with my outright Hoopla. I'd drawn another double-circle, this time containing a triangle, with various letters or sigils I'd borrowed from a Coptic manuscript I'd found reproduced in the college library. I wondered if perhaps I'd found the inspiration for Fraser's perverted ritual, for underneath that I'd copied from some source:

LVI.vii Rouse yourself for me, spirit, whether male or female, and go into every place, into every quarter, into every house, and bind Kopria, whom her mother Taesis bore, the hair of whose head you have, for Ailourion, whom his mother named Kopria bore, that she may not submit to vaginal nor anal intercourse, nor gratify another youth or another man except Ailourion only, whom his mother named Kopria bore, and that she may not even be able to eat nor drink nor ever get sleep nor enjoy good health nor have peace in her soul or mind in her desire for Ailourion, whom his mother Kopria bore, until Kopria, whom her mother Taesis bore, whose hair you have, will spring up from every place and every house, burning with passion, and come to Ailourion, whom his mother named Kopria bore, loving and adoring with all her soul, with all her spirit, with unceasing and unremitting and constant erotic binding, Ailourion, whom his mother named Kopria bore, with a divine love, from this very day, from the present hour, for the rest of Kopria's life.

I was startled by a light tapping on my door. In fact it made me jump. I laid down the manuscript and got up. I opened the door to find that there was no one there.

I peered down the long corridor. The entire building was deserted. The cleaners hadn't yet reached the Lodge in their daily rounds, and all of the other students were at lectures, except for me and Fraser.

"Fraser?" I shouted. I went downstairs to his room and knocked on the door. "Fraser?" There was no answer. I pressed my ear to the panel of the door but I could hear nothing at all from inside. Then I thought I heard a tiny footfall on the stairs behind me.

There was no one there. A second set of stairs led up from the back of the Lodge, obviously a hangover from the days of servants in the old house, and I thought that if I nipped up that way smartly I might be able to catch whoever was messing around. But when I reached the top of those stairs, the landing was clear and the house remained in silence. Further down the shadowy corridor the door to my own room stood slightly ajar, as I'd left it.

I heard another tiny creak of steps. This time, though, it was from the winding staircase leading up to the attic. I went to the foot of those stairs and looked up. The gloomy stairwell was clear. My head was throbbing now in competition with my pulse. I set a nervous foot on the first step and began to ascend the attic stairway.

I hadn't been in the attic since I'd gone up with Dick Fellowes, after which the door had been securely locked up all over again. Now the door stood open a tiny crack. I touched my finger to the door, but I didn't apply any pressure. Instead I listened.

I listened hard. What I heard from behind the door was the most terrifying sound I have heard in my life. I had to strain hard to hear it.

The only possible way I can describe it is to say that it sounded like grains of sand. A very few grains, falling on a plastic or metal sheet. A faint sprinkling, and then a sudden spitting of the gritty sand at its target. Then it would stop altogether. In that moment I had the horrible impression that something was listening to me on the other side of the door: listening to me listening. The sprinkling of sand resumed again. Then stopped.

I turned on my heels and hurried back to my room. I grabbed my jacket and my keys and I locked my door behind me. Then I dashed out into the sunlight, and went looking for Mandy.

Chapter 18

"This is nice!" Sarah said, sitting down and unwinding her long, long scarf in a manner that reminded me of myself. She wore a pullover, threadbare at the elbows and with the over-long arms reaching down to her black-painted fingernails. My eldest daughter, home from Warwick University, was very keen to see me. She also wanted me to meet her boyfriend, who was called Mo. I tried not to think about why. Anyway, I offered to treat them to lunch in town. I suggested a Thai place in Soho.

Sarah was a joy to be around. Always was. Always will be. I think I'm in love with my own daughter—not in any erotic sense, my name's not Sigmund Freud—but in the sense that I love her company best of all people and miss her when she's gone.

"Is it okay for you, Mo?" I said

"It's more than okay," said Mo, settling in and grabbing a menu card. "It's good of you to bring us here."

Mo didn't look like Nosferatu at all. Well, he had the shaved head and either he'd been working down a coal mine or he applied a bit of black eye-liner. But so what? Same with the two silver rings through his eyebrow: so what? He wore what we used to call a donkey jacket over a white t-shirt; that and some very impressive Dr. Martens boots, just like Antonia did at GoPoint.

"I'm ordering wine," I said. "I bet you'd rather have a Thai beer, Mo."

"No, wine's good for me."

"You've got something in common," Sarah said. "Mo is a connoisseur of the grape."

I set down my chopsticks in surprise.

"I pretend to be working class," he said apologetically, "but my dad owns a vineyard in France." There was something wonderfully kissable about Mo, the way puppies are kissable.

"He is working class," Sarah said. "His dad's a bookie. Shall we get loads of dishes and share?"

"Really? A bookmaker? They are kind of the aristocracy of the working class, aren't they? Yes, order loads. I'm all for it. How's Mum?"

Sarah shook her head rapidly and made a vibrating noise with her lips. Mo snorted. A tiny, sweet waitress with scintillating black eyes came, and Sarah sang out the names of several dishes. "Is it too much, Dad?"

"No, keep going. You both look like you need a good meal. Ah, here comes the wine. Thank God."

I let Mo taste the wine and imitated the thing she'd just done. Shivering my lips. "What does that mean?"

Sarah shrugged. Mo pronounced the wine acceptable and said, "Sarah's Mum gave me the impression you were a kind of down-and-out. You don't look like that to me."

"A down-and-out?"

Sarah shot him a warning look, but he ignored it. "So did Lucien. Well, he said you were a loser."

"Mo and Lucien didn't exactly hit it off," said Sarah.

"No?"

"Lucien keeps having a go. About his clothes, anything he says. He can't seem to resist having a dig."

The food arrived, steaming, scented with glorious spices. I wondered if the pair of them were doing a number on me. Mo liked wine. Mo didn't like Lucien. I do tend to gulp at my first glass of wine, and I noticed that Mo was carefully keeping pace.

"Well, tuck in," I said.

We all did, and were pretty soon emptying our second bottle of wine. Behind us one of the Thai waitresses attended to the spirit house at the rear of the restaurant. She rearranged the model birds on their perches, relit a candle and put a tiny vase of flowers inside it. Mo was interested. I told him that in Thailand most people have a spirit house somewhere in the garden, and that tending it regularly keeps the spirits in good favour.

"So are there spirits in this restaurant?" Mo asked lightly.

"Yes, several," I said. "In fact there's one standing right behind you at this moment."

Mo dipped his fork and looked behind him. Sarah glanced up at me and shook her head quickly, a warning.

"Ha!" said Mo. "Ha ha!"

"Do you know what that tattoo on your forearm represents?" I asked Mo.

"What, this one?"

"Yes, that one."

"No. I just thought it looked good."

"It's a protective amulet."

Mo looked at it now as if someone had tattooed it on his arm without his permission. Sarah stepped in. She didn't seem keen on the way this conversation was going. "Mum thinks you're having some kind of breakdown. I'm supposed to report back."

"Well, as you can see I'm a fully integrated, high-functioning human being who is ready to order another bottle of wine. With the approval of you young things, of course."

Mo drained his glass, and so did Sarah. I only had to mention more wine and they behaved like it was their birthdays. Though neither of them could hold it well. By the time we hit the fourth bottle Sarah was getting her *gang kiew wan gai* all over the tablecloth.

Suddenly she tossed down her fork. "For fuck's sake, Dad, we can't stay a fucking day longer with that fucking awful pastry chef. We'll just have to crash at your fucking place. Won't we, Mo?"

Well, that was that. I must have agreed. Then this lunch that was going so well, so swimmingly, took a nosedive when Sarah blurted out, "Mum says you've got a fancy woman."

I said nothing.

"Have you?"

Mo, who was less pulled around by the wine than Sarah, registered the irritation on my face. He looked a little nervous.

"Well? Have you?"

"No, I haven't. Okay?"

"It's no big deal, Dad. If you have or you haven't."

"Can we drop the subject?"

"What's to drop? I mean, it's not like it's a big deal either way! I mean, why be so cagey? Why be so secretive? I mean, fine, if you have you have if you haven't you haven't; I mean, it's not like world news; I mean it's not like anyone gives a damn; I mean, I'm old enough to be told, but if you don't want to tell me what the hell do I care if you tell me or not?"

Mo kicked her under the table, but in a way that I was meant to see.

Sarah turned on Mo. "Why are you kicking me? He's my fucking dad! He's always like this. Big secret out of nothing at all. Am I in the wrong now? Am I?"

I threw down my napkin. "I'm just going to the loo," I said.

On my way back to the table I went to the cash register to settle the bill. My credit card failed. I hadn't made the repayments. I had to pay on my debit card, and every time I did so I was going deeper into overdraft. When I got back they were both silent. I explained I had to get back to work.

Outside the restaurant they asked me to direct them to a decent pub. I suggested coffee might be more in order but since they were having none of that I showed them the French House on Dean Street, where Dylan Thomas once famously inserted his middle finger up the anus of someone's pet monkey. No, that doesn't sound right. Anyway, before I left them and without saying anything about our spat, Sarah embraced me mightily. I left them wobbling along Dean Street, having doubtfully entrusted them with a key to my place. They had threatened to return home to get their stuff.

I promised I'd square it all with Fay.

Well, that's one way to describe the shrieking, high-decibel telephone call I got from Fay later that evening. It seemed that Sarah and Mo had returned home in a state of total inebriation, airily gathering up their bags while making insulting remarks about Lucien's pastry. Words were exchanged. Doors were slammed. Parting shots turned into grenades.

I was to blame, apparently, for "winding Sarah up." I protested that this was unfair. Fay asked me what I thought of "Nosferatu" and when I reported that I found him to be a very personable young man she became even more enraged. She wanted an apology, from someone, and so did Lucien.

I promised that I would ask Sarah to call Fay when she and "Nosferatu" had slept off their afternoon.

In fact, I'd arrived home from work to find my kitchen looking like a badger had rifled through the rubbish bin. A half-finished attempt to make a sandwich lay on the floor along with the knife used to butter it. A quarter-pound of cheese lay on the table bearing the impression of someone's teeth. Sarah and Mo had found their way to my bed, upon which they both lay snoring heartily, having been unable to remove their boots. I felt not unlike I was in that story about the girl and the three bears.

I wasn't *too* bothered by this mess in my otherwise rather obsessively tidy home. In fact, the sudden appearance of a little chaos was almost welcome. It reminded me of the time in my life when the kids were toddlers and I couldn't get out of bed without screaming as my foot descended on a sharp Lego brick or some other unnecessary plastic toy. But what did upset me was that my bookshelves had been ransacked.

When I say ransacked, I mean that four or five books had been pulled out of the middle shelf and had been opened or casually tossed on the sofa. The secret hiding place for the scribbled exercise book written by Seamus had been disturbed and the exercise book itself dislodged. It lay on the sofa, open, on the third page. Whoever had started reading it—Sarah or Mo—had abandoned it early before dragging their monkey boots onto the snow-white duvet of my bed. I returned the books—and the exercise book—to the shelf. Then I made some strong arabica.

They were still fast asleep when I went into the bedroom with the steaming coffee. *Who shall I rouse first?* I thought. Yes, Nosferatu.

He woke with a sudden snort and sat upright, sweeping a large hand across his shaved head. Sarah blinked her eyes open, too. "Oh God," she said. "Oh God."

Mo looked deathly. He blinked at me. "I'll leave this here," I said. "See you downstairs."

About half an hour later Sarah appeared having showered. She was wearing my white towel-robe and she'd fashioned a turban from another towel, in that provoking way that women do. She blinked at me.

I raised my eyebrows at her. "Your mother wants you to call."

"Oh God."

"Something about an apology."

"Oh God."

Mo joined us. He didn't say much. Just kept touching the ironwork in his eyebrows, as if to check no one had removed them while he'd been sleeping.

"You've tidied up," Sarah said. "You shouldn't have. We left a mess."

"It's fine."

"No, it's not. I know you: you'll put us in a taxi and send us back to Mr. Pastry."

"Really, it's okay. Look, I have to go out."

"Where to?" Sarah whipped off her turban towel and started to vigorously dry her wet hair.

"Help yourself to anything in the house. There's wine under the stairs. Just don't touch my books, okay? I'm very fussy about my books."

"Cool," said Mo.

"That was me," Sarah confessed. "Sorry."

"What made you go for those books in particular?"

"No idea. Where are you going?"

"I have an appointment. I mean, why grab those books out of all of them? I'm just interested."

She shrugged. "Maybe they were sticking out. What appointment?"

"They don't stick out. Not a centimetre. I'm an obsessive and I keep them all in line. It's a kind of illness."

"Look, it's fine by me if you're going to meet someone," she said.

"Shut up," I said rather sharply, "or I really will send you back to your mum's." I wondered if some demon had guided her towards that particular bookcase.

"Cool," she said, chastened. "Cool. No problem."

I reached the bathroom door and closed it on her. I let the shower run and run.

Chapter 19

We met next at the Windsor Castle in Notting Hill. Her choice of venue, though it was familiar enough to me. In fact, I know all the pubs. I could tell you everything about the recent history of London by its inns and hostelries, but you wouldn't want to hear it. I could explain its geography by the routes picked out by draymen. I'm a bit of a connoisseur of the alehouse shadow, too, so I knew perfectly well, before she mentioned it, what's buried in the cellars of the Windsor Castle.

Every pub has a shadow. Well, not every pub; but if it doesn't have a shadow it's not worth drinking there. I have a theory that all the pubs in aggregate are themselves an encyclopaedia of demons. The Windsor Castle is indeed shadowy, moody; all wood-panelling and sectioned off with bulkhead-type doors chopped out of the wood, through which one has to step.

I waited for her in the second section, at a corner table under some framed pictures. As soon as I saw her enter I felt a flush of holy terror. The demon within her was no longer hiding.

They become brazen, you see. When they know that you know.

She arrived in a high-collared black silk cheongsam dress embroidered with red. Wonderful red, like the lipstick on an oriental courtesan glimpsed through the flimsy veils of a passing sedan chair; the red of the victim's torn throat in a grey, fog-bound Victorian London. That red. She stepped through the bulkhead doors in sheer, platinum-grey nylons and spike heels. Over all this she wore an ankle-length double-breasted gold-buttoned Cossack coat. If I had previously persuaded myself this was not a date, the illusion was now over.

I got up too quickly to greet her, aware of other men's heads turning. Their eyes raked her but I was gratified as I helped her off with her coat that she failed to reward them with a single glance. Maybe they were speculating about the mythical secrets of an older man. If she were to even peep in their direction they could relax and believe that money, or fame, or power or some other trite formula had her yoked to me. But these men knew nothing of the ways of the demon. They had no idea what was at stake.

"I'm so sorry I'm late."

"You're not late. It's fine." I draped her coat on the bench and she swayed into a chair across the table from me. "You look stunning."

"You've made an effort, too."

Maybe I had. I'd gone out and bought a linen jacket and a powder-blue shirt. I'd trimmed some of the wilder hair of my eyebrows. These were all things ridiculous to me, but I suppose one has to groom the inner troll. "I started drinking already." I felt tense and she picked up on it. "You hungry?"

She nodded. She couldn't seem to stop herself smiling at me. The demon of a woman's smile: they smile too much. I tried to sound casual. "You know what? I fancy the wild boar and apple."

"Me too. And oysters."

When she said "oysters," she looked up at me from the menu, briefly, as if it were a code word. Behind my pretended fascination with the menu I was observing her minutely. I just didn't want her to know it. Demons, you see, are clever. They flash in and out. They don't enter someone and take up residence. Like a bird on a wire they startle quickly. Then they re-alight. They may be there for months. Or just a few seconds.

Over the years I have become expert at looking for the signatures of the demonic presence. You might see it in the drumming of fingers on the table; or in what looks like a casual self-preening gesture; but mostly it is available in the face. There it is, sometimes in a moment of increased mobility in the features. Loaded into a tic of the eyelid, maybe. A flaring of the nostrils. But mostly it's in the eyes.

Of course, it is easy to mistake any normal activity deep in the folds of the human face as a sign that a demon has taken up residence. But over the years you can become quite expert. In her case it was like a sudden match-flare behind the eyes: not a reddening or hot embers or anything so unsubtle, but a honey-coloured brief flare, the combustible elements of which could easily be separated out as: empathy, pity, hunger.

It was all happening too fast. I was going to have to put her off, and I thought that in order to do so I would maybe that night tell her everything. All of it.

"I was nearly late myself tonight," I said after placing our order with the waiter.

Two men were drinking morosely in the corner. They had no interest in each other's company, and the fuckers couldn't take their eyes off her. It insulted me. I wanted to get up and tell them to pull themselves together, but she didn't even seem to spot it. Could she really be so unconscious of the effect she was having on men? At last I turned and gave one of them a very cold stare. He looked away guiltily.

"Why was that?" she asked. "Why were you almost late?"

"My daughter and her boyfriend. They're down from university, staying with my wife, though it's not working out."

"What's your daughter's name?"

"Sarah. She's dragged her boyfriend along with her, too, and they've upset the ex-wife's bloke."

"Ex-wife. Last time you said 'wife.'"

"Ex-wife. Yes, the ex-wife's bloke."

"The cake man?"

"Yeh, old cake-hole. They're both at Warwick University. Where did you say you went to university?"

"I didn't."

"Didn't say, or didn't go?"

"Didn't go."

"Really? I'd have sworn you did. You would have had me fooled."

"Why would I want to fool you about that?" This came out rather sharply. Then she softened it to, "No, only the University of Life."

"Ah, that superior institution. I think you've been an attentive scholar."

It was the wrong note. She said, "That sounds just a tiny bit patronising."

"Does it? I'm sorry!" I was sorry, too. I'd been paying too much attention to the movement of shadows and the tiny indicators flitting across her face, looking for demon-sign, and I hadn't been careful enough with my words.

"Just a bit. Over and over in my life I've run into men and women who are less intelligent than me but more highly educated. Educated people wear their qualifications like a club tie; it's pretty obvious if you're the only person at the table who doesn't have one. It used to bother me; then I found out how easy it was to learn the codes, the language."

"What I meant was, you seem as sharp as anyone else I know."

"Shall I tell you about some of the subjects in which I've graduated? You might not believe me. I have a doctorate in depravity. How does that sound to you, William? A PhD in addiction and recovery. Trained in the fellowship of the gold-diggers, and the liggers, and the dancers and the hangers-on—"

"Whoa! Slow down!" There was something wrong here. I was the one determined to find a way of putting her off, but here she seemed to be hell-bent on playing the same game. "What are you saying?"

"I want you to know where I've been. What I am."

I know that, I thought. *I know all about it.* That feeling as if I'd known her for years. That odd impression of waking up in the middle of a novel, as if you share a history or a back-story that hasn't been fully revealed to you. Like reincarnation.

But these were dangerous thoughts. I was already folding her into my destiny. It also confirmed for me that the demon inside her was making me think that I was falling in love with her, which could not be allowed to happen. But it was my own voice speaking in the lover's whisper, saying exactly what I didn't want to say or hear. "It's odd. I feel as if I've known you for years." I almost bit my tongue off, because it sounded exactly like the kind of thing that weak and wretched lovers say.

"You have known me for years."

I came to my senses. "What?"

She shook her head. "What I mean is," she said, "I feel exactly the same way."

But I had the feeling she was retreating, like someone who goes to make a chess move and then thinks better of it before taking their fingers off the piece. We exchanged the mildest of all smiles. Her hand rested on the table and I wanted to reach out to stroke, with the lightest touch of my finger, the vein on her wrist. I had no doubt that I could make a shiver run up her arm. But instead I retracted my hand, perhaps too suddenly.

Like most men I have made advances in my life, skilful and clumsy, artful and inept. But I'd never had such a terrifying compulsion to stroke a vein on the inside of a woman's wrist. It was proof that my senses weren't jaded. It also told me that my feelings were insanely out of control.

The food arrived. I ordered another bottle of wine. I know I was taking it at a clip. Maybe I thought I could pour wine on the demon; that it would become sleepy and passive. I refilled her glass and said, "You know, there are some men in this bar who can't take their eyes off you."

"You mean there are other people in this bar?"

She made me laugh. We were falling down a tunnel, a rabbit-hole, and again it was all happening faster than I had suspected it would. I wanted to tell her that it was no good, that she was inhabited by a demon and that I was onto her and that it couldn't go anywhere. I even thought about addressing the demon directly, through her, as it were. "How are the oysters?" is what I said instead.

"Good! Here, try one." She tipped the contents of the shell into my mouth. "Why did you get married? Was it love?"

"Partly. But I was also hiding, I think. My years immediately after college were a little crazy. I think I was a sort of casualty. Got married as part of that."

"Funny. I did the same."

"You've been married, too? What was your craziness?"

"Oh no. You haven't told me yours."

I set down my knife and pinched the flap of skin between my eyebrows. I wondered how much of it I might tell her, and how much I would be able to leave out.

Chapter 20

Term ended and I was glad to leave college, to put some distance between myself, Fraser and the events of the last few weeks. My parents were divorced and as usual I was faced with the choice of staying with my father in Daventry, who didn't want me there, or my mother in Rugby, who wanted me there too much. At Dad's there would be no conversation and no food in the house; at Mum's there would be lashings of home cooking but all of it spoiled by interminable questions about where I did my laundry and at which supermarket I did my shopping. Answering any of these questions generated five more, and each of those five generated five further questions. I see now that my mother's fraught wittering was a kind of illness but at the time it just made me want to go out and find a kitten and drown it.

Mother and I ate Christmas dinner together. We each had a table cracker and we pulled them in turn. A blue paper hat tumbled out mine and an orange hat plopped on the table from hers. Not putting them on seemed more of a desperate statement than wearing them, so we did.

"What does your motto say?"

I fumbled for the curled scrap of paper. Printed in green ink so faded I could hardly make it out and so banal I could hardly bare to repeat it, mine read: "*A day without a smile is a day wasted.*"

"There you are, then," said my mother.

145

"What?" I said, cross and nonplussed at the same time. "What?"

But she didn't answer me, pretending to be intent on hacking a leg from the small cockerel crowning the table.

After that we settled down on the sofa. Mother liked to watch the Queen's Speech on TV, and at least it shut her up for a short while. After it was through she sniffed, as if she were a connoisseur of the Queen's speeches and said, "Not so good this year." Then she quizzed me about which brand of washing powder I tended to go for.

I think I lasted until the Boxing Day TV special before I called Mandy and begged her to let me come and spend the rest of the holiday with her in Yorkshire. She got her parents to agree to me staying, on the understanding that I would sleep on their sofa-bed and not in Mandy's bedroom; whereas I would willingly have slept on a razor blade in the coal shed had that been all that was offered.

Mandy and I spent the holidays holding hands and walking the beautiful freezing Yorkshire moors under sensational stainless-steel skies. The wind swirled and twisted and tormented hosts of roosting rooks, blasting them from the trees like scraps of black paper. We hiked to pubs along wet, leafy lanes, and under the flaking, inspirational light I slowly felt my head clearing.

When I was alone with Mandy I felt safe and far away from Fraser and all notion of harmful demons. She was happy, too. Without knowing anything about the events of recent days she'd felt she was losing me, that I'd been drifting away from her. Here, under the blustering skies and tumultuous clouds, we climbed inside a protective bubble of intimacy. We were Heathcliff and Catherine but with nothing to take us away from each other.

One night I got so drunk I felt myself dissolving under Mandy's gaze and I asked her to marry me. She said yes, and I was ecstatically happy. The walk home took hours because we kept stopping to soul-kiss. I felt as if the dramatic rolling landscape either side of the road was filling me up.

But the next day we both pretended it hadn't happened.

Okay, so we were drunk, and maybe that made it not count. But neither of us broached the subject or even dismissed it as a bit of tipsy foolishness. Neither of us said, "*Hey, were we so drunk that...*" Instead we engaged, without a word, in a conspiracy to pretend that it was never said.

To this day I don't understand why.

It's not as if I forgot what had been said. And though I never asked Mandy, I'll stake my life that she didn't forget either. Because that moment of tipsy foolishness or whatever it was always stood between us. Yes, like a demon, if you like. It was as if we'd made something, hatched something, breathed life into something; and although we'd tried to abandon it, it followed us and made any hope of a future together impossible. We travelled back to Derby together and she returned to her shared digs and I went back to the Lodge.

Back at college, the buzz was all about a girl called Sharon Bennett who had gone to Australia for the Christmas vacation. Australia, that is, via Columbia after swallowing six condoms stuffed with cocaine, and with a further dozen secreted in her vagina. Her arrest had made the national news.

The story was all the more acute for me because not only was she another former girlfriend, she was also one of the five girls in the photographs in the attic. I could quite believe it of her: she was a space cadet, a serious recreational drug user. Her catch-phrase was *down the hatch* and I couldn't keep up with her. All the same, it was a dismaying story.

In the Students' Union bar I was about to order a pint of bitter for myself and a vodka and coke for Mandy when a girl in an army combat jacket and a pink scarf reached out her arm and gently fingered my lapel. "Have you heard about Rachel?"

Rachel Reid was another of the girls in the collection of five. The girl in the combat jacket was her room-mate.

"No, what about her?"

"She died over Christmas."

"What?"

"It was a potholing accident."

"Potholing?"

Rachel had been an enthusiastic caver and climber. She'd initiated me into the potholing game. After joining the caving club, I'd spent two Saturday afternoons worming around cold, wet passages underground before calculating that it wasn't a game I particularly enjoyed.

Rachel and another caver had been trapped underground by a flash flood that had inundated a cavern in the Derbyshire Peak District. They'd been brought out dead. The girl couldn't tell me much more than that. She was herself still stunned by the news and her way of dealing with it was to tell everyone who'd known Rachel.

Mandy brought me out of my paralysis by taking the glass of vodka from me. She squeezed my hand. "Wasn't she another ex of yours?"

"You know perfectly well she was."

"You're a curse," said Mandy. "Come on, let's find a seat."

I didn't think I was a curse. I thought it was all just a rather unpleasant chain of disasters that had befallen three of the girls in the photographs. The other two—Mandy beside me, and Lin cheerfully pulling pints and dispensing cut-price vodkas at the bar—seemed in good enough sort.

My initial response was to find Fraser and tell him what I'd heard. But in fact I'd already determined not to have much to do with him at all. I had just two terms left to go before emerging with my degree. I planned to divide those few months between catching up on my studies in time for the final exams and getting Mandy naked as often as she would let me.

I rationalized it all thus:

One: Sandie had a nut allergy, and a careless caterer had failed to label the sandwiches. As Fraser said, it's not unheard of.

Two: Sharon was smuggling drugs and had got caught. As the Buddha says, shit happens.

Three: Rachel participated in a dangerous sport and had run slap bang out of luck. Right.

Without ever mentioning the photographs to Mandy I discussed it all with her. "These things come along in threes," she said.

"Do they?"

"That's what they say."

"They? Who the fuck is 'they?'"

"No one knows who they are. We don't talk about they. And it's bad luck to use foul language when talking about they."

"Oh yeh."

All right, I thought. Just so long as they don't talk about things coming along in fives.

The days passed, and then the weeks, and Fraser failed to return to college from the Christmas break. While I was certainly not in a state of grief about this, I couldn't help wondering what had become of him. My thoughts did stretch to wondering whether he too had become another victim in the series of disasters. I could have made enquiries—maybe got a telephone number from the college authorities—but I didn't. Oddly, even though one of the cleaners confirmed that he hadn't been in his room in Friarsfield Lodge since the beginning of term, I did find myself on more than one occasion poised outside his door, listening.

I don't know what I was listening for. I had this irrational idea that Fraser was fooling everyone and that really he had come back to college but was hiding. I thought that if I stayed with my ear by the door for long enough he might make a sound that would give the game away. And there were sounds. Nothing that would confirm his presence or activity in the room, but odd punctuations in the silence behind the door.

Once I heard what I thought was the sound of a piece of paper—like a paper dart—hitting the floor. One day I heard a zip rasp, but for a split second only, and not long enough to represent a real zip. Another time there was a very brief flapping, like the sound of a carpet being rolled, but just two turns. I would press my ear to the door, hardly breathing, straining to hear more; but there never was more.

"What are you doing?"

I know I jumped. I actually had to put my hand on my heart. "Oh. I was just seeing if Charles was back yet. He hasn't returned from the holidays."

It was Dick Fellowes. He must have crept up on me. I had no idea how long he'd been watching me with my ear to Fraser's door. "It appears not. We'll have to make some enquiries about him."

When my beating heart recovered, it suddenly occurred to me to wonder what Fellowes was actually doing there. He certainly had no habit of dropping in at the Lodge. He had no casual business there. His presence always related to some particular purpose. He gazed back at me, either expecting a reply or waiting for me to leave. "I'll go back to my room, then," I said stupidly

"Yes, you should."

I did go back to my room, with my cheeks flaming, but I left my own door ajar. I wanted to know what Fellowes was doing. I couldn't actually see him, and the damndest thing about it was that I think he just stood there for several minutes. I believe he was waiting to see if I would come out and check on him. Or maybe my presence had stopped him from doing something like going into Fraser's room, or whatever. I have the feeling we were trying to outwait each other. After maybe twenty minutes of this nonsense I couldn't stand it any longer, and I collected some coins together on the pretext of going to call Mandy from the payphone in the hallway.

But when I stepped out of my room and into the hall I saw that Fellowes had gone.

I called Mandy anyway, and went round to her place. We hadn't fucked in something like six hours and I wanted to be inside her again. With my tongue in her mouth and my dick in her pussy I could feel as if the world was right. Or if the world wasn't right then at least I could hide from it.

When I got to her place she'd just had a bath and was still wrapped in a towel. She squealed when I whipped it off her and threw her on the bed. I buried my tongue in her pussy and she was pulling me with both hands by my hair, deeper into her, when I suddenly lost my erection. I don't know why. It just collapsed.

"You okay?" she asked, pulling me to her.

"Yeh. I just… I dunno."

"I love you, William. Come here."

"This is real, isn't it? Me and you?"

"Of course it's real. Why do you have to ask? Let's get under the covers."

We got into bed and we lay holding each other. Outside the windows the twilight deepened, and then the amber streetlights outside her window came on. After a while there was a flurry under the lights.

"It's snowing," she said.

I barely heard her. I was busy thinking about what Dick Fellowes had said when I offered to go back to my room after he'd caught me eavesdropping at Fraser's door. *Yes, you should,* he'd said. Now why would he say that?

Chapter 21

Fraser did return to college, rather late in the term, but I had as little as possible to do with him. For one thing he actually stank worse than he did before—worse than anyone I've ever known. I failed to imagine why such a clever person—there's no question that he had a fine brain—couldn't be bothered to wash his face and clean his teeth in the morning. I avoided him.

In fact, I even avoided staying in my own room as much as possible, shacking up at Mandy's place for as long as I could get away with. Whenever I returned to my room I would find notes from Fraser: scruffy bits of paper shoved under the door, requesting that I see him. Then I ignored his notes altogether. I found further notes from him in the college pigeon holes. I pretty much knew his movements and he was easy enough to dodge.

Over the weeks, the notes started to take on a more desperate character, scrawled and littered with javelin-like punctuation marks inveighing me to *get in touch!!!!!!* I ignored all of these notes and remained holed-up with Mandy, working hard on my final essays and fucking into oblivion.

We fucked until we were sore and then we fucked again. We barely went out, mainly because I didn't want to run into Fraser, but also because we spent a lot of the time stoned on weed. I was mad for the smell of her. Were it not for Fraser's example I would never have washed her off me. The smell of the weed and the smell of her pussy became commingled in my mind. I think I was stoned on both.

One time we were naked on the bed and she was rolling a joint for me. I stuck my finger inside her and I smeared her juices on the cigarette papers and on the mixture of tobacco and grass; and I smoked it. I smoked her. Mandy just shook her head at me.

Mandy folded her soft wings around me. She knew something was chasing me, though she never asked what. I started to let her make decisions for me. I stopped going out at all. She did my shopping and turned in my college essays. I thought she was my salvation. I just wanted to get through college, finish my degree, get a job and yes—ask her to marry me all over again. I knew I was in flight, but it didn't matter. I loved her and I wasn't faking it.

Then one evening she persuaded me out of my pit. She was getting cabin fever. Mandy wanted to go down to the Students' Union bar, breathe the air outside of her room. Reluctantly I agreed.

When we got down to the bar we plunged into the usual high-energy and low-IQ noise of student life. Mandy saw some of her friends grouped around a table and dispatched me to the bar to get drinks. I don't know why, but I felt nervous, on-edge. I'd hardly ventured out of Mandy's room for three weeks and I felt dislocated.

After I'd fought my way to getting served at the bar, I ordered drinks for Mandy and myself. I noticed that Lindi wasn't there pouring pints that night, so I asked about her. The girl serving me looked at me strangely. She dropped Mandy's empty mixer bottle in a big plastic tub and approached me from behind the bar.

"Lindi is in Good Hope," I thought she said.

I remember sniggering as I reached for a banknote to pay for the drinks. "Where the fuck is that?"

The student barmaid had a heavily freckled face and washed-out blue eyes. "She was on a bouncy castle and it blew up in the air."

"What?"

"It wasn't pegged down properly."

"What?"

"It was a kid's party. Well, after a kids' party."

"What?"

"She was just having a bounce at the end of the day and it blew up in the air. She fell on her head. Terrible."

The girl looked at me with her pale, washed-out blue eyes. Then someone else wanted serving. I stood there appalled, stupidly holding my pint in one hand and Mandy's vodka and coke in the other.

After a while Mandy appeared. "Are we getting a drink or what?" she said.

What I couldn't tell Mandy, of course, was that Lindi was the fourth on a list of five; Mandy was the fifth.

We sat with her friends, though as they chatted in high spirits, Mandy catching up on the gossip, I remained silent. They just thought I was morose, whereas I was stunned by the news about Lindi's freak accident. It's not that Mandy and the others were unsympathetic. It's just that they couldn't see the mathematical equation in all of this, or Mandy as a factor in that occult equation.

After the bar closed we went back to Mandy's place as usual. I rolled a joint when she went to the bathroom. The alcohol had made her frisky, and she got naked, dancing around me to try to snap me out of my mood. I was sitting on a hard chair where I'd constructed my joint at the table. Mandy put some music on and made a lap-dance around me, the smoke rising from my joint but my mood not lifting with it. Mandy took the joint from me, had a draw on it and reinserted the joint between the v of my fingers before blowing the smoke in my face.

She climbed on me, grinding her crotch into my thigh. The music came to a stop. Mandy climbed off my lap and looked hard at me, hands on her hips. Then without a word she switched off the tape player and climbed into bed.

I sat in my hard chair for maybe an hour. By the time I joined her in bed she was asleep. I switched off the light and inched my way between the sheets, not wanting to wake her. But I couldn't even lay down my head. I just stared at her, wondering what kind of suffering or curse I had called down on her. Yes, it had been Fraser's doing, not mine, but I'd created the frightening ritual out of scraps of arcane knowledge. I was seriously implicated in it, and in ways in which I couldn't begin to tell her. I wanted to defend her, to stand in the way of the evil shadow that had fallen over her, but how?

I remained poised above her lovely, frail sleeping body, watching over her, feeling ugly yet protective, a stone gargoyle leaning out from some buttress against the night, my face contorted in the dark.

I knew what I had to do.

Chapter 22

We'd finished desert. Crème caramel, and the sweetness of it just made me want to give in, to kiss her. I wanted the sugar from Yasmin's lips. Her hand lay flat upon the table, and I still wanted to stroke it, to touch it, but without penalty. I looked round for the waiter.

"Don't order more wine," Yasmin said.

"No?"

"No. Do you know why I suggested this pub?"

"Tom Paine's bones are supposed to be buried in the cellar."

"That's it. *The Rights of Man.* Tom Paine is my hero. The landlord of this building at the time had Tom's bones brought back from his pauper's grave in New York. He was going to give him a heroic burial, but then he lost his money. The building was sold and Tom's bag of bones was left in the cellar. And walled up."

"And what has this got to do with me?"

"Nothing really. Except that you're walled up in the cellar. Like Tom."

I laughed, but I felt the furrowing of my own brow. "What? I think I *do* need another glass of wine." I waved to the waiter.

"I've added another basic right to Tom Paine's list."

"What would that be?"

The waiter, a handsome young man with a head of dark curls and raisin-coloured eyes, appeared, smiling at the table, hands clasped before him, leaning in to the table. She didn't even acknowledge him. "The right to be fucked within an inch of your life by a beautiful woman who has the hots for you."

I blinked. I couldn't help it: to avoid the intensity of her gaze I looked at the young waiter, as if for his comment on the situation. Perhaps he saw a kind of pleading in my expression, because he looked away from me and stared down at the table.

"If that's what *she* wants," she added. "And she does." Then she turned to the waiter and smiled. "We just want the bill. Thank you."

The waiter went away and I fumbled for my credit card. "Well, that'll give him something to tell them in the kitchen."

"I don't care what they think in the kitchen. Take me home."

But I couldn't take her home, even if I wanted to, because my daughter and her boyfriend were there.

"My place, then," she said, "but I warn you, it's not up to much."

I tried to think of a way of resisting, but she'd taken charge and wasn't even listening to my feeble protests. Outside the pub she confidently hailed a hackney cab and while its diesel engine ticked over she held the door open for me. She gave the driver an address just south of the river.

In the rear of the cab she leaned in to me, kicked down the seat in front of her and laid a heel on it, exposing from underneath her coat a leg clad in that elegant grey nylon. I was forced to admit to myself that I was a little bit scared of her. "Look, I don't know how much good I'm going to be to you."

It was true. I meant my remark both sexually and emotionally. I was completely out of practice. I felt targeted; I wondered if women had suddenly become much more predatory since I was last in the game. When I was younger I remember chasing girls; I don't much recall them ever chasing me.

She lifted a lazy finger to her lips and placed her other hand inside my coat. "Shhh! I'm taking you home to tell you something. After you've heard it you might not want me anyway."

The cab carried us across London. The amber streetlamps bathed her lovely features, and as they did so I was able to search her eyes without her seeing me. With the streetlights rising and setting over her at intervals, the cast of her eyes made her look like a jungle-cat. And after we'd gone a few miles I saw that thing I was looking for. She was half-squinting through the cab window as the city flashed by. It was the tiny match-flare, behind the iris, a brief instant of terrifying luminescence.

"Stop the car," I shouted to the cabbie.

He pretended not to have heard me.

"Stop the fucking car, will you?"

He heard that. He screeched to a halt. "Jeshush!" he said.

"What is it?" she asked. "What's wrong?"

I threw the door open and stepped onto the pavement. She scrambled out after me, astonished. I said, "I can't go home with you. It's as simple as that."

I ran a hand through my hair and happened to catch sight of the driver who was regarding me with an expression of distaste. "What's the game?" he shouted.

I flashed a couple of banknotes at him. "Take her home."

She paid the cabbie with my money and stuffed the change into my pocket. The driver sped off.

"Well," she said, "that was a surprising development."

"Sorry. Panicked."

"It's okay. Look, we're close to the river. Let's walk. We don't have to go back anywhere."

We'd stopped pretty near Westminster Bridge. The truth is I wanted to go directly home; but I owed it to her not to end the evening on quite such a dramatic note, so I agreed to walk alongside the river up the Victoria Embankment.

It was chilly and I allowed her to huddle in against me for warmth. The night sky was heavy, almost polar-blue. The tidal river had the scaly quality of a dragon's back where the Embankment lights rippled its surface; and it had a low voice to which you should never listen but to which you do. I'd always associated the Thames with the flux of life, and not with death; but right at that moment it looked obstinate and cruel with a regal disregard for any of our small lives. It also looked cold and deep.

"Are you okay?"

"Yes," I said. "I'm okay."

"My fault," she said. "I rushed you."

"No, it's complicated." She seemed happy to leave it at that, at least for the time being. I looked in her eyes, and that flare, that illumination, had gone. I had scared off the demon with my sudden action. But I knew it wouldn't be far away.

I was right.

When we approached the Hungerford Bridge, a shadow moved under the cross-hatched girders and a voice called out to me, "Terrible, ain't it? I'm trying to get a cup of tea."

My scalp flushed. I stopped. "Seamus?"

Shuffling forward in his greatcoat was the old soldier from the Gulf, his head shaved, his eyes like black caverns. I heard a ringing in my ears. My tongue froze to the roof of my mouth.

I felt Yasmin's arm urging me forward, but I was cemented to the spot. As the figure came into the light I saw clearly that it was indeed Seamus; then in the next moment a light travelled over his face and he was not Seamus at all, but some other beggar looking for a handout. But I was too chilled at heart to respond to him.

Yasmin stepped forward and handed him a few coins. Then she linked arms with me. "Come on," she breathed.

"You're not having a good night, are you?" she said to me after we'd passed on well beyond the vagrant. "What did you see back there?"

"The old soldier. The one who blew himself up outside

Buckingham Palace."

"You hallucinated?"

"Yes," I said. "No. You know what? I'd really like to go home now. I don't feel good."

She looked concerned, but didn't argue. We crossed the road so we could each pick up a taxi to our respective homes. Finally one drew up and I insisted she take it. She climbed inside. I closed the door on her perplexed expression, and the cab pulled away. *Well,* I thought, *at least now she knows what she's dealing with: that's the last I'll see of her.*

Chapter 23

Fay telephoned me at work. There had been some trouble: Robbie had been beaten up at school. She wanted me to go round to the house, which I did.

Claire hugged me as she always does. Claire is the most uncomplicated person I have ever met. She is utterly free of demons. They can't find a kink or a bobble or an abrasion to hang on to. They slip from her like water slides from porcelain. She's not the brightest of souls but she is mercifully free. I don't have favourites; but she's my favourite.

Lucien was in the kitchen, uncorking a bottle of wine as I went in. He's had the kitchen completely remodelled, even though Fay and I had had a new kitchen just twelve months before he moved in. The new kitchen has lots of stainless-steel wine-racks and spice-harbours and pan-hangers and utensil-ports and condiment-docks. Lucien is a fucking tart. I don't like to see pear-shaped, middle-aged men with their long, greasy grey hair flapping over their collars. He also has massive balls of ear-hair. Even if he hadn't stolen my wife and family I think the mildest of men would feel compelled to pummel him with a cricket bat.

It was with great pleasure that I rejected his offer of a glass of Mouton Rothschild, opened especially to impress me. "It's a little early for me," I said.

He made a funny noise. It sounded like the word *ewe*. Drawn out. Fay looked like she wanted to strangle me, especially now

161

that the cork was out of the bottle. "Where's Robbie then?" I said.

"He's in the living room."

I don't know what I expected. Maybe to see him with blood on his shirt front, or with a split lip. He was playing some computer game called *Kill the Bitch* on the vast flat-screen TV Lucien had installed there. Not a scratch on him.

"Been in the wars?" I said.

He didn't look up from his game. "Bit."

I sat down and watched him for a few minutes as he exacted unspecified revenge on some prancing female electronic ninja, the blue light reflected from the LCD screen washing over his face.

"Are you okay, Robbie?"

He shrugged.

He wasn't letting me in. I couldn't do anything, and the truth was my heart was in shreds. When and where had I lost him? I'd worshipped the boy for the first dozen years of his life, and he'd worshipped me. Sometimes the thing between a father and his boy can be even more tender than the thing with his girls. And then one day he stuffed a lot of attitude into a kit bag and ran away to sea in some distant geography unknown to me.

"Well, so long as you're okay, I'll go, then."

He shrugged again, his thumbs working feverishly on his game-pad.

"Sarah is staying at my place. Come round and see her any time."

"Right."

I went back into the kitchen. Fay and Lucien were waiting with a sense of expectation. Claire was perched in the corner on a high stool, trying to read my face. "He's fine," I said.

Fay bristled. "You didn't see the state he came home in."

"What happened?"

"Some brute pushed him into a wall."

"He looks in pretty good shape to me."

Fay folded her arms and turned her back on me. Lucien intervened and said, "William, we have to talk."

"Go ahead. I'm all ears."

"We've got to pull him out of that hellhole."

"Pull him out? You make it sound like pulling out of Iraq. It's a good school. I checked the stats. It's one of the best state schools in all of London. I wouldn't send him there otherwise."

"We should send him back to Glastonhall. Give the boy half a chance."

"Am I stopping you?"

"It's about the money, of course."

"What did you pay for this kitchen?"

"Oh," Lucien said. "Puh-lease." It was one of his catchphrases from his TV programme.

I made a bit of a show of looking at my watch. "I have to be in town for seven," I said.

Fay turned round to face me. "You gutless worm," she said.

"Mum!" said Claire.

I stared hard at my ex-wife. "Fay. I've never ever laid a finger on you or mistreated you, or even abused you verbally like that in twenty-two years. But if you insult me again in front of Claire or any of our children I'll slap your face very hard."

Lucien made to speak, but I turned to face him and he got a sudden blast of the heat of my rage. He thought better of opening his mouth and he was right to. I was boiling. "Claire, come and see me to the door."

Claire kissed me before I left the house and I walked down the street trembling. I was on fire. Christ, I could have done with a glass of that very fine Mouton Rothschild.

How many coincidences are we prepared to tolerate, how much synchronicity, how many flukes, chances, twists of fate, what degree of happenstance, how much weird correlation will we be prepared to ignore before we finally throw up our hands and say that cause and effect is not the only ballgame in the universe? When do we admit that rationality is just something useful we made up to help us along? A map and compass don't hold back the night. How much disastrous scientific progress do we make before we stop calling it progress? When do we stop pretending that instrumental reason has no dark side? I was a student at the time, and I hadn't even been awarded my degree: I wasn't posing these questions to myself, I just wanted to figure out how I could save Mandy.

Four girls out of five. Lin, Sandie and Rachel had been snuffed out like candle flames and Sharon's life had been blighted. I stacked it up and resized it this way and that. I told myself it was a coincidence. A freak alignment. I wished I hadn't burned the photographs of them all that I'd taken from the attic. I wondered if there was some way I could undo it all.

I nursed murderous notions about Fraser. I actually did contemplate ways in which I might kill him and try to make it look like an accident. I really did. I wondered if he might be taken in a trade-off. Of course there was never a possibility of my coming close to doing him any real harm. Just because I harboured these thoughts didn't mean I was about to enact them. But the more I thought about Mandy, the more I needed to protect her.

It occurred to me to try to offer myself.

I was winging it. I didn't really know what I was trying to do, or undo, or re-do. All I had was the fake manuscript of rituals that I'd concocted only for Fraser to get his diseased hands on. That and the attic venue.

I stopped having sex with Mandy: I felt like I was a contamination. I made up some excuse about having the flu. Then I made up some other lie to put her off the scent: I said I was going home to see my mother for a couple of days. In fact

I went back to my room in Friarsfield Lodge and pretty much locked myself away from everyone for three days.

There was a plague of notes pushed under my door, all from Fraser. I didn't read them. I didn't even want to touch anything he'd touched. I scooped his notes into the metal waste bin, squirted them with lighter fuel and incinerated them. Then I washed my hands.

I only left Friarsfield Lodge on one occasion, and that was to buy a loaf of bread and some tins of soup, all of which I could eat cold in my room. I had such little appetite anyway, and I'd genuinely developed a light fever that was preventing me from sleeping well. Each morning I'd wait for the Lodge to empty as the students went off to lectures before I would use the bathroom. The cleaners only entered our rooms on a weekly basis, so they were easy to dodge. Of course, there were always a couple of malingerers who couldn't be bothered to get up for lectures but even these tended not to hang around the Lodge during the daytime.

I spent my time studying the manuscript I had forged. I also made a few preparatory visits to the attic. The door was locked still, but of course I knew how to get in by the side panel.

The place was creepy and stale. Each time I stole in by lifting the panel a kind of desperate sigh of fresh air went around the attic room. I re-chalked the pentacle and set candle holders and my ceramic pots of salt and sandalwood, etc. on the points of the star. I couldn't stretch to a goat. I didn't know whether the head was necessary or just ornamental in these circumstances.

On the third day I was coming down with a touch of the flu I'd lied about to Mandy. I didn't like the thought that I'd wished it on myself, but I knew that I had. Despite running a fever I knew I had to go ahead. It was a Friday, and my last chance for a few days: the Lodge would be busy and active over the weekend and I wouldn't have the quiet to get on with things.

A night of terrible dreams of utter carnage had mostly kept me awake, so I was up and about long before my fellow students were making their way to breakfast at the refectory before lectures. I propped a mirror on my desk and looked hard at myself. I had planned to cut off all my hair, before very carefully shaving my head. There is a very strong ritual argument for this. Given the state of mind I was in at the time, I wanted to take all precautions and follow all instructions to the letter.

But at the last minute a kind of resolution, an abandonment to the inevitable, washed over me. It hit me with unstoppable conviction that the ritual stuff was all window dressing, or at the most a kind of training for the mind. I felt beyond all that. I believed I was so connected with the forces at large that all I would have to do was sit down and wait for them to come to me.

After I heard the last inmate of the Lodge slam the door closed behind him, I changed my clothes for a thick woolly dressing gown. My head was throbbing so I took three aspirin tablets and washed them down with a big glass of supermarket whisky. Then I went up to the attic.

I think it must have been quite cold in the attic, but with my fever I barely felt it. I lit the candles around the five points of the pentagram star and I placed a photograph of myself in the place where I'd found the photographs of the five girls. Then I lowered myself to the floor, sitting cross-legged in my dressing gown, in the middle of the pentacle.

You have to understand that I was merely going through the motions of ritual in lighting the candles. I'd lost all faith in the improvisations of my fake manuscript. I was committed to summoning whatever entity I was about to encounter by mental force alone. I had some mantras I planned to use simply to stop me from losing focus or falling asleep.

I'd taken off my watch, but the church clock sounded a dull nine bells from somewhere near the town centre, and it was at that time that I began to repeat to myself the mantras, or rather the incantations that I had either been given or I had devised (by now I'd forgotten myself which was which). I knew that persistence was the absolute law, and that while I might be allowed a moment to pause for, say, the taking of a sip of water, any serious break or punctuation would send me right back to the beginning of the process. My faith in all of this was that something that had no basis in authentic ritual—if there is such a thing—had worked for Fraser; therefore something similar would work for me.

I had in my knowledge a *key*, which was not something of my own invention, but which I'd stumbled across in at least two different sources. It is very difficult over the course of several hours to stop the mind from wandering from its focus. There come moments of distraction, blankness, instances of almost forgetting what one is doing. These lacunae can be plugged or turned by the key I'd discovered, which is to repeat the numbers *five, six, seven,* and in any language. Five being the number of Man; six being the number of Hell; seven being the number of Heaven. I could do so in Greek, Latin, Hebrew, French, German and of course simply in English. And in those moments when the mind has strayed from its purpose the key is a great comfort, and one almost hears and feels, distantly as it were, the tumbling of the chambers of a lock of cosmic proportion.

Fünf, sechs, sieben.

This device becomes an important reassertion of brain rhythms, and the use of different languages reawakens the supplicant out of the trance which is inevitable but counter-productive.

Pende, exi, efta.

This three-beat count was a lifeline whenever I felt myself coming adrift. It was a yardstick. It was like coming up for air. It was also a numerical amulet.

I broke my chanting only for an occasional sip of water, and used the key to restore the rhythm of the chant. After two or three hours of chanting the mantras and repeating the movements and gestures, the mind becomes open to the most terrible visions: ugly, leering creatures climbing from the silt of the bottommost reaches of the unconscious mind. I was led to understand that the chants and gestures were each a knot in a silver rope that would stretch out until the appointed moment, and that these loathsome creatures represented the weakening of resolve in the psyche, an attempt to loosen each knot, and the numerical count held them at bay before the tying of the next knot.

Cinque, six, sept.

The perspiration was pouring from me. I felt it trickling along my spine and down my neck and in my groin. I sneezed heavily, and became frightened when I thought there was no one to say "bless you." Here I was abasing myself before demons and worrying if my sneeze would open the door to them.

I heard the church bell toll at midday. It felt comforting but enormously distant. Somehow a great, mountainous landscape with brooding skies had opened between me and what should have been the urban location of the church. But it had receded, fallen back deep into inner space; or I had. I persisted.

At one o'clock I heard the bell again, a far-off single toll. My bones were aching and my brain was on fire. I thought I couldn't go on. My throat had swollen and dried. I struggled to swallow a teaspoon of water.

At two o'clock I was brought back to my senses not by the church bell but by the slamming of a door somewhere in the Lodge. By now I was hallucinating. Just across the attic floor I could see another version of myself, speaking the mantras, seated cross-legged inside a pentagram, candles burning at all five points. This other version of myself suddenly became aware of me, mouth horribly agape, tongue waggling lasciviously in its mouth.

In the next moment there was a woman—or a naked creature, for although I want to think it was a woman, it might have been a fat maggoty creature—copulating with him, sitting in his lap, gazing lovingly into his eyes. I remembered to make the count.

Quinque, sex, septem.

And the nightmarish vision disappeared.

I reapplied myself. Then at three o'clock I heard the church bell clonk, hollow in the distance, like a bell that had cracked in the casting. At four o'clock the sound wasn't even a clonk; more like the sound of a creature trying to clear its throat. My skin flushed horribly; not mere goosebumps but a rippling as if some live things had found their way under my skin and were racing around trying to get out. Then the sensation suddenly stopped instantly.

It was over. The sky outside had gone dark. I knew the ritual was done.

The moment was almost one of anticlimax, but not quite. There was no sudden or dramatic event; the candles neither guttered nor flared; the temperature didn't dip. But something about the attic had changed, beyond my comprehension but not beyond my apprehension. Something about myself had changed, too. Some weight inside me had shifted. Some density had realigned.

And something swarthy was gently pouring itself into the room, like black sand through the neck of a timer, as if through the tiniest fissure, a crack forced in the fabric of the world by my concentration alone.

There was a sense of slow decanting, as if some presence had dissolved in one space and was reconstructing itself in another. My apprehension of it was more intuitive than it was visual, and even so, there was a smokiness to my vision, as if something unclean had been smeared on my retinas. The room became denser with what I want to describe as soot particles, and this sootiness began to resolve itself into a set of frightening chevrons pointing like a dart right at me. I felt a huge pressure, an enormous solidity of the air. The pressure on my ears was similar to that experienced in an aircraft cabin.

I began to shiver, not from the cold but from terror. My blood dried in my veins as if it had become salt; my banging heart wanted to shatter my ribcage. I felt the migration of warm piss on my leg. I had been warned about this by Fraser, about loss of bodily control. He'd told me it was important to speak, to reassert control of my bodily functions. He said it was vital to sound commanding.

But the words were like wet cement on my tongue. I had to fight them up and out of my larynx and my voice was shaking. I was like a little girl trembling at the sight of a huge black dog.

"No," I said firmly, surprising myself. "You have to find another form or I can't speak with you."

The congealing of sooty particles stopped abruptly. The smokiness in the room began to lighten. The pressure lifted. I'm certain my ears actually popped.

Within moments it had gone.

My steady breathing recovered. Then I heard soft footsteps on the stairs leading to the attic, making an almost stealthy approach. I listened hard. The footsteps climbed another couple of steps, then halted. I listened again. The footsteps seemed to ascend two more steps, and halted again.

My breathing was so shallow I thought my head was going to explode. The footfalls finally reached the top step outside the attic door. I knew that the door was locked, and I held my breath again. But with infinite slowness the door swung open. A spectral figure took a step inside.

With his face to the skylight window, the figure was a silhouette. But I knew who it was who had come. His eyes, lodged in the wreath of shadows that was his face, were starbursting. It was Dick Fellowes. He gazed at me for a long time.

He moved his jaw, as if trying to search for command of his words before speaking. I've seen that gesture since. It is a kind of signature of momentary demonic occupation.

"We need an understanding," he said finally. "You can never walk away from this."

I nodded.

"But the only way out for you," he said, his voice a tense whisper, "is to leave the college. You can't stay around here."

I nodded again. I knew that. "But do we have a deal?" I said.

"A deal? Yes. We have a deal."

* * *

By the time I reached the Crown near Seven Dials in Monmouth Street I had almost recovered from my altercation with Fay. Almost. The Crown is a tough place to find a seat. I've been there many times on my own and usually it's standing-room only at the bar. Yet traditionally whenever the Candlelight Club choose to meet there we always find an empty table at the rear. Stinx says it is because we were part of the fabric in the 1820s when it was called the Clock House and its clients were the worst kind of pimps and murderers. Here the "King of the Pickpockets" held court and they divided the spoils of any lunatic stupid enough to enter the district after dusk. Stinx thinks of us as a reincarnation of all this villainy, what with our book-forgery business.

No seats on this night, however. I arrived first and stood at the bar, calling for a glass of Cabernet and studying the paintings of cut-throats and thieves that would have grogged in this very joint a couple of hundred years ago. You could feel their ghosts. No, really, you could. The reek of bad blood has never been washed away from this part of the city.

I once went to see a shrink with nicotine-stained fingers at his surgery near this place. Told him all about my demons. The lot. Held back nothing, and paid good money for the privilege.

He listened very carefully, made notes and asked how long I'd been seeing these demons. Then he threw down his pencil and said, "There's nothing wrong with you."

"Uh?"

"You display the symptoms of schizophrenia yet it doesn't seem to impede you or even overly distress you. You're what I'm tempted to call a *functioning schizoid.* "

"That's a very nice phrase," I said, "but I know that other people can see these demons."

"So you tell me."

"You think I'm lying?"

"Look, did you think there is a line you cross that makes you a schizophrenic? It's not like having an infection that can be seen with a microscope. Schizophrenia is a ragbag term we apply to all the forms of disturbing mental behaviour we can't explain. And even if there were such a 'line' to be drawn, you would have to draw it believing that at least half the population was rational. I see no basis for that."

"I don't know. I'm just not very keen on being labelled a schizophrenic."

"Look, let's assume for a moment that these demons you see are real. If you could persuade me to see them, would it change your life in the slightest?"

"No."

"And if you were unable to persuade me?"

"No."

"In which case, Mr. Heaney, if you want we could discuss this philosophically for an hour once a week at my standard rates."

I left him; I could see he was dying for a cigarette. I felt like I'd been offered the choice between a blue pill and a red pill, one of which would change my life forever. I know he was just trying to save me my money, but I wasn't sure if he'd helped me or made things worse.

Diamond Jaz ambled into the pub, perhaps half an hour late, wearing shades and a beautiful camel coat. The broadsheet newspaper folded and tucked under his arm might have been there to skilfully offset the expensive chic of his impeccable style for all I know. A photographic accessory. Every head in the Crown turned briefly, as they always do. And in the same moment a table cleared itself.

Jaz dropped his newspaper on the table to claim the space against the dozen or so other customers who might have wanted it. Effortlessly securing a third seat for Stinx, he smiled at me and sat down as I called in his usual tipple.

"Why the shades?" I asked as I settled down next to him.

He lifted them briefly. A small but angry blue bruise formed a crescent under his right eye, which he covered again with the shades.

"You want to watch that rough-trade thing," I said, clinking glasses with him.

"Yes, I think I might be ready to try a woman again."

"Careful."

"I've seen what it's done for you. You keep trying to wipe that smile off your face but you can't."

"I don't know what you're talking about."

"She's hot, isn't she? Gets you hard just by sitting across the table from you?"

"Where's Stinx? He should be here by now."

"What are you afraid of, William?"

It was no good trying to tell Jaz to shut up. If he knew he'd got to you he would tease all the more. So I said, "Falling in love with her, that's what."

He took off his shades the better to look at me. "It's not going to fuck up my poetry, is it?"

"Oh, I've got you a couple here for you." I reached inside my breast pocket and withdrew a few folded sheets. They were samples for his new collection. Less cynical; less miserablist, as requested.

He snatched them up and began to read avidly. As he did so I flicked open the newspaper he'd brought in. There was a photograph of a suicide case on the front page. The man in the photograph looked familiar. He was a footballer. "Hey," I almost shouted, "this guy used to drink in that god-awful club you keep taking us to."

Jaz looked up from my doggerel. "Yeh. Topped himself. He was being blackmailed."

"What about?"

"Queer." Jaz went back to perusing the poems.

"The poor guy. Surely no one bothers about being gay in this day and age."

"Get in the real world, William. Can you imagine the chants from the terraces? Hey, this is a love poem!"

"Sort of."

Jaz went on to study the second poem. My thoughts were still with this poor young man. He'd tried to reach out to me in the nightclub. Not that I could have helped him in any way—Tara the good-time girl had misled him about that. But I'd seen his demon in the men's room. His sad, squat, suffering demon. Even then it was a demon of no hope. Waiting. Like all the other demons I see. Just waiting.

"I like the new phase I seem to be entering. This is good stuff."

"I should think so—it took me a quarter of an hour to write."

It was true. I'd spent three hours thinking about Yasmin and this poem—which ostensibly was not about Yasmin at all, but really was when I came to look at it later—flowed from my hand in an act of automatic or almost unconscious writing. Granted, it was bad; but it was effortlessly bad.

"No, really, William, this is fine stuff."

"Oh shut up. I'm going to give Stinx a call. See what he's up to."

But I couldn't get hold of him. I left a message for him to call me back. I tried to put a little urgency into my voice.

While we waited for Stinx we talked about our other book

project. The forgery. Not the forged poetry, the antiquarian forgery. We would be needing a new mark. But Jaz had spooked. He said there was still someone poking around asking questions. He had no idea who this person was, but it had come to him via a third party: someone had been asking how Jaz and I knew each other.

"No problem," I said. "After this one we just freeze all activity for a while. Close down. Give them nothing further to go on. We start up again in a year."

"Why not just close down now?"

I could hardly tell him that I'd loaned myself to GoPoint and needed the money to pay off my debts. "No. We'll complete this one. If Stinx comes through."

Jaz looked at me hard. "You seem to think he might not."

"It's more complicated than usual. Remember the original we took to model our copy on? Stinx spoiled one volume of it in a studio accident and I'm under pressure to return it. So he has to come up with two copies. And pronto."

"He hasn't let us down before, has he?"

"No. But where the fuck is he? That's all I'm saying."

We speculated a bit about who might be asking the questions but drew a blank. We had another round of drinks. Jaz told me a few fun things about his poetry tours. He was being commissioned by Lambeth Council to supply a short poem which was to be set in stone around the base of a sculpture outside a new community centre. The project was funded by Lottery money. The penniless buy their tickets of impossible hope and the government rake-off is partly returned to them in the form of bad artwork and fake poetry. How the poor get roughed up. Twice.

Cold Chisel Press were also avid for a new collection and Jaz was very keen for me to write it fast. We agreed as usual to hand over the spoils, which admittedly were not likely to be very much, to GoPoint.

Apropos of nothing, Jaz said, "Write me a sex poem."

"Bugger off, Jaz."

"Please. Write about this woman you're in love with."

"Ha," I said. "I'm not in love, you ponce."

"Go on. Write me a really deliciously sleazy sex poem. I'd say you *are* in love, actually."

"Ha!" I said again. "Ha!"

Chapter 24

Jaz was right, of course. My worst fears had been confirmed. I was in thrall to Yasmin, right up to my neck. My head, ears, nose and throat, however, were still trying to resist. My rational, clonking, battery-dead misfiring-calculator-like brain was trying to summon up numbers other than those shown on the screen. Because I did not wish to acquiesce. Did not wish to go under. Because I lived in mortal dread of transitory love, winged and fiery, principal amongst all the frightening demons.

You think I'm speaking in metaphor. I'm not. Of all the demons most difficult to describe, the demon of transitory love is the easiest to identify or to witness. You are humbled in its presence. You are awed, mortified, trounced, pissed on. Still your mortal heartbeat quickens, your skin flushes, your eyes fix and re-fix and deliquesce. You lose all faculty of good judgement. You mismanage all sensible emotion. You become an ape, led by the demon on an unbreakable golden chain. And then when the subject of your fascination is just not ready for it any more and departs, you are left only with the company of yourself.

How do you know when it has gone? You just know. There is a radiance lost; a glamour fades; a soft focus resolves itself into sharper lines. A certain pressure in the air recedes. The demon that carried you in its wings to the glorious heights has dropped you like a stone.

And then all hell breaks loose.

A long time ago I resolved never, ever to give this demon such power over me again.

When I left Mandy at the college, I quit the course without a word to anyone. I didn't tell Mandy; I didn't let my mother know—in fact, to this day she still thinks I completed my degree and I see no reason to disillusion her; and I didn't bother to inform the college.

I just packed up my bags and I left. It made me physically sick to do it, but that's what I did. I threw up in a rubbish bin behind the bus station on the morning I left Mandy forever. I came to London because it's a city of refugees. Pretty much everyone who comes to London to live is fleeing from one demon or another. Some of them even know it.

My actions regarding Mandy might have been cowardly, but they were not selfish. I was trying to save her. I knew that her fate would be the same as those four other girls unless I made the trade, the deal, the exchange. I was still passionately in love with her but I wouldn't allow myself to be the instrument of her destruction.

Yet I hadn't managed to completely cheat the demon. It's one thing knowing when the demon will flap its wings and go; it's quite another thing to leave before the demon has done with you. That particular demon followed me to London and wrecked my life for three years before it was through with me. I hurt over Mandy. I cried. I tried to destroy my life with drink and drugs and reckless behaviour. But for three years, when I woke in the morning the first thing on my mind was Mandy; and she was the last thought in my head when I went to sleep at night, no matter whom I was with nor how much I poisoned my system.

For a thousand nights, I shredded myself. My demon flogged and flamed me. Old London Town is a fine place to burn. There is so much company, also on fire.

When the demon was done with me I promised myself never to let it approach me again. I devised a kind of mental yoga to keep it away. A system of disciplined thinking and alertness. And it worked! The side effect of this yoga was to roll back the surface of the world, and to make plain to me the astonishing array of demonic activity exacting a pull, like the moon and the tides, on every single human life in the capital and beyond.

There are thousands of them, and in multiple forms, living at our shoulders. Hosts of them, malign and benign, swarming or singleton, some fascinated by us, others disinterested. All utterly unseen except by the initiated.

The truth about demons is shocking to those who cannot see them. For those of us whose eyes are opened once, we can never go back. And the fact of it, their constant presence in the ether, would become almost banal were it not for the constant discipline required to keep them from attaching.

I have medicated my life with vigilance.

When I met Fay I liked her a great deal, and I knew that I wouldn't fall in love with her. Not in the kicking and screaming, biting and scratching, weeping and wailing manner. I saw that she would be a fine companion and a good mother should we be blessed with children. But also that neither of us would be open to the demon.

They are so clever. They enter our lives at a tangent, as it were, staying only for as long as it suits them, for as long as they can feed on our emotions. Maybe for a few seconds, maybe for years. Those who know about these things talk about spectacular interventions for good or ill. I met a man once who told me that a demon was the inspiration of Christ, entering him when he was a young man and abandoning him on the cross. These stories should not be repeated.

But since the day I saw one of their number enter Dick Fellowes in the gloomy attic room of Friarsfield Lodge to make my contract, the world was a changed place for me. There are so few cognoscenti. So few with whom this fact of life can be discussed. I knew Fraser, of course. And over the years I had occasionally sought out one or two authorities in the field. Those who were not charlatans were spectacularly eccentric or even unhinged. Then there were the accidental encounters with people who knew. Seamus the old soldier who was no older than I am: he was a good example. But he didn't know what he was seeing and they fed on him mercilessly. I could have helped him. I should have helped him.

And now there was Yasmin, who hosted demons, but who didn't know it. They flew in and out of her, like dark birds in and out of a tree.

I neither expected nor wanted ever to see Fraser again. I always regarded him as the chief architect of my suffering over Mandy. I know I wrote the fraudulent book that summoned the demon, but it was he who conducted the first ritual and it was he who had placed the photographs of Mandy and the four other girls around the goat's head.

Young people are obsessed with remaining cool, and it is always good advice anyway not to scare away the object of one's love with excessive displays of ardour. I had loved Mandy passionately but had never really told her. The nearest I had come to any serious declaration was that drunken night in the mist-draped dales of Yorkshire. But I blew it. And ultimately I made the sacrifice that protected her. Isn't this what love, genuine love, is supposed to be about?

Well, I did see Fraser again, but not for over fifteen years. I was in a café in Ealing—one of those earnest brown-rice-and-holistic-happiness joints where demons never bother to go—when on a cork-board between notices for flat-shares and Anarchist meetings my eyes fell upon his name. He was involved in one of a series of workshops organized by something called Karmic Insight. His workshop was titled *How To See Spirits*. I almost fell over.

It had to be him. It was too much of a coincidence. I looked at the other workshops. His was sandwiched between a workshop on Holistic Drumming (Intermediate) and another one about something alarming called Ear Candling. The workshops were being conducted at a nearby Adult Education Centre on Saturday afternoons. I glanced round the café. Everyone was intent on their tofu so I was able to snatch the notice from the board and stuff it in my pocket.

I was in a state for the days leading up to the Saturday afternoon of the workshop. I was going to see him; I wasn't. Was; wasn't. It's not that I was afraid of Fraser, but I was scared of what he represented. By now I was married to Fay with three small children. I had my job with the youth organization and I lived quietly. But there he was, in my neck of the woods, muddying pools, poisoning wells.

The Saturday came round. I dithered. I finally made up my mind to go along.

I deliberately arrived late to his workshop. He had a class of about eighteen or so, arranged in three rows on plastic chairs. He was writing some words on a large flip-chart with a day-glo marker pen, so he had his back turned when I slipped into the room and took a spare seat at the rear of the group. I hoped to go unnoticed.

And indeed I did, for several minutes, because Fraser was utterly absorbed in what he was saying. His lecturing style was to prowl and stroke his chin as if deep in thought, making little or no eye contact with his class. He wore a black silk shirt and black trousers belted at the waist and secured with a piratical silver buckle. He was carrying a lot more weight than when I'd last seen him. The fingers of his large, pale hands were be-ringed with silver and gaudy stones, and he fiddled with these rings whenever his hand dropped from his jutting jaw. He had another silver ring through his left eyebrow. I noticed a very slight stammer. He was a bag of nerves.

I didn't think he could possibly recognize me. For one thing

I myself now sported a trim beard and neat moustache, which although it rightly engenders universal hilarity today was fashionable at the time. What's more, my head was covered with a beanie and for good measure I was wearing dark glasses.

And yet with all of this amounting to a disguise, he clocked me. He was in the middle of describing some esoteric process of mental preparation when he looked up at me and stopped dead. He stared hard at me. One or two of the members of his class coughed or shifted in their seats, so long was the hiatus as he stared at me unblinking.

He was obviously a professional at this teaching game, because he recovered his stride, managing to pick up where he left off. For the next hour he talked complete balderdash to his group, recognising full well that I was sitting there knowing it was balderdash; and yet he betrayed no shortage of commitment to his teaching.

I don't know why it was called a workshop. It was actually just a lecture, with fifteen minutes of Q&A at the end. A lady with a chopstick through her hair asked him if he thought the Spiritualist Church might help; an intense young man with bad skin asked a question about the Kabbalistic Tree of Life and then proceeded to answer his own question, sort of.

Two or three people, including the lady with the chopstick, lingered to quiz Fraser after it was all over. I hung back, waiting for them to clear. When they'd gone he collected up his papers, ignoring me. I waited patiently by the door with my arms folded.

Eventually he approached me. I thought for some reason that he was just going to breeze through the door but he didn't. He planted himself squarely opposite me. "A surprise," he said.

I nodded. "Do you do a lot of this?"

He sniffed. "Brings in a crust."

"I didn't think you'd recognize me."

"I wouldn't have," he said with a nod to the side, "but I saw your demon first."

"Oh? How many do I have these days?"

He looked around the room. "Just the one as far as I can see."

"Okay. Just testing."

"You were always testing me, William. Always."

"A drink," I suggested, "for old time's sake?"

He had to pick up his coat and hat from the cloakroom. The coat was a long black leather trench coat. The hat was a black fedora with a white band. I thought he looked a complete tit, and as we crossed the road to head for the pub, I said so. "What's with the Halloween get-up?"

He stopped in the middle of the road. "Do you have to be so fucking insulting?"

"Come on Fraser, let's get off the road. You'll get run over and then where will you be?"

No sooner had we stepped inside the Red Lion opposite the Ealing Studios than Fraser said, "Trust you to choose this place."

Fact is I didn't choose it. It was the nearest available watering hole, and I told him so. "Sometimes these things have a way of choosing us, don't you think?" He gave me what is often described as an old-fashioned look.

It's true though. The place is crawling. I mean *crawling*. All those photos of dead comedians don't help either. Where do you think all that comedy comes from? It's certainly not from happy folk, is it?

"We could go to the Drayton," he said. "Ho Chi Minh worked in the kitchens there."

I told him I didn't give a flying fuck about Ho Chi Minh. I ordered myself a glass of red wine and he had a pint of Fuller's. Someone at the back of the pub made a piss-taking remark about his hat so he took it off. He got halfway down his pint before he spluttered, "Why the fuck did you never respond to my messages?

Messages message messages! You never answered."

"It's all so many years ago," I said, wiping the spray from his mouth off the lapel of my jacket.

"And where did you go? You never told anyone. It was the talk of the college. Where is William Heaney?"

"Well—"

"You never even told that Mandy, did you? Did you?"

That Mandy. "No."

"You broke her heart. You know that, don't you? She couldn't believe that you would treat her like that. I don't think you can guess how disappointed she was."

"I can guess."

"Well, don't feel too pleased. She got someone else pretty damn quick, that's for sure."

It was very easy to remember why I bloodied his nose that time. "Did Dick Fellowes ever say anything to you?"

"No. Why?"

I didn't give him an answer. I glossed the whole thing: said I'd had to get out of college, that it was driving me mad, that it all got too complicated. I don't know if he accepted my blandishments. He talked a bit about how he scraped through his degree. He made no reference at all to the business in the attic at Friarsfield Lodge. We bought more drinks. Then he went banging on about Mandy again and I started to hear myself getting cross with him a second time.

"Look, Fraser, you know perfectly well why I left. You know what happened to those girls. You of all people."

His face flushed a shade of beet. Flecks of white spittle appeared on his lips. He slammed his beer down on the table. It sloshed dangerously in the glass. "But that was just it! That was the whole thing!"

"What whole thing?"

We were attracting too much attention from other drinkers in the pub. Fraser didn't even seem to notice. "That's what the messages were all about. All those messages I sent to you, which you ignored!"

"What about them? What was in the messages?"

And when Fraser finally told me exactly what was in those notes of his, I almost fell out of my chair.

Chapter 25

At the office, Val and I were getting the papers ready for the forthcoming Annual General Meeting of our organization when I received a surprise visit from Tony Morrison—that's Commander Morrison of the Metropolitan Police Force to you, but Tony to me. Truthfully I never know whether to address him as Commander Morrison or as Tony, which he much prefers. It depends on whether he drops by in civvies or in his impressive serge uniform with epaulette silverware of crossed tipstaves in a laurel wreath. I looked up from my desk to see him standing in the doorway in full panoply. A little flutter of guilt stirred my heart, as it always does when a policeman looks at me; even when I've done nothing wrong.

"Any chance of a coffee?" he said.

Val scuttled away to the kitchen at once. Anyone in authority and she practically curtseys. "Tony! What brings you here?"

"Just passing. Can't stay long—my driver is on double-yellow lines."

"Careful—the police round here are keen as mustard. Have a seat."

It's true that Commander Morrison did sometimes "drop by." He'd been an immensely useful servant to our organization. He'd helped set up funds for projects to work with teenage joy-riders and runaways and young single mums, giving up some of his own time as well as official police time. We got along famously well. He was always trying to get me to play golf with him, and apart from that small detail he was genuinely one of the good guys.

"Let's sit in the meeting room, shall we?"

As soon as he said that I knew he hadn't just "dropped by" at all. He had something to say to me that he didn't want Val to hear. I got up to go through to the meeting room when the phone rang. Val picked up, then put her hand over the receiver. "Home Office," she mouthed.

"Do you mind if I take it?" I asked Tony.

"You'd better."

They were inviting me to chair some new committee. Recent figures showed that the number of homeless children in the country was around 130,000. I wanted to say why not sack the entire committee and use the fucking committee's considerable fucking expenses to build a few fucking emergency homes and fucking shelters. Of course, what I really said was: yes, I'd chair the committee.

"How many homeless children?" said Tony when I told him the reason for the call. "Well, I suppose I can believe it."

"But this is the year 2007," I said. "Not 1807."

"No." He took off his peaked cap and blew out his cheeks. I could tell he didn't really want to talk about the figures for the homeless. Tony has a strong widow's peak and very pale complexion. The temptation to invoke vampire references is only just resistible and I wondered if his staff managed not to. But he has a warm smile to offset this physical affiliation to the undead.

Val brought him his coffee. She always remembers just how he likes it: no milk, two sugars, and he always makes a point of saying *sweet as sin, black as death*. He flirts with her. She loves it. I smiled benignly as we went through all that and when she closed the door after her, he got to the point.

"William, your name has come up in an odd place."

"Really?" *This is it,* I thought. *The books. They've tumbled to us. That's what all this snooping has been about.*

"Yes. An odd place."

"What odd place?"

"Look, I'm here as a mate, not as a copper, okay?"

"What did I do? I'll cough to it."

He seemed to think that was a good enough joke. "Nothing. But enquiries have come my way. I'd go to the wall for you, William, you know. I would. But I just thought I'd see what you have to say."

"And?"

"This case with the terrorist. Outside Buck Palace."

"Seamus? He wasn't a terrorist. He was a desperate old soldier. His mind was completely fogged."

"A bomb is a bomb. Anyway, that's not the point. The thing is you lied to the investigating officer about something the old soldier handed over to you."

"I did lie. It's true."

"Why? Why did you lie?

I looked him the eye. "Tony, I've no idea why I lied. You must know what happened: I was there on the night because of my association with GoPoint—"

"They're a bloody nuisance those GoPoint people. Someone should close them down—"

"And he gave me this…scarf, and, I dunno, I just wanted to somehow protect the old boy from the world. It's stupid. I can't explain it."

He nodded thoughtfully. He had sympathetic, soft brown eyes but his gaze was unnerving. He scraped his cup in the saucer, over and over, as if trying to dislodge a drip of coffee. "Okay." At last he took a sip. His Adam's apple bobbed in his throat. He put his cup down again and sat back in his chair. "But why was that, William? Why did you lie to the detective when he came to your house?"

How was I going to tell him? The truth was not going to come out well however thin I sliced it. *Well,* I could have said, *it's like this: I lied about Seamus because he was one of the few people who can see demons, like I can, and I wanted to know what he'd made of it, so I kept the scarf because it had a book in it, which incidentally you don't know about. See? It's all perfectly clear. Forget it; I'll even play golf with you.*

Right.

I'd known Tony for over seven years. Not once during our friendship had I ever alluded to demons or anything like it, and for obvious reasons. Of course, I could have tried it on him. I'm sure he's heard some pretty unlikely stories in his long service as a police officer, but in the scheme of things I had no doubt that somewhere in the shells of his experienced ears it was going to sound just a teensy bit ragged. Even if it happened to be the truth.

"I can't explain, Tony. I know I'm an idiot. Maybe I've got a guilty conscience but whenever a policeman interviews me I have this tendency to resist, to equivocate, to—"

"To lie."

"Dammit, I know you're cross with me. I'm sorry I can't explain it. I was there. Send your guy back and I'll tell him."

"He's not my guy, William. Nothing to do with me. It's just that your name and my name got connected up on a SO13 computer. So they came and asked me to vouch for you."

"And did you?"

"I vouched. But once you've started lying to them, well it doesn't look good, does it?"

"I suppose it doesn't."

"They think there's more to it, you see," Commander Morrison said, getting up to leave, refitting his peaked cap. "There isn't, is there?"

"No," I said. "You can tell them that Seamus was just what he appeared to be." I wanted to add that he could say the same for me, but I didn't want to lie all over again.

I walked him to the lifts. In many ways being caught out for lying felt worse than if the police had uncovered our antiquarian books racket. We shook hands and he said I'd probably hear no more about it. As the lift doors were closing on him he pointed at me and said, "Have you thought any more about a round of golf?"

I went back into my office feeling quite shaken. I had to wipe my brow with a tissue.

"Are you all right?" Val said.

"No," I said. "No."

I was late getting home that night because we had to finish off the papers for the AGM, but when I did get back I found Stinx sitting at the kitchen table nursing a cup of tea. Sarah and Mo were with him and appeared to be in counselling mode.

Stinx looked terrible. He had three days' grey beard stubble and his eyes were bloodshot. There was a bit of blood on his ear. His clothes carried the pungent rot of stale Guinness and tobacco. He didn't have to tell me what had happened, but he did.

"Lucy left me again."

Needless to say he hadn't brought me the finished forgeries.

"You want to get that Lucy," I said, "and give her a hard kick up the arse."

"Dad!" went Sarah. Mo sat back in his chair and blinked at me.

"No, I mean it. She keeps doing this to you, Stinx, and I for one am fed up on your behalf. Really, you've got to show her your toecap."

"But I love her," Stinx wailed. He may have been drinking tea but he was still pissed. "I loves the gal!"

"Don't listen to my dad," Sarah said. "He's not exactly an expert."

Stinx got up off his chair, slightly unsteady, and wobbled

towards me. "No, but I loves your dad, too." He put his arms around me and gave me a bear hug. "I know I missed you the other night. Should-a been there. Is Jaz all right?"

"Yeh, he's all right."

"He's all right, is he, that Jaz? All right? Not mad with me?"

"No one's mad with you, Stinx. Sit down."

"Lucy is. He's all right, is he, Jaz?"

"He's fine, Stinx. Siddown. Drink your tea."

"Cos I loves him, too. Both of you. You and Jaz. You know that."

"Look, just siddown, will you?"

"I've nearly finished, you know. The book. Almost done."

Yeh, I thought. *Yeh yeh.* "We'll talk about it tomorrow, Stinx."

"I have. Almost."

"Tomorrow."

I finally managed to extricate myself from his bear hug to manoeuvre him back into his seat. Tears were streaming down his face and into his beard stubble. He pulled out the filthiest handkerchief from his pocket, put it to his nose and blasted three enormous charges into it. I don't know why but to see him snorting into this dirty old rag gave Sarah and Mo the giggles. Even though I was still seething about Stinx's failure over the forgeries, it somehow transmitted to me. We worked hard not to let him see us sniggering, but see it he did. He looked from one to another of our faces.

"Fuck it," Stinx said. "I'll go home, then, if I'm to be laughed at."

"No you won't," I said. "You're staying here."

He'd taken the hump. I had to fight him down and explain we were not laughing at him, but at his dirty old handkerchief. He relented. I told him he could sleep over and I asked Mo to run him a bath, but while it was filling Stinx fell asleep on the couch in the living room. I took off his shoes and spread a duvet over

·

him, and we left him there, returning ourselves to the kitchen.

Sarah had cooked a chilli sauce. We ate in the kitchen and I told the two of them about Stinx and Lucy, and how he was a great artist but he'd never been recognized.

"He says someone is following him around," Mo said.

"He said that tonight?"

"Yes. I think that's why he came to see you. But it had gone out of his head by the time you arrived."

I left the kids sitting up and I went to bed. It had been a tiring day and I soon drifted off to sleep. But at about two o'clock in the morning someone was by my bed, shaking me awake. It was Stinx.

"What is it, Stinx? What's up?"

"I'm sorry to wake you," he whispered. "I don't feel good."

"Are you sick?"

"No. It's that room downstairs. Where I was sleeping on the sofa. I keep thinking there's someone in the room with me. I've put the light on three times and there's nothing there. Then when I switch the light off again it's like I can see someone watching me."

"I'll come down."

I threw on my dressing gown and together we went downstairs. We went into the kitchen and I set milk on to boil, to make cocoa. It's what I always used to do when the kids were small and they couldn't sleep. I put a side-light on and we kept our voices low so as not to wake Sarah and Mo.

"I'm being a bloody nuisance, mate. I should leave you alone."

"No, you're not. Stick around here for as long as you want."

"I don't know what it is. Maybe I've done too many drugs and drank too much booze over the years. But it was like that moment when you're just dropping off to sleep again, and then it moves. Tell you what, it made my skin crawl. Turned me over, it did."

"Here, drink this."

"How about a splash of rum in it?"

"You don't need it, Stinx, believe me."

I left him grumbling about drinking chocolate milk. I pretended to need the toilet, but really I just wanted to check out the living room for myself. I pushed open the door. The room was in complete darkness. I listened to the silence for a while. Nothing.

Then, just to satisfy myself, I switched on the tall standard lamp. What I saw made me rear back. It doesn't matter how many you've encountered, it always hits you like a thump in the gut. It was a demon. They can be seen in certain light but not in others, and now with the standard lamp on I could see it slumped in the corner of the room, against the book case. It looked desperately unhappy; it was covering its face with its hands, and peering at me from behind its fingers, waiting.

I stepped back into the hall and closed the door. I had to take a deep breath to compose myself before returning to the kitchen.

"Awwight?" said Stinx.

"Fine. I'm just popping upstairs a second."

I had to go and check on Sarah and Mo. Sometimes demons bring others with them. It's like a low-level virus. I opened their bedroom door. There was enough light from the landing for me to see them sleeping, and to see all round the room, but after what had just happened downstairs I had to be sure, so I switched on the bedroom light.

Sarah stirred in her sleep; Mo slept on. Nothing had got in. Nothing was attending on them. I was relieved. It wasn't that I expected it; it was that I had to reassure myself. The demon in the living room had come in on Stinx.

Sarah and Mo lay on their sides facing each other, unthreatened. Their light, sleeping breath on each other kept them safe. They reminded me of Mandy and myself when I was the same age as they were now. They were on high ground. They hadn't yet fallen. Their innocence made me want to smile, to weep.

I went back downstairs. "Look, there's a box room. If you're not comfortable in the living room you can get your head down there instead."

"No, I'll be all right. I must have been dreaming. Couldn't drag myself out of it, sort of thing."

"Whatever you say."

It would make no difference where he chose to sleep. The thing would simply reappear in whatever room he chose to be in. The demons wait you out and leave when they're ready. That's all they do. I didn't like the shape of the thing I'd seen in the living room, but I knew from bitter experience there was nothing I could do about it. Nothing nothing nothing.

Chapter 26

Yasmin's persistence was quite surprising. She emailed me. I ignored her. She emailed me again. Why, I didn't know. After my behaviour in jumping out of the taxi cab and later on the Embankment she should have learned that I'm a poor nutter and left me alone.

But of course I wanted to see her. I just couldn't handle being alone with her. My social movements were pretty much limited to the Candlelight Club and I couldn't take her out for an evening with the boys. For one thing, women were not allowed in the Candlelight Club, and for another thing, no woman in her right mind would want to spend an evening with us. But then a solution presented itself.

I called Yasmin. "Do you want to come to a book launch with me?"

"A book launch?"

"Yes. An old friend of mine is publishing a book. Chap by the name of Charlie Fraser."

"Never heard of him. What should I wear?"

If the invitation to the launch of *How to Make Friends with Demons* by Charles Fraser had taken me somewhat by surprise, I surprised myself even further by the idea of taking Yasmin along with me. Anyway, my curiosity had been piqued enough to want to go, and I thought it offered a good opportunity to be with Yasmin, but not be alone with her. We had some trouble finding the place. The venue for the book launch was a small New Age store in Hampstead and the wine they served was unspeakably New Age, too. It had been fermented from English blackberries and positive thinking, but everyone in the place was holding their glasses up to the light and saying, *How to make friends with demons? Not by offering them this footwash, haw haw haw!*

There was a small tower of Fraser's books by the till near the doorway. Yasmin lifted a copy from the pile and leafed through it. "You're mentioned at the front," she said.

She showed me an acknowledgements page, where I was included in an unnecessarily long list of names. In fact, I was referred to as "the inspirational William Heaney who triggered the search." I was taken aback to be so feted. That is to say, I didn't at all want to be feted.

"Fame," said Yasmin.

I shook my head and flicked through the book. It was a lot of hooey, but sandwiched between the spiritual waffle was a ritual laid out for the reader to follow. It looked rather familiar.

"Bugger!" I said to myself, but aloud. "He's only gone and published it."

"Published what?" said Yasmin.

I didn't want to answer. I didn't want to tell her that Fraser had published a half-baked ritual that I'd composed out of fragments of arcana and magical lore a quarter century ago. A fraudulent, unfinished ritual that had been successful in the summoning of dark entities for which *demon* was the only available word in my vocabulary. He'd only gone and encouraged the spiritual tourists amongst the general public to have a go for themselves.

I was still flicking through the pages in astonishment and displeasure when a transsexual publicist from the publishing company pointed out that the ones on display had to be paid for. I returned the transsexual an evil grin and restored my copy to its pile with a slap.

"I'll buy one," said Yasmin.

"No you bloody well won't."

I could see Fraser at the back of the shop. He was ebullient, glad-handing everyone, tipping back the wine. He wore a black shirt with too many buttons open and the fabric was soaked with sweat as he worked the small room. I knew that he had clocked me and Yasmin when we came in because he looked away too quickly, deliberately burying himself in an intense one-to-one conversation with an anorexic lady in beaded headgear.

"Come on," I said to Yasmin. "I'll introduce you."

I went back to the pile of books, grabbed one, and made a direct approach to the Great Author. Taking out a pen, I loomed over him. I had to break up his conversation with the girl in the beaded hat. "Sorry," I said, "but would you?"

His jaw slackened, and then he pretended to be glad to see me. He signed the book with a flourish. Huge loops in his signature. Best wishes. "Can I introduce you? This is Yasmin."

Yasmin held out her hand and he shook it and enclosed it with his other hand. "William was always so lucky with women."

She glanced at me and then said something to him about looking forward to reading his book. Finally he released her hand from between his paws.

"I acknowledge you in the book," Fraser said.

Such largesse.

"So I see. I'd like a word when you get a moment," I said.

"Well, not now. Obviously."

"When?"

"What about?"

"Well, I won't say that now. Obviously."

He looked around. For a moment I thought he was going to call over his transsexual publicist to strong-arm me out of the shop. Then he decided to write down his address. At first he was going to write it in the fly-leaf of the book, but he thought better of it. He produced a dead betting slip from his pocket and scribbled on the back of it.

"We'll talk at length another time, William. I have so many people to see here right now." He turned to Yasmin. "A thrill to meet you."

"And you," said Yasmin. "Good luck with the book."

Fraser quickly turned to someone else.

I backed away towards the till, paying for the signed book under the baleful eye of the publicist. Fraser tipped back another glass of gut-rot, glancing at us out of the corner of his eyes. I waved cheerily, effusively even, not needing to sour his evening any further.

We stayed another few minutes at least. Then Yasmin set down her glass between a dish of peanuts and a display of books about self-hypnotism. "I can't drink any more of that," she said.

"Me neither. Let's go."

We slipped out. Just as we were leaving, a cab pulled up, spilling a couple onto the pavement. Yasmin dug me in the ribs. "Look who it is!" she whispered. It was the poet Ellis with his new squeeze. They were clutching invitations for the book-launch. *What a small world publishing is, I thought.*

I ducked back into a neighbouring doorway. Yasmin must have thought that I was embarrassed for him to see us together. It wasn't that: I didn't want him to tackle me about his copy of *Pride and Prejudice* because I had nothing to tell him.

Though he hadn't spotted us and we didn't stick around to say hello.

Yasmin and I adjourned to the Dove, a seventeenth-century riverside pub with an open fire to take the chill off the tongue after the blackberry wine. Graham Greene drank there. So did Hemingway, but not with Greene. Oh, who cares who drank there? I was more preoccupied with Fraser. Seeing him in the flesh had triggered it all off again.

"You're not quite with me tonight," Yasmin said.

"Am I not? I'm sorry. It's that wanker Fraser. He stirs up memories."

"Want to tell me?"

No, I bloody didn't. I was thinking about what he'd told me that day after I'd cornered him while he was lecturing his class. I distinctly remember him using the back of his hand to wipe creamy foam from his upper lip. "That's what I was trying to tell you," Fraser had said to me in the Red Lion in Ealing. "That's what all the messages were about."

By "messages" he meant wads of paper stuffed in my pigeon hole, and the confetti of folded notes that had been shoved under the door. I'd scooped them up and binned the lot without opening a single one.

Fraser had drummed his fingers on the table. "I mean, it was a nasty accident, that business with the bouncy castle blowing away."

"But we were told she was dead!"

"Well, we were told she was in a coma. Or at least I was. That's not the same thing. Anyway, Lin made a complete recovery. Shortly after you left the college she was back, pulling pints behind the student bar, none the worse for it."

"Well, I'm glad to hear of it; of course I am," I told Fraser. "But what about Sharon? What happened there?"

"Ah," he said. "Well, that was different. The Sharon Bennett who ended up doing time in Australia wasn't the same Sharon Bennett we went to college with. I mean it's a common enough name. Somehow it got reported back wrong. Chinese whispers and all that."

"So what did happen to Sharon? Our Sharon? I mean the Sharon I used to go out with?" I didn't want to give Fraser the satisfaction of saying "the Sharon in the photograph above the floor-chalked pentacle in the attic at Friarsfield Lodge."

"She'd just dropped out. Bit of a case, wasn't she? You said yourself she was space cadet."

I remember biting my fingernails—not normally something I do. "But the other two?"

"Sadly, that was…"

So two of the girls had died. Rachel and Sandie. But two don't make a pattern, do they? One swallow doesn't make a summer, and neither do two. You need the full five swallows, I figured.

I had to ask. "Did you ever hear anything of Mandy?"

He tugged at his earlobe before answering. "Occasionally I'd hear from her over the years. Then all contact stopped."

"Did you see much of her after I left?"

"Oh, for God's sake, William! You just upped and left her without a word. She was in a terrible state."

I couldn't bear the thought that Fraser had been the one to "comfort" her after I'd left. But I couldn't stand to press the matter with him, either.

That day I didn't tell Fraser anything about my last actions before leaving college all those years earlier, and perhaps I should have done. If there was anyone in the world who would have understood and even supported my actions it would have been him. But I never alluded to my farewell ritual; I never hinted that I'd tried to save Mandy from what I'd thought was certain disaster; and I made no reference to the fact that a demon had appeared to me in the form of Dick Fellowes to strike a bargain.

The nearest I ever came to raising the matter of our attic adventures was to ask, "Did you ever get any more visits from Dick Fellowes?"

"He had the attic scrubbed out, fumigated and redecorated. He even performed some kind of blessing on the place, apparently. But then he left under a cloud himself."

"Oh, what was that about?"

"Well, you know these religious types. Nude boys or some such thing."

Chapter 27

Strolling by the Thames with our coat collars high, blinking at the lights: this had become our favourite activity. Being part of the city but safe from its currents and its tides; watching the commuters, watching the commerce, watching the passage of people and the burden of bridges spanning the great river.

It was a way of being with Yasmin and yet hiding from her. We talked: for God's sake we talked interminable talk, but I never told her anything. She knew nothing about my twilight activities. She never even asked about my odd connection with Fraser, and why I was acknowledged in his recently published book. Of course I wanted to tell her but I had too razor sharp a sense of how it would sound.

With our fingers interlaced as we strolled the Embankment the cold didn't seem to reach us and the damp didn't penetrate. And if we did need to rest or to get warm there was always the cheer of the London pub. We walked, we drank, we talked.

Sometimes I would stay out just so I didn't have to face the mess Sarah and Mo were making of my house. One night I got home to find a lot of trash and papers gusting around the rubbish bin. I decided I really was going to have to speak to them about it.

I was tidying up the rubbish when the front door opened and Sarah appeared in her socks. "Oh, you're back! Someone has been trying to get in touch with you."

"Can't you keep this place tidy?" I had to shoulder my way past her just to get into my own house. "Who was it?"

"He wouldn't say. He tried twice, though."

I went through to the kitchen, ignored the unwashed dishes and the piles of laundry and opened a bottle of rather handsome and spicy Brunello di Montalcino. I was in that sort of mood. Mo was at the table eating breakfast cereal. It was seven o'clock in the evening, for goodness sake. "Did this person say what he wanted?"

"Well, he wanted to speak with you."

"Yes, obviously he wanted to speak with me, but what about?"

"He didn't say."

"Did he leave a name?"

"No."

Did he leave a number?"

"No."

I looked meaningfully at Mo, who was busy spooning milk and cereal flakes into his cherubic mouth. "So to all intents and purposes he may as well have not have called, you may as well not have answered and you certainly may as well not have told me about it."

"Sort of grumpy this evening, aren't we, Dad?"

"Not at all. Would you like wine with your cornflakes, Mo?" I asked.

"Yes please."

I poured three glasses. I didn't like the way Sarah was looking at me. "Dad, why don't you bring your girlfriend here?"

"Oh, that would be nice. She could see you guys in your nightware mopping up milk with breadsticks."

"Ooooo," went Mo.

"Are we crowding you, Dad?"

"Look, a lot seems to be happening, that's all. Are you sure he didn't leave a name?"

"Who?"

I gave up, took the rest of the bottle into the living room and went to put some Tangerine Dream on the turntable. Someone had been going through my vinyl collection—Mo, I suspected. The album sleeves were out of order and though I felt an irrational burst of annoyance I managed to avoid making a fool of myself over it. It wasn't about the sequence of the discs, it was that my life was being put out of order on every front. I was emotionally stretched. I felt an unseen hand reaching into my little world and messing up my kitchen and moving Jazz-Rock-Fusion A-E and putting it in Electronic-Trance G-M after replacing it with Blues-R'n'B P-S. Just for a laugh.

I wanted to return to my orderly world, with my debts squared, with my wine collection and my record collection and the bed corners all turned down. And then again the biggest threat to this world was not Mo at my records or Sarah dumping her laundry, nor the police at my door, nor the threat of the bailiffs chasing up on my defaulted loan: it was Yasmin

I felt like John Barleycorn: I was being ploughed, harrowed, sown, harvested at the knee, threshed, winnowed and ground between stones. The sudden intrusion of Yasmin into of my life had left me reeling. As indeed had the "friendly" visit from Commander Morrison and the fact that I'd been exposed for lying to the Security Services. A further trouble to me was the paranoia riding on my certainty that someone was onto us about the forged books. Now that Lucy had left Stinx I despaired of him ever coming through with the forgeries. Normally he was a rock, but I thought his binge-drinking—quite apart from sabotaging the forgery project—might lead him to talk about our modest operation to the wrong person. Then there was the fact that my son hated me. Added to all this, I had Sarah and Mo turning day into night and habitually leaving the cap off the toothpaste tube. Oh yes, I almost forgot: there was also the small matter of the proliferation of demons.

This is when they come, when you are feeling like a wounded stag at bay. These are the anxieties upon which they attend. I looked around the room for my old demon. I sensed he was close. But he wasn't there yet.

I poured wine on the thought. And still more wine. I don't know whether I dreamed this or just thought it, but I saw myself as a circus plate-spinner. As we all know, those fabulous plate-spinners cheat by engineering dimples into the underside of the plates to keep them aloft; in my dream the dimples had inverted into nipples and I couldn't even get the plates started.

Meanwhile in real life one of those spinning plates was about to come crashing down. "Wake up, Dad. There's someone on the phone for you. Wake up."

It was Sarah, shaking me. She was holding the telephone, her hand muffling the mouthpiece. I must have fallen asleep in the chair. For a moment I didn't know where I was. I had to glance around the room to pull my senses together. "Whisit?" I managed to slur.

"It's that guy who's been trying to get hold of you."

"Wassewant?"

"Talk to him and you'll find out!" Sarah held the phone out to me.

"Hello?" I said, looking at Sarah.

"Am I talking to William Heaney?"

"You are."

"My name's Mathew Stokes. I'm calling from the *Sunday Observer.*"

"Yes."

"We have a story and we'd like to give you a chance to comment on it before we run it."

"Comment?" Sarah was hovering, searching my face. I shooed her out of the room with a gesture. "Hold on a moment." For good measure I closed the door on her, because I knew she'd be trying to listen. "Comment on what?"

"It's about your publishing activities, Mr. Heaney."

Right, this it: we're finally knackered, I thought. I went straight into denial mode. "My publishing? That sounds interesting."

"We've pretty much got the full story. You can say nothing or you can put your own side of things."

"May I say nothing?" Somehow I'd become Oscar Wilde.

"You can. This is a courtesy; a chance to get your side in."

"My side? My side of what?"

"Look, there's no point you pretending. The story is going to run whatever you say. We've got a statement from Michael Ellis. You're not going to deny you know him. And though Jaz Singh is refusing to say anything, we know that he's a regular drinking friend of yours. In fact—"

"What has Ellis said, exactly?"

"He's behind the original allegation. We investigated and now we have proof."

"Proof. What proof? What proof do you have?"

"We found some discarded manuscripts in your handwriting. Actually we still have them."

"What the bloody hell are you gibbering about? What handwriting? What allegations?"

Matt Stokes sighed at the other end of the line. Like he was very, very tired. "Michael Ellis alerted us to the fact that you are the actual author of Jaz Singh's poetry."

I almost dropped the telephone.

I'd thought this was about forged antiquarian books! Whereas it was about this other game. The thing I never gave a moment's thought. I was torn between manufacturing a few sobs to make a clean confession or switching lanes into a new track of complete denial. I opted for the latter. "Yes, and I'm the author of that new Shakespeare folio that just turned up. Plus a couple of William Blake engravings"

"You're going to flatly deny it all?"

"You seem to know more about it than I do."

"Look, Mr. Heaney, we have the manuscripts in your handwriting. We got them from your rubbish bin."

"You've been going through my rubbish? This gets better and better!"

"Look, you haven't done anything illegal. You've just conned a few people who are too far up their own arses anyway. Off the record, I suggest you claim it was a literary hoax. There's a long tradition of this sort of thing. It's almost a genre in itself. And the fact is we're going to run this story in the Arts Review section whether you like it or not. It would be a much better story, both for you and for me, if you were to fill it out. Offer a cheeky grin, sort of thing."

"I'm not big on cheeky grins. Give me a minute will you?"

I needed to think. After a few seconds I asked the journalist if he'd spoken to Jaz. He said he had, just a few moments before calling me, and that Jaz had refused to comment. I asked if he would promise not to run anything until I'd got back to him. He told me he'd give me to the end of the week, but no longer.

I made a call to Jaz but his line was engaged. I was able to leave a voicemail asking him to call me back. I went back into the kitchen. Sarah and Mo looked at me expectantly. There seemed to be no point keeping it from them.

"So let me get this straight..." Sarah kept saying.

"I've got one of his books!" Mo told me.

"Tell me you didn't pay good money for it."

"Yeh, Jaz Singh, he's like, really cool with all the students right now. Ultra-hip. Totally. I mean he's a genius. What I mean is, his poems... those poems... your poems... are really *really* good."

"Oh, for God's sake, Mo, it's gibberish."

"No they're like... hot... and very cool."

"They can't be both hot and cool, now, can they? They're crap. I should know: I write them."

"So let me get this straight..."

"They're not crap!" Mo said. His eyes had gone moist with earnestness. "All that stuff about demons sitting just behind your emotions, it's, it's…"

"Mo! Stop, please! I come home, I open a bottle of wine and when I've finished the bottle there's another shit poem ready to give to Jaz. It's a joke."

He wasn't having it. "No way." He shook his head very slowly. "No fucking way."

"Look, I wrote the fucking things! I'm the ultimate living authority on them! They're crap if I say they are!"

"Just let me get this straight…" said Sarah.

The telephone rang and the front doorbell went at the same time. It was Jaz in both cases. I mean, I answered the door while Sarah got the phone, and there was Jaz speaking to Sarah on his mobile phone, somewhat pointlessly instructing her to tell me that he was at the door. "We've been blown open," he said, patting me on the shoulder and stepping into the hall.

We all regrouped in the kitchen, which everyone seemed to think the proper place for a crisis. I opened another bottle. Jaz drank a glass straight down, as if it were Lucozade. Mo stared hard at Jaz. He couldn't get his head round the fact that he was meeting someone who had been an idol up until five minutes ago. But who wasn't any longer

"Thank the b'jesus," I said to Jaz. "At first I thought it was about the books."

"Right. Right." He dragged his hand slowly across his face, as if he were washing it.

"What books?" Sarah wanted to know.

"We need to get a story together, Jaz. There's no other way out."

"I'll be a laughing stock," he said.

"No, we'll put a spin on it. That's what government ministers do all the time."

"You once told me that spin is the same as lies," Sarah said brusquely.

"Yes. We're going to lie. We say the poems were written jointly. We say that, because poets prefer the company of their own misery, there has never been a tradition of collaborative poetry, and we've sought to change that. We claim the poems would never have been taken seriously as such. And since I'm a rather retiring person, I wanted no truck with the demon of fame so I was happy for Jaz to take on the persona of the poet. We say that T. S. Eliot and Ezra Pound did much the same thing."

"Is that true?" Mo asked.

"Who cares if it's true?" I said.

We all drank more wine, and with my kitchen cabinet to advise me, we constructed a written statement. Mo contributed a travel phobia for me. Sarah got some books out and checked that Ezra Pound had indeed chopped Eliot's whining verse at least in half before it saw the light of day. Jaz, who had changed the title of one of the early poems, was eager to describe that as a process in which I wrote the first draft and he the second. By the end of the evening I actually started to believe the whole farrago.

When we'd got our statement together I tried calling the journalist but I reached an automated switchboard. I guessed that he'd gone home. So I emailed our statement to an address he'd given me, and then I went to bed, leaving Jaz to drink more wine and chill with the kiddiewinks into the early hours.

"You haven't heard from Stinx, have you?" I asked Jaz before retiring. I was starting to sound desperate.

"Not a peep."

Jaz had his photo printed in the papers a lot more than I did. Why not—he's much more handsome. I had a photo taken outside my house with me looking wistful and suburban. It was in the Arts pages of the *Observer*. If you look closely you might be able to make out the shadow of a new demon manifesting in the corner of the shot. Well, it's either that or just a normal shadow because the photographer came late in the afternoon when the sun was going down. No one noticed either way.

Jazz had a few performance dates cancelled and one or two people seemed to think they'd been made a fool of. I didn't see how that worked: as far as I was concerned they were already fools when they initially went giddy over my doggerel. On the other hand, if they'd argued the case for it being good poetry originally I'd have thought they'd want to maintain their position.

I confessed all to Yasmin. All about the poetry scam, I mean; not the other stuff, for God's sake.

"Is that all?" she said. "I thought you were about to tell me something important."

The worse thing for me was that I became associated with the poems I'd written. The last thing I wanted at my time of life was to be taken for a poet. It was deeply embarrassing. Especially when it came to the content of the explicitly sexual ones. Val in the office wouldn't look at me for two days. I suspect she'd read somewhere the one about secretaries who wear plaid skirts. Which she often did.

Chapter 28

Well, at least we finally knew what all the snooping was about. What with my habit of lying to the police, the last thing we wanted was for *them* to come and ask me about forging antiquarian books, and at least that threat seemed to have cleared.

But to keep this plate spinning I desperately needed to find Stinx again to speed up the operation. I also needed to see the detestable Ellis before he lost interest. My problem lay in contacting him when I had no progress to report on *Pride and Prejudice*. I couldn't exactly call him to say that I had nothing to report, so I decided to let him in on one or two other gems that had appeared on the scene. A nice little first edition of Dickens, I thought. Maybe *A Christmas Carol*. Or perhaps Sterne's *Tristram Shandy*. Maybe something from the lucrative children's market

I didn't exactly rub my hands at the thought of seeing him. Something else was gnawing at me about that bastard Ellis. He'd put the *Sunday Observer* on to us, the little shit. I couldn't think what his motives were, apart from jealousy. Jaz after all was the poetry world's pin-up boy, and Ellis was never going to be more than an also-ran with a big hooter. No, I owed Brother Ellis a visit.

I also owed a visit to Antonia at GoPoint. I anticipated that she might have already got through the last donation, and anyway, with only a few days to go before Christmas I liked the idea of a seasonal announcement that there might be more to come later.

I was seeing Yasmin pretty much every evening after work by now. We would eat early, stroll by the Thames and stop for a drink. That's as far as the evenings went and it did puzzle me as to why she hung in there, but she seemed content not to push it. The idea that she might be Ellis's spy did still trouble me, but I so relished every minute spent with her that I pushed that notion to one side. Anyway, because my evenings were crowded with her I took a long lunch-break during which I was set on seeing Antonia and Ellis both.

The Christmas decorations had been set up in the streets and even though it was only lunchtime the lights were on in all the stores as I jumped aboard a red bus tilting down Oxford Street towards Bloomsbury. A fellow passenger kept trying to talk to me about something impenetrable, and I nodded vigorously without really understanding. No, it wasn't a demon, just a red-bus nutter. There are hundreds of them.

When I got to GoPoint, that very same Mancunian woman with the bad teeth and the padded jacket was hanging round the doorway, shivering. "Do you know when it will be four o'clock?" she asked me as I rang the bell to gain admission.

"It's definitely on its way," I said. She seemed happy with that.

One of Antonia's assistants let me in and told me that Antonia was in her office.

There was something odd about the place, but I didn't have time to register what it was because Antonia, whose cubby-hole "office" faced the door, looked up from her computer. She greeted me with her usual smile, but it seemed to me slower in its delivery than usual. She got out of her chair and embraced me in her normal way. But there was something missing.

"No William Blake poetry today, Antonia? You usually have

some clever and obscure line to throw at me."

She released me from the embrace. "I'm a little tired." She cleared a space for me and drew out a plastic chair. "Have a seat."

"Tell me something, Antonia. Who does it for you?"

"Does what?"

"The selflessness. The sacrifice. The patience. All this endless giving."

She looked at me with cloudless eyes. "If you ask that question, you've lost the point."

"Aren't you going to ask me why I'm here?"

"No, but you're going to tell me."

"Right. I'm reasonably confident that come the spring we might be in a position to make another donation."

She shook her head and looked away. Then she looked back at me again, searching my face. There was a smile on her lips, but it was strained. The lines at the corners of her eyes were engraved deeper than ever. The wrinkles around her lips seemed today to be claw marks. "It's great, William, but it's redundant."

"What! They're trying to close you again? But they've been trying that for years! So what?"

"It's not that. We've come to the end of the project."

"The end? Why?"

"It's me, William."

What? What about you?"

She offered me that thin smile again. "O Rose, thou art sick."

"What?"

"The invisible worm has found out my bed. I'm ill, William."

"What?"

"I have an advanced cancer. I've known for a while. I've had some treatment, but it's flaring up everywhere. They treat it in one place and it pops up in another. They've done everything they can."

I found myself standing up. "But we've got to get you good treatment. We'll find it for you, Antonia." I heard myself shouting, as if it were someone else's voice.

"William, William, you sweetheart. Sit down. Come on, sit down. I've got a brilliant oncologist. There isn't anyone better. It's just the cards that have been dealt. Now listen, I'm making arrangements about closing GoPoint."

It felt like news that a war had been lost. An empire crumbling. "You mean it's really all over?"

"There's no way it will stay open after me. Everyone knows that. I've been given three months, four at the very outside. We'll sell the lease to property developers and donate the proceeds to a similar organization. The work goes on. You won't stop giving, will you? They all still need it."

There she was. Dying of cancer and still thinking of other people. I felt utterly ashamed.

"Don't cry over me, William! I'll only feel worse."

"I'll squeeze out a fucking tear if I want to!" I shouted.

Then she hugged me once more, and we didn't let go for a long time. Finally she pushed me away and told me she had lots of work to get on with. I kissed her again and scanned the tiny room. There was no trace of anything. Nothing demonic could find the tiniest finger-hole or the smallest foot-hold around her. She burned too brightly. She'd chased them all off with a glowing white heat that had ultimately turned inwards upon herself.

When I left the building, the padded woman harangued me again. She took a thin roll-up ciggie out of her mouth to have a go at me. "Oi! When will it be four o'clock? Oi!"

"Oh, fucking well shut up,' I barked back.

She straightened her back, indignant. "No need to be like that," she shouted after me. "No need at all."

I was already a ticking bomb when I marched across

Bloomsbury towards Holborn to meet with Ellis. I was angry with Ellis and I was angry with everything in this dirty world. I looked at the hardness of my own heart and I looked at this great capital city, where we have no leaders and no one to admire. Our government ministers are fraudsters, liars and deceivers without conviction, whose only ideology is to cling to power; our captains of commerce are wolves dining out on blood and bone; our religions prey on small children and feed us stories of nightmare; our media poison us with consumerism, a hideous bloated worm eating its own tail; our football heroes beat their wives and rape young girls; our movie stars and our models are junkies and drunks; our poets are incomprehensible.

I rage! I do! I rage when I see the lives of ordinary people squandered. The lives of young men and women, weak like me, going under the tidal sludge of drugs spilling across the sink-estates of the nation; the homeless drifting like wraiths; people eating themselves into oblivion and doping themselves with bad television; brave boy soldiers sacrificed in deserts for the ambitions of the insanely rich. I do rage! I weep! To see life held so cheap! And all I have as antidote as I stand lost in the middle of these leaders who are not leaders, these demons hidden in the souls of men and women, are my humanity and my rage.

Demons feed on us at every compass point. They lap, they slurp. They devour us in cruel slow motion. And the illusion of love is the only promise of defence, and even that will crumble. And I know that even Yasmin, coming to me in the guise of love, is inhabited by the cruellest of demons, just there to get my hopes up.

And in this state of rage I crossed down to the pub where I'd arranged to meet Ellis at the Cittie of York, one of London's oldest inn sites. Rumour has it that in this pub... Oh, fuck rumour, that's where he wanted to meet me, through the gloom of the great-hall bar and at the back where there are intimate drinking booths; though why anyone would want to be in an intimate space with Ellis defeats me. It also rankled because I knew that he'd once taken Yasmin there.

He was waiting for me. "Billy," he said dryly, urbanely, ironically. He waved his empty glass. "Get me a large whisky. Plenty of ice."

My real purpose in meeting him had been to stall him on *Pride and Prejudice* while I pretended to sound him out about whatever antiquarian book he might be on the lookout for next, so that I could possibly "find" him a copy; or maybe plant a couple of titles in his head that I "knew" were being offered on the market. My purposes in raising money from this game had now been confused by Antonia's news so I had even less relish for his company than usual. But I needed to keep him sweet and in place to complete the sale so that I could pay off the loan I had given over to GoPoint.

"What a piece of work you are!" he said as I planted his scotch on the table. "You and that Paki bum-boy. Hey, you forgot the ice."

I raised a single eyebrow at him. Not only was he a shit poet; he was also a racist homophobe. "Nice suit, Ellis. Armani?"

He shrugged his shoulders deeper into his jacket. "How long would you have kept it going? The pair of you?"

"Years, probably, if someone hadn't shopped us."

"Good luck to you, I say." He averted his eyes to take a sip of his scotch. "A shame the cat got out of the bag."

I looked at him. Could it be he was unaware that I knew it was he who'd tipped off the journalist? "I've no idea how the truth got out. Then they found scraps of paper in my wheelie bin."

"Yes, I read all about it in the Sundays. I was astonished."

It was true. He thought I didn't know! "Thing is, I didn't tell anyone myself. Not a soul."

"Really?" he said. He gave me an earnest and wide-eyed look. "Then it was probably someone very close to you."

"Why do you say that?"

"Well, they would probably be familiar with certain of your phrases. Signature remarks. Verbal tics. If they made a note of them they might have found them cropping up in Jaz Singh's odd vernacular style." The scumbag was actually revealing to me how he'd found us out. He was enjoying himself. Taunting me.

"Perhaps you're right." I wondered if I could trip him up over Yasmin. Get him to reveal that he knew we were seeing each other. I decided to chance my arm. "How's that lovely girl you had with you in the Museum Tavern?"

"Oh, her?" He stifled a fake yawn. "Yasmin? No idea. She was pretty enough but a bit deranged."

"Really? That's alarming."

"Yes, one of these dangerously promiscuous types. Come on then, have you got it for me?"

"A few more days."

"Oh, for God's sake. I've had enough of this."

"We arrange for full technical proofing," I said. "All part of the service. You don't want to be paying out that kind of money without being one hundred per cent certain of what you're getting. But it takes time."

He regarded me steadily. I changed the subject and started talking about the business in general. At first I suggested that the market had gone very slack and that not much was coming into view. Then I mentioned a few names. Dickens and the rest. Dropped a few hints about what I'd heard was about. Or what might be about.

"How come," he said, waving his large, putrid poet's finger at me, "how come I never hear about these? I scour the Internet and I ask other dealers all the time but I never hear about them. What are your sources?"

I took a sip of my wine, which wasn't half bad. Then I treated him to a delicious and murderous smile.

"Any prices mentioned with those?" he wanted to know.

"I never discuss prices until I know what's genuinely available. You know that. And it depends on other buyers."

"Other buyers," he said with contempt. "Do you think I'm an idiot? There is no other buyer on this deal, is there?"

There had been of course. But no longer. "I think I told you a bit about him already."

"What, this fucking toyshop owner? He doesn't exist, does he? You think you're smart, Billy Boy, but you're transparent. You know that? See-through. If he's real, give me his number."

"Obviously I can't do that."

"You give me his number or the deal is off. Simple as that."

He was in a sour mood and I do believe he meant what he said. I didn't know which way to play it. If I gave him the number, Otto wasn't going to be there. Someone might even tell Ellis that Otto was dead.

I took a sip of wine. Then from my wallet I took out one of Otto's business cards and handed it to Ellis. "Fair enough. If he confirms that he's prepared to beat your latest offer the book will go to him. Final."

Ellis snatched the card from me and took his mobile phone from his pocket, flipping open the case. He said he was going to bloody well check Otto's bid. He tapped in the digits and I waited with my arms folded. Ellis tried to stare me down as the phone rang.

I have no idea whether someone answered or whether Ellis connected to an answering machine. Either way, Ellis rang off. He clipped shut the cover of his phone and dropped it back in his pocket. I raised a single eyebrow at him. He'd lost. If I could just get Stinx to come through the sale was secure.

Then Ellis raised the matter of the vellum, a sample of which I'd already used to tempt him. He demanded that it be included in with my "outrageous" price. When I flatly refused he spat a unique kind of poetry at me, remarkable for its metrical brevity and industrial language. Punchy, I think literary critics would call it. Muscular.

"And what exactly is your commission on these deals, Billy Boy? I think I ought to know how much you get out of it every time I buy a new book from you."

"That's *information*," I said smugly, "that you don't need to know."

And then he launched into an unprovoked rant. About his publishers. About his agent. About his *translators,* for God's sake. About me. How we were all leeches and parasites and vampires sucking his vitality and living off his talent. After a while I stopped listening and marvelled at how his jaw worked the air and how his lips parted and mashed and how he bit at some of his words. It was like watching a dog chewing on a huge uncooked steak; spittle flew from his lips across the table as he found the choicest of remarks to describe all of us who had come within his orbit.

I remember thinking: How dare you say all these things when just up the road a saintly woman is dying of cancer; and how dare you refer to Yasmin in that way; and how can you sit there and pretend that you didn't betray Jaz and me to the Sunday newspapers; and what makes you think you can taunt me in this way?

He hadn't finished. "And don't think I don't know that you're tupping that slut Yasmin. Did you think I didn't see you coming out of Fraser's book launch? Hiding from me! That was pathetic!"

And in the next moment it was as if some spirit had got inside me, because I had Ellis by the throat. I'd pushed him back on to the bench in our private cubicle and I was throttling him. My fingers had sunk into his neck like talons and were squeezing his windpipe. I was choking him within an inch of his life and I was enjoying it. He was making these absurd spluttering, wheezing and sobbing noises; his face had turned pale blue and he was kicking out his leg and struggling in a feeble effort to drag my fingers from his throat.

Still with my hands at his throat I became conscious of other drinkers in the pub watching us. I looked up. The exertion had made my hair fall across my eyes. Two men at the bar were staring at me. A third, standing away from the bar, was Seamus, the old soldier. He watched with casual interest.

The truth is I wanted someone to stop me. But, shaking from exertions, when I looked them in the eye the men at the bar turned away and continued with their conversations. One of the bar staff was interrupted in the act of ringing a sale into the till. He looked horrified at what was going on, but when he saw me glowering at him he merely wiped a finger under his nose and continued with the transaction.

I thought it pretty appalling that no-one would intervene in a public place to stop a man from being choked to death. Indicative of our modern and uncaring society.

I let Ellis go.

"You're a fucking lunatic!" he rasped at me, fingering the bruises on his throat. "What's got into you? You fucking loony!"

I sat back and said nothing. I straightened my hair. I was surprised by how out of breath I was.

Ellis got to his feet and grabbed his coat. "Loony!" he bellowed at me again. "Fucking loony!" Then he marched towards the door without looking back.

"That's for being a shite poet," I bellowed after him.

After a few moments I went to the bar and ordered myself a glass of 1997 Château Pichon-Baron, 2nd-growth Pauillac.

"Large or small glass, sir?" said the barman who three minutes earlier had watched me strangle someone.

"Large, I think. Leave the bottle there, would you?"

"Certainly sir. Coming right up."

I didn't return to work after my attack on Ellis. I drank heavily at the Cittie of York all afternoon. I felt I was in a dangerous place and that I needed to sedate myself with wine. My sudden violence with Ellis hadn't satisfied anything. It had just started off a process.

I'd lost my purpose, my *raison d'être* in the manufacture of fake antiquarian books, and I'd lost our best customer, too, all in an afternoon. Worse, I'd just throttled the only means by which I intended to pay off my serious debts.

The barman kept a wary eye on me but my behaviour was impeccable until I got stuck in the Gents. I don't know how it happened. I remember standing against the porcelain urinal, pissing away. I must have fallen asleep for a few minutes because I woke with my cheek sticking to the wall tiles. There was some graffiti. I was sure it hadn't been there when I'd started pissing. It read:

Five, six, seven.

Just that.

"Ha!" I went.

I tried to find my way out of the Gents but I couldn't locate the door. On my knees I went round the room, pressing the walls, looking for egress. I did a complete circuit of the room, but still no door. Slumped against the wall, I called Yasmin on my cellphone. I was supposed to meet her after work, but I asked her to come and get me.

Someone came in, pissed and went out again, so I felt reassured that there was a door.

After a while the barman came down. "I got worried about you," he said nervously. "Shall I help you up?"

"I wish you would."

So the barman hauled me to my feet. Mercifully he discovered the door and we went out, me unsteadily, him with his hand guiding but barely touching me. He wanted to call me a cab.

"No, I've got someone coming for me," I said.

"Honestly?"

"Young woman. Coming for me. I know what you're thinking."

"I'm not thinking anything," said the barman.

I found a seat. The bar's custom had thinned out during the afternoon, but the after-work legal crowd was starting to fill it up again. They gave me a wide berth. I don't know why but I started to think about Seamus, and his document.

Eventually Yasmin arrived.

She stood over me, bemused. "You're sozzled."

My God, she was beautiful. I wanted to have her, there, in the pub. The barman came over and they exchanged a few words out of my earshot. He looked at me and then he looked back at her. He stuck a finger in his ear and shook it, as if to de-wax. I knew what he was thinking.

Yasmin got me into a taxi. I had no idea where we were going. I kept trying to figure out the route, but couldn't. I had a dreadful thought. What if my name were Seamus? And she was taking me to GoPoint? A kind of panic rose up in me.

"Where are we going?" I said.

"I'm taking you home. To your house, I mean."

That seemed acceptable.

There was a ridiculous fuss when I did arrive. Sarah and Mo were still in their pyjamas—again—but came to the door to see what was up. It was totally unnecessary that Yasmin had her arm around me as if she had to support me up the path. I couldn't have been that drunk because I was fully sensitive to the exchange of looks between Sarah and Yasmin. They did that thing women do: rapid calculation, processing a thousand small details into a hundred different boxes, all marked, stamped, appraised, indexed, judged and scorned. All in a heartbeat. Anyway, there were no formal introductions. Behind Sarah I remember Mo's grinning jackanapes face.

Yasmin said, "He needs his bed."

Sarah turned on her heels. "This way."

"I'll help him upstairs," said Mo.

"I don' need the shelp of a jackaschnapes," I said cheerily.

They got me to my room and laid me on my bed. Sarah took off my shoes, but Yasmin said, "I'll deal with it."

"He's my father," Sarah said. "I'll do it."

"Come on, Sarah," Mo said.

"What?" she said sharply.

"Leave them!" Mo said.

Sarah looked cross about something. I smacked my lips at her, and she left with Mo. Yasmin quietly closed the door. "Do you want me to stay?" she asked.

"Of course I do."

She took off her coat and flung it on a chair. After pulling off my shoes she unbuttoned my shirt and lifted my left shoulder and then my right to pull it from under me. Then she undid my belt. I tried to undo hers in return. It was all rather undignified.

"No," she said. "This isn't the time."

That sobered me up, a little. Quite right: sex was the last thing I wanted at that juncture. I sat upright, blinking at my reflection in the mirror. I didn't know what I was doing in the bedroom. I certainly didn't want to go to sleep. I stood up and gently pushed Yasmin aside.

"Where are you going?"

I went to my office and took from its hiding place Seamus's exercise book. I needed to know it was there, that no one had stolen it. Seamus had entrusted it to me. In my confused and drunk condition I even believed for a moment that he had written it for me.

Chapter 29

This is the last will and testament of me, I, Seamus Todd, ordinary soldier of the Queen and very little else is my guess. Not that there is anything to laugh about in the way of *will* and that leaves only the *testament*. But which is honest, true, factual and everything I have seen with my own eyes. If I haven't seen it with my own eyes, or if I maybe just thought it or heard it said second-hand by another soldier or anyone else, then I have left it out. There's more than enough cheap talk and I don't want to add to it.

I done my twenty-two. Born in 1955, I joined the army at eighteen. Then the last couple of years haven't been so good, but I'm not complaining, that being my own fault, and the few thousand pound give me by the army when I was discharged I have not used wisely. This is my own slip-up, no one else to blame, and I don't like a moaner. Never have.

I don't have much to say about my time before the army but most of it weren't good. I never knew my father and my mother, bless her, was a bit simple. I can say that, she being my own mum, though if another soldier were to say the same I would easily break his back. Even before I enlisted I heard things said about her and I always paid back the badmouth. All I know regarding my father was that he was a soldier. I don't know what regiment. The thing that steered me to the army was when one badmouth did say my father was not a soldier but an entire barracks. I paid back the badmouth for that, too, but I was touched by the Law for it. It was my probation officer at the time brought up the question of the military and I went sharpish to the recruitment office in Halford Street and the army saved me and squared me with my PO.

Though she died from a fall after drinking in 1988, I still won't have things said about my mother. I was given compassionate leave from serving in Belfast to come back for her funeral. I had a sister somewhere but she never even turned up. There was some talk of a half-brother, but if there is one, I never met him. The army was my family, and after the cremation of dear old Mum I went straight back and signed on for another seven.

I started off as a private in the Staffordshire Regiment and I worked my way up to colour sergeant. Three tours of duty in Northern Ireland and then joined the landing assault as a battle casualty replacement in the Falklands. I was already well seasoned when the Gulf War came along in '91. Most of my squaddies were little pink-nosed boys of eighteen or twenty-one. I was their big angry Daddy, and I looked after every one of them. They all said I was hard but fair. What else do you want? I stand by that. I looked after my boys. They knew it. I told them "loyalty and a sense of humour" is what I want, "but you can fuck the sense of humour" and it always got a laugh. I don't know why. Well, you're not laughing when you're under fire.

I had the tip of one finger shot off in South Armagh bandit country on patrol, while another soldier was telling me a joke about three nuns out picking mushrooms. Wedding finger, left hand. Lucky for me the IRA sniper was a shitty shot. Also broke my leg in the Falklands, but this was in a game of football after we'd taken the islands back from the Argies. Slipped on sheep shit. That's the only injuries to report out of all my combat experience.

When the Gulf War kicked off it was just another posting, except that now I was looking after all my little lads, and it was my job to tell them how normal everything was. You know: war is normal.

And it is normal. That's why it's a paid job. You don't ask: Why are we in the Gulf? Why are we in Ireland? Why are we in some sheep-shit South Atlantic island that no one's ever heard of? You don't argue with the Queen. You form up. Move out. Press on.

And in January of '91 I came to be in the desert as a member of the coalition forces lined up against Saddam Hussein's Iraqi cohorts to drive them out of Kuwait. According to Saddam it was going to be "the mother of all wars" and him saying that put the wind up everyone. But that's not how it turned out.

We knew we were going long before Christmas. They haven't told you but you hear the drum. I can't explain. You're on active duty and there's a drum beat, an echo, maybe it's your own heart beating very quiet, and it thuds on until something happens or until you're stood down. Hear the beat, get the order. Form up. Move out. Press on.

With the heavy armour already at sea we were to be airlifted after Christmas so I was able to tell my boys: go shag your girlfriend and kiss your wife and get ready to go. It's what I always said and it always got a laugh. But the family men, those of them with little sprats in the homestead, there was always a quick switch off behind the light in their eyes. Yeh, better get the lad that new bike this year. Yeh, better get that little gal a big teddy bear.

But I didn't have that to think about, and no family to make Christmas with. Preferred my own company. Nuke a leg of turkey, pull in a crate of brown ale, feet up, watch the telly. I did get invites, I did. One or two of the lads would have had me come and sit down to Christmas dinner with them and theirs. Poor old fucker's got nowhere to go type of thing. Nah, didn't want it. Only makes the evening darker when you have to get up and leave.

So Christmas Day I'm feet up and supping beer from the

bottle in my mess watching the Queen's Speech. Outside is definitely not a White Christmas. It's lashing it down with rain. I'm listening to her talking about looking back to the past and wondering if she's going to mention us lot off to the Gulf, and I don't know if she does or she doesn't because I fall asleep in my chair.

I'm woken by this tiny tapping. At first I think it's someone beating on the window with a coin or something, but I can't see anything. My empty bottle has fallen to the floor and the Queen has long finished. Some comedy programme is gagging away on the telly and I hear the tapping again but its coming from the door. Well, the upper half of my door is frosted glass so if anyone's jogged over to wish me a happy Christmas I would see their shape through the glass and get ready to thump them. But there's that sound again: a tinny little rapid tap tap tap.

I knuckle my eyes, get to my feet and open the door. But there's no one there. Or at least no person there. Because I look down and I see what's making the noise. It's a crow. He's been tapping on the door with his beak, see.

I don't know why but it makes my skin flush to see this crow there, black as you like. His feathers are a mess. He's dishevelled by the rain. Then he lifts up his head and looks me right in the eye.

—What the fuck are you doing there? I say to him, out loud.
—What's goin' on, then?

And he shits on my doorstep and hops over my foot, and inside.

It's a big crow. A very big crow. I'm standing there with the door held open, not knowing what to do. I want to leave the door open for it, but it's perishing outside and all the warmth from my gas fire is escaping. So I shut the door.

—That's sorted you, ain't it? Now what you gonna do?

Crow hops a bit further in. I'm scratching me head. Don't want a live bird in there for the rest of the day. The crow makes some clicking noises at me. Then it hops over to the telly.

Now my telly is already a beat-up thing and the on-off switch is hanging out of the front panel by its wiring. Well maybe the crow thinks one of these exposed wires is a worm, because it goes for it, grabs a thin cable in its beak and it pulls; and then there's an almighty bang and smoke and sparks from the telly.

And I'm in my chair.

That's right, I'm back in my chair. The telly has blown up. There's no crow. Nowhere. Been dreaming, haven't I? Dreaming.

Only one thing. *Only one thing, my son.* The door, though not open, is ajar. And there's that little worm of birdshit, just past the threshold. And you know what? That's two things.

I never told anyone this. I've written it down here in my will and testament, that's all. Because I stopped thinking about it, what happened on that Christmas Day. You can let a thing like that play on your mind. If you're weak. And if you're off to war, and you've got boys to look after, you don't want that shit playing on your mind and jogging your elbow. You don't want it.

I pushed it to the back of my mind. Anyway the drum was beating. Form up. Move out. Press on. Within a few days the tinsel and the Christmas cards and the Brazil nuts were all just another check-box on last year's calendar and we were in the Saudi desert.

Now the desert held no fear for me, but it wasn't the kind of fighting I was used to. Street to street, house to house, urban shadows, that's me, and that's where I learned my Ps and Qs in Ireland; and that education served me well in Bosnia when I was the blue hat; or before that even your coarse terrain, yomping over the bog-fields of the Falkland Islands. Give me rough cover, half a shadow, I'm your man. But the flat, trackless desert: not my arena.

Tanks for the desert is the thing. Line up your tanks. Get your air power to fuck over as many of the enemy's tanks as you can before you roll him up. It ain't complicated. But then when you do hit a settlement or defensive position you've got to have your infantry—me—keeping pace with the tanks in armoured Warriors, so's we can dismount and engage at the battle line, mopping up with bullet, grenade and bayonet. That's me. See that bayonet? Don't get to use it very often but I do love to keep it shiny and sharp. That's where I'm happy.

But this was mostly going to be settled by the tanks, not by a bayonet's length. And for the first time since World War One there was serious threat of gas and chemicals. We drilled and drilled and drilled, fixing those spooky chemical hoods in place. Stinking. Hear yourself heavy breathing. All your buddies bug-eyed, trying to see your face behind the mask. Get your jabs at the ready. That's not fighting. But you got to do it.

And it's the fucking boredom of it that can get to you.

We'd finished up the drill one evening and I was standing, dripping with sweat and getting my breath back from bellowing at the lads from behind the mask. The lads were dismissed and I was standing with my hands on my hips looking out at the sky over the flat desert sands.

—What you looking at, Colour Sar'nt? This was a lad called Dorky. Good lad but wouldn't shut up. Used to keep following me round like a little dog. Always asking questions. —What's this? What's that?

—Come 'ere, Dorky. Look out there. What d'you see?

—Nothing, Colour Sar'nt. Nothin' there. Desert, only desert Colour Sar'nt.

—Look again, son.

—Can't see anything. Nuffink.

—Look at that sky. You ever seen a sky that colour?

—No, Sar'nt.

—Not Sar'nt, Colour Sar'nt you little toe-rag. What colour is it, Dorky?

—Pink, Colour Sar'nt.

—It ain't pink, you muppet. Look again.

A few of the other lads trudge by, clutching their sweaty chemical masks, wanting to know what we're looking at.

—Dorky says it's nothing, I says to 'em. —Then he says it's pink, but I says it ain't pink. What colour is that sky?

—Lavender, says Chad, a Black-Country kid. —Innit.

—No, ti'nt lavender, says Brewster, a Liverpool scally, good lad in a fight. —Ti'nt lavender.

Next thing there's seven or eight lads looking into that nothing, trying to decide what colour that nothing is. The truth is I don't know what colour it is. It's the most beautiful sky I ever seen in my life and I don't know what colour to say.

—See that sky, lads? That's why you joined the army. It ain't just to have it out with the Iraqis. It's so you'll see miraculous things. Like that sky.

And I walk away; leaving them scratching their heads. They don't know if I'm taking the piss. Truth: I don't know either. Though I do remember thinking: look at the sky now, lads, cos it's gonna get dark.

Waiting, drilling, waiting, drilling. Saddam has used gas against the Iranians and the Kurds and the marsh Arabs, so we're expecting him to fling a pot of gas in our faces. Real Soon Now, as they say. But it doesn't come. There are a few more sunsets while the air assault makes softening-up runs over the Iraqis occupying Kuwait. It turns out the enemy has no decent air assault to answer with and I'm already thinking this might be a short war.

Where is their air assault? Where is their artillery, lobbing gas and chemicals at us? This is supposed to be the biggest army in the Middle East. What are they doing? Lying in their trenches and sharpening their swords? The waiting is getting our boys nervous. There's only so many times you can tell 'em to look at a pink sky. Lavender.

When they boys talk, all they talk about is what size TV screen they're going to spend their service wages on; and since this is the first war properly televised how they're going to watch it on these big TV sets when they get home. Drives me mad.

—What the fuck for? Like living it ain't enough for you? You want the Hollywood version? The boredom taken out? The dozy rosy ending? You think it's a fucking game show, doncha?

—No, Colour Sergeant.

—Yes you fucking do. Don't *no colour sergeant* me, you muppet.

The serious aerial bombing starts in the middle of January and while that goes on we just have to train and wait. There are a few duels with the artillery but the only attackers are helicopters. The MLRS units are pumping out rockets and with these little bug things—unmanned RPVs—whining in the sky to send coordinates back to our computers so we can throw still more rockets I start to think: that's it, mate. Your type of soldier is redundant, get cashiered, hang your boots up. See—there's nothing coming back. One-sided war if they don't have the technology. Then at the end of January the Iraqis start to stir and they move across the Kuwait border and into Khafji. That don't last long. We're getting rumours that the Iraqi prisoners picked up in Khafji have no stomach for the fight.

By the third week of February the Iraqi divisions have all their supply lines across the Euphrates River bombed to fuck and they are low on food and water. Huge numbers of their tanks and artillery have been smashed. And we're still practising with masks and watching sunsets. It's all good news for us. The ground offensive might be easier than we first thought. But I don't like it. Not war, is it?

I never like it when it's too easy. If it's too easy, it ain't worth it. Ever.

Nobody is more relieved than me when they tell us we're on. Hear that drum? I don't have to be told. I've been listening to our artillery increase its bombardment every day. No one has to tell me. We're going up the Wadi al Batin and then swing right into Kuwait City and even though my lads are looking a bit sick except for Brewster who is well up for it I'm laughing and singing; *Wadi, Wadi, we're going up the Wadi,* and my boys are going: *You're cracked, Colour Sergeant, you are.*

Not cracked. It's just that when I know that I'm doing what I'm supposed to be doing, that's when I'm happiest. Form up. Move out. Press on. 24th of February 1991 and the British 1st Armoured of which we are a part is rolling. Hear the noise of war engines. And guess what? It's overcast, cold and raining. British weather, in the desert. Staffs ride in the hulls of Warriors, just behind the tanks and even though the desert is trackless we move, we bounce and we move.

I'm disappointed not to be part of the first wave. Yank Marine forces have gone under cover of darkness to make paths through the minefields and barriers and first layers of Iraqi defensive positions. After sunrise I begin to hear the gun reports of tank engagement. What I don't know is that the Yanks and the French have struck north to slam the back door on the Iraqis. The enemy have no air reconnaissance by now so can't have known this. No reinforcements and no way out. They've been popped in the oven and we're just about to turn it up to Mark 200. How d'you like your turkey cooked?

It isn't until later in the first day that we swing back eastwards to engage Iraqi armoured troops around the Kuwait border. I have the strange feeling that the war is already over after the first day because we just keep going. Black puffs of smoke drift across the sands and the crump of engagement ahead isn't getting any nearer. We stop to mop up a few emplacements, but besides a few rounds fired off the resistance is feeble. We pick up a few of their troops—conscripts, kids trying to smile at us—and they are all passed back down the line as prisoners of war.

There is no conflict. We can't find it. Just deeper into the desert and thick black smoke billowing around, and a weird stench. I keep thinking: I can see the smoke, I can hear the guns, but where's the war?

We roll on for hours, past burned-out shells of tanks and beetled armoured vehicles, all Iraqi. Flame is still licking from some of the gun turrets, smoke is winding from the guts of engines. Metal is buckled and bent. Vehicles are lodged in the sand, caterpillar wheels buried deep, and dust covers them like they've been there for years. It all has the feel of a battle long over. The only thing that makes you certain it's recent is the occasional burned corpses of soldiers flung from a bombed vehicle. Or half a corpse still in a vehicle, like the bit of the sardine you can't get out of the corner of a sardine tin. We put rounds into every burning tank we pass anyway, either with the 30mm Rarden cannon or we strafe them with the chain gun. Just to be sure. Well, not even that; more out of frustration of having nothing to shoot at.

Doesn't look much like there's going to be any kind of role for us boys. Not that I'm hungry for it, like some of the kids looking for action. I'll do it if it's there to be done, but I've learned enough about the bookkeeping of war. You don't want to get yourself in the red column just by staying too long.

I'm in the turret with the driver. Weird phosphorescent flashes keep popping from miles up ahead, and they're followed by what I want to call a flutter; it's like your eye goes a-quiver for a moment. And there's a smell in the air, nothing like the usual reek of burning and high-ex. And I don't like it. When it comes to combat I don't much like anything I haven't seen or smelled before.

Anyway I'm just thinking we're not going to see much action, and that this war is far off the radar, when we come under fire. Mortar and small arms.

—Rag-heads, 'bout five hundred metres, quarter left, goes my driver Cummings, a snippy little hard-case Bristolian with shit tattoos all over his neck.

—Shove in that dip, quarter right.

There's a dune we try to snuggle in behind. Our vehicle stops dead in the sand and the engines power down. I drag my knuckles across the side of Cummings' head.

—Do not repeat do not let me hear you refer to the enemy as rag-heads towel-heads sand-niggers or any other fucking thing other than the fucking enemy, right Cummings? Right?

—Colour Sar'nt!

They should know that by now. I won't have it. Not in the middle of combat. Down the pub, in the mess or in the whorehouse you can call 'em what the fuck you like. But not here. Won't have it.

—Why not? I ask him. —Why fucking not?

Another mortar falls and there are a couple of pings as bullets strike our AV. The boys in the back think I'm mad. We're under fire and I'm giving them parade-ground drill. But I know the mortars are well short and the bullets are spent when they hit the sides of the Warrior. —Come on! Let's hear it!

—Underestimation of enemy, Colour Sar'nt, says Brewster, at the top of the class.

He's going to say more but I cut him off. —Under-fucking-estimation of enemy! I don't know what we've got here but sitting just behind them is the National Republican Guard. More fucking highly educated than you are, Cummings. Crack fucking soldiers, you cunt. Loyal to Saddam. They are not towel-heads rag-heads or sand-niggers, they are the fucking enemy and you will respect their capacity to blow your fucking balls off, right, Cummings?

—Colour Sar'nt! goes Cummings, red in the cheeks. Another round of bullets ping the Warrior.

—These fucking people invented reading and writing while we were still living in mud huts and dancing round Stone-fucking-henge with blue faces, you got that, Cummings?

—Colour Sar'nt!

Well, that's enough of that. All the lads in the back are looking at me, so I swing down and give 'em a nice big smile, like really I'm just lemonade. —Good lads. Now then, what we got?

Turns out there is a little emplacement dug into the sand, still active behind our front line, and this is just what we're here for. Clean up. Mrs. Overalls. Get the Marigold gloves on, out with the bleach and polish, make the world shine. Our infrared should be able to tell us how many bodies they have dug in but it's on the fucking blink which is normal. All this gear works fine until you need it to run with sand in it; though I suspect these phosphorescent flashes might have something to do with the malfunction. Doesn't matter. Our AV is well equipped to take the enemy out.

The terrain suits us. There's a slight rise on our eastern flank so I can get a couple of lads out there to attack the position while we give covering fire with the cannon. Brewster and Dorky volunteer, as do one or two others. I give them the nod, and then for some reason—I don't know why—I decide I'll go and hold their hands. It's not that they need me. There's just stuff bothering me. Can't put my finger on it at all.

I order the driver to power up and move on fifty yards to fire a couple of white phos-grenades to make a smokescreen so's we can drop out and flit over to get behind the rise, hopefully unnoticed. When we reach the rise we can see a burned-out Iraqi tank on the sand maybe just another hundred yards away. We scope it out. There are bodies, or bits of bodies, lying around it. No life. It's all clear. It's a bit of useful cover and we go up behind it to set up our gear to help the Warrior make its fire on the Iraqi bunker.

—Fucking hell, says Dorky.

He's looking at a torso nearby. Or at least I think it's a torso. But it still has its arms and legs. It's a weird shape. Shrunk. Nasty.

—Never mind what's around you, I bark at him. —Get operational!

But Brewster and Dorky are paralysed by this thing. Mesmerised. It's an effort for them to look away.

—Come on lads, I say, a deep low growl.

Training kicks in, they go to it, fumbling a bit, fidgety, hyper, but they set up. And I look at this thing, but out of the corner of my eye because I don't want the lads to see I'm freaked by it, too. And I am. I'm freaked.

It's a corpse—of a kind—of an Iraqi soldier spilled out of the tank. Part of his head's gone but most of the rest of him is there. Well, I can't see hands and feet. None of that bothers me. I've seen enough bits of bodies in my time and after a while it's no different to what's in your burger. But this thing: it's a body but it's shrunk to maybe a third of the size it should be. It crossed my mind it might be a kid, but it's bearded and anyway it's not like it's a kid, it's like the whole thing has twisted like a plastic bag when you set fire to it. And it's left a spooky shadow behind, a man-shaped shadow on the sand.

The boys are set up and ready, but I've got to shift this bloody mess. I step over to the thing and I try to side-foot it under the tank, out of eyesight, but my foot passes straight through part of it. Nothing turns my stomach. My guts are cast iron, but for the first time in years and years my bowels soften. Some of the thing sticks to my foot. I scrape sand and debris and push as much of it as I can under the tank.

I turn back. Dorky and Brewster are watching me now. —All set up, lads?

—Colour Sar'nt!

Brewster radios the Warrior and we watch the slow elevation of the canon before it locks. There's a pause before the Warrior launches its bombardment of the Iraqi emplacement. Dorky watches the results through binoculars and reports what's happening. I have to make a mental effort not to think about this goo stuck to my boot.

—Give 'em a strafing.

—Chain gun! Brewster tells his radio.

There's not much more. After the cannon and chain gun have softened them up they come out and all we have to do is point our weapons. These are not Republican Guard. These are conscripts; they've had enough and they're stumbling out with their hands on their heads. They seem to think we're the Yanks. Their idea of being a prisoner is to try to talk to us in Iraqi.

After the prisoners are passed back down the line the mopping -up pattern is repeated. The only thing that's changed is the dust. The tanks and the armoured vehicles are kicking up so much dust and sand that it's getting hard to see further up ahead. We're proceeding pretty much by radio coordinates and infrared activity. We stop a couple of times to check out a destroyed tank or other vehicle and we keep spotting these shrunk plastic bodies, with their shadow-casts, and all the time I'm thinking: what weapon is it that shrinks a human being but doesn't destroy a tank? I mean, the tanks are burned but the shell is intact. I have to break up little groups of boys standing mesmerised over these shrunk bodies.

—Don't look at it, lads. Press on.

About another ten kilometres ahead we get radio directed to another clear-up. Same as before: a few salvoes to loosen the sand around them then in we go. The Iraqis are pouring out like ants from a poisoned nest, but I don't want my boys to get complacent. There are always die-hards, and I want no rush. By the book, me, and I'm dedicated to bringing all my boys home with their trousers on.

The dust and the sand are being swirled around by a strong breeze coming from the east. It smells of spice and engine smoke and this other stuff I don't like, and it's choking so we have to go in now with scarves over our faces, just to stop your nose and mouth filling up. This time I peel off with five of my boys,

Dorky and Brewster amongst them. From somewhere up ahead there's sniper fire coming at us, but it's being fired pretty wildly into the dust. We get down behind an escarpment.

They know the drill. I'm going out very wide; they're going to crawl on their bellies at spread intervals but stay in visual range, using the dust-storm as cover. Meanwhile I've got my other boys noising up the Warrior's chain gun to draw fire and support our attack.

I yomp off maybe three hundred metres wide. I can hear the report of the sniper as he fires on the Warrior, but I can't see him. The dust gets thicker. There's a strong breeze picking up and I can't tell how much of this dust is generated by vehicle movement and how much is a natural wind-blown sandstorm, but it's swirling and lashing about like a sand-lizard's tail.

I look across the line. The dust is so strong I can barely see Brewster, who is my nearest support. I wave at him. He sees me and I point to my eye, warning him to stay in visual range with me and the next man. I don't want to be shot by my own troops: happens all the time in combat. Brewster gives me the thumbs up to show he understands.

We make slow progress towards the Iraqi emplacement. They're still firing, infrequently and wildly. I have an instinct there's only one or two of them, maybe three hundred metres away. I'm going on my belly.

Then the dust whips up again suddenly and aggressively. You can actually see the sand in the air turning in spirals, a whip-o'-will, a dark thing, like a live creature, part smoke, part sand. And the dust is so thick I've lost sight of Brewster.

If he remembers his training he'll stay exactly where he is until we re-establish visual range. But at the moment I can't see more than maybe seven or eight metres ahead of me in the gritty yellow fog. We're all radio disarmed: nothing like somebody squawking through your set when you're on your belly six inches away from the enemy. Maybe I could use the radio safely with

238 · Graham Joyce

this wind and racket going on but I don't want to risk it. We wait. Behind the wind I can hear our artillery pounding the Iraqi dugouts a few miles ahead. Then I can't even hear that.

After a while the sandstorm begins to ease. I have a thin cotton scarf over my mouth and it's almost stiff with the dust logged in it. My eyes are stinging and sweat is dribbling along the curve of my spine. I'm scoping out the spot where I last saw Brewster, but even though the dust is clearing I can't see him or anyone else.

What I can see is the Iraqi dugout, and I'm way nearer to it than I should be. There's no activity. The dugout has taken a direct hit and there are bodies spilled. There's still no sign of Brewster and should one single rifleman remain in the dugout, I'm exposed.

I have two grenades. An L2 high-ex, and a white-phosphorous grenade. I decide to use the phos-bomb because as well as clearing anything within fifteen yards of where it lands it makes a good signal. I chuck it at the dugout and get down, keeping my eyes averted from the flash to avoid the after-dazzle. The thing goes off and the smoke rises pretty quickly. Anything coming out of the dugout is going to walk straight into my line of fire.

But there's nothing there.

I hang in, still waiting to make eye contact with any of my boys. Visibility in the dust is fluctuating at between maybe twenty to thirty yards, no more than that, and after the shock of my phos-grenade everything is quiet. I can't even hear the artillery up ahead and the flyovers have stopped altogether. I decide to wake up the radio.

My radio, like all of them in our unit, is a piece of shit twenty years old and it's fucked and we've reported it fucked and got no replacement gear. I have to make several calls before someone in my Warrior picks me up.

—Who's that? I ask.

—Fox, where are you?

—I'm at the dugout. Where's Echo and Valiant? These are the call signs for Brewster and Cummings: normal names are prohibited over the radio.

—They've lost you, Cobra.

—Did you see my flash?

—Flash?

—Phos-bomb, you fucking idiot. You couldn't fucking miss it. If you can't raise Echo and Valiant send me two other lads to clear this dug out.

This is bad radio procedure. Normal conversation is also prohibited but we're on a closed net at short range and I'm getting mighty irritated with everything.

—No flash, Cobra. Give me your last coordinates.

I sit back and wait. The thick yellow cloud of sand and dust is like a gas, a sulphurous fog, and I still can't see more than about thirty yards. No one comes. I radio again.

—We can't find you, Cobra.

—For fuck's sake. I'm gonna lob my high-ex. Follow the fucking bang, you useless twat!

—Colour Sar'nt.

I do just that. If there was anything alive in the dug out it's probably mince by now. I radio again.

—No bang, Colour Sar'nt.

—What?

—No bang. We're looking. We're listening. Sit tight.

I wait for another half an hour. What bothers me is that there is no sound from anywhere in the desert. Pretty unusual, I'd say, what with a war going on. The distant artillery has stopped. It doesn't make sense. I radio again but this time I can't get a signal at all.

My instincts convince me that the dugout is clear up ahead. I do what I tell my boys never to do and I make a solo approach. Not because I'm feeling brave but because I'm bored. I'm in the middle of combat and I'm bored, and when I'm bored I start thinking too much and that scares me more than the enemy.

The dugout is well sandbagged and there is a big, black broken gun blasted halfway over the sandbags. I can smell the oil and the ripped steel. I approach silently, slowly from the rear. The dugout is clean. When I say clean, I mean there are no live enemy. Plenty of dead ones. Nothing done by my grenades though, because they're all shrunk, shrivelled bodies like I've seen before. Shrunk with their original shadows scorched into the dust. Scattered particles of my WP are still smoking, but no one's going anywhere.

I kick over the mess cans and check round. There's nothing of useful intelligence and I need to return to my unit. The problem is I don't know where my unit is and my radio is still on the blink. I go outside the dugout to climb the rise to see if I can get a better signal. Maybe ten yards from the sandbags I hear a click.

Things that never happen in real life: you see those war movies, maybe Vietnam, where a soldier steps on a mine and they cut to the expression on his face as he realises what he's done. There's a pause. Boom!

Nah. Doesn't happen. You step on a modern mine and there's no pause and you've no face left to have an expression. You know nothing about it.

But I step on something and there's a loud click. I don't know what it is, but I can feel a metal plate under my foot. I've trodden on something and I've triggered a spring-release mechanism.

I have no idea what this is. It may be a mine, it may be an improvised booby trap. But I know that if I don't keep my foot down on it, it's going to blow my leg off, and maybe a lot more. The point is I'm stuck. I'm not going anywhere.

Now this is an interesting situation. With the yellow smog, visibility is still down to about twenty yards or so, but should any Iraqis come stumbling through that dust I'm a dead man. Should I lift my foot I'm a dead man. I can't see what it is I've trodden on but I can certainly feel the hard metal shape under my size-nine boot. Maybe it's a mine that has malfunctioned. Maybe it's some old piece of crap the Iraqis had left over from their desert war with Iran, and it's not going to blow. I have no way of knowing.

I feel a maggot of sweat run along my spine. My mouth is full of dust. Keeping my foot in place I get on the radio. Miraculously I patch through at the first attempt.

—Cobra. Where are you?

—Listen carefully. I've stepped on a mine.

—Fuck! Are you all right.

—No, listen. It hasn't gone off. I've got my foot on it and I can't go anywhere or it will detonate.

—Fuck! Don't move your foot.

—You dickhead! I'm not moving my foot anywhere. But I need you to find me pronto. I need someone to work out how to get me out of this.

—Colour Sar'nt. What are your coordinates?

—Exactly what I gave you last time.

—Can't be, Colour Sar'nt. We've been all over there looking for you.

—Speak with Brewster. He was the last man I saw.

—Exactly what we did, Colour Sar'nt.

—Well fucking do it again! I'm getting a bit fucking warm out here, Corporal!

—Colour Sar'nt!

—I'll fire three rounds, wait fifteen seconds and then fire a further three rounds. You listen for me.

—Won't be easy in this noise, Colour Sar'nt.

And I'm thinking, what noise? There is no noise. The desert is completely silent. Then I realise at the back of Corporal Middleton's radio voice I can hear artillery booming. I end radio contact and I fire three rounds into the air. I count to fifteen and do the same again. I try to radio Middleton to get confirmation but all I get on the airwaves is angry static.

Hoping they can locate me from my gunfire I wait. With my hot foot on the mine.

In the heat and dust of the desert, in full combat gear, with the sweat trickling inside my helmet, my vest and in my groin, I wait and I wait. And no one comes.

I'm on alert and my automatic rifle is primed in case an Iraqi turns up out of the dust and spots me standing there. I think about getting down on one knee to give my limbs a break; but I'm afraid that the slightest easing of pressure from the spring-mechanism will detonate the mine. Eventually I have to do something and I do lower myself on one knee, but only by resting my gun arm across the thigh bearing over the mine and forcing my entire weight down on that leg.

I stay in this position for over two hours. The radio crackles with static but nothing else. At one point I lose my patience and bellow out loud. —Brewster! Where are you, you little shite-hawk? Brewster!

Nothing. No one. Not even a sound. My leg is cramping up badly so I return to my standing position. By now I've run through every possibility for getting myself out of this. I have the weight of my pack, equipment and weapon, but I can't risk manipulating it all onto the mine in the hope that it is heavy enough. With gear weighing roughly fifty pounds I even try to make a calculation, but I have no way of knowing what force I'm currently bearing on the mine under my foot. I reckon that if and when the boys turn up they will have the gear to clamp the mine, or to weight it, or to get me out of my boot somehow without the thing triggering.

I take off my helmet. Even though my head is shaved it's caked in sweat and grit. I have weird sensations running up and down my leg. A horrible feeling of lightness is in my foot, as if it's threatening to float up quite against all my intentions for it to stay bearing down on that metal plate. Then a Red Admiral comes by.

I mean a butterfly. One of those beautiful, rare ones you sometimes see in an English country garden. I didn't even know you got them in the desert and I think, well, there ain't much green round here for you, is there? I'm glad to see it. It takes my mind off the situation for a few seconds as it flutters by. Then it turns back towards me and it settles on my wrist.

Beautiful. I wonder if this is the last thing I'm going to see. I do believe it drinks the sweat from my wrist. It opens its wings and just stays there quite happy. There you are. Drinking sweat from a man with his foot on a mine. What's that all about?

That's not bad, I think. If that's the last thing I'm going to see, a Red Admiral. I can think of a lot of things lower down my list. Have you ever looked hard at one? They are strange. They look like they're looking back at you. Like they're holding this cloak open for you to see.

Rubbish, I know, but I start to think about keeping the Red Admiral alive. —You don't wanna stay there too long, old pretty. You're in the wrong place. You don't wanna stay there.

I flex my hand, gently, but it doesn't move; it's still drinking my sweat. When it beats its wings to fly away I watch it go. I track it for several yards, to the vanishing point where the yellow dust closes in around me. But it seems to stay, fluttering in the air, the tiniest red dot; and then the red dot changes and I realise the red dot I was looking at isn't the tip of a butterfly's wing at all; it's the red dot of an Arab's *shemagh*, the traditional headscarf, and the Arab wearing it is making his way towards me.

Chapter 30

After my attack on Ellis in the Cittie of York, I began to brood. I read Seamus's manuscript over and over. Of course he never targeted it at me—no, I'm not completely paranoid—but it seemed to speak to me directly. He hadn't written it for me, but he had written it for people *like* me. And what I began to brood on was what I'd done, back in Derby, in my youth.

After everything that had happened I was ready to take my foot off the mine. But I needed a little help.

All those years ago, I'd walked out on the great love of my life, a grand gesture in which I'd made a fool of myself. It sat heavily with me. I tried to put it aside—and for long periods of time I would manage to do so—but it always came back. Another demon for me: I seemed to be collecting them. But I knew that if I didn't confront this particular demon head-on it would always be waiting for me at the gate.

I started to make my own investigations into what had become of Mandy. I'd always been in dread of some terrible confirmation of my earliest fears, suspecting that something bad had happened to her; that my pact, my deal, had been ineffective. But over the years—not least from Fraser—I had learned that no such bad fate had befallen her: at least no worse than that which befalls many people, in that she'd married, had two children and got divorced. Then it seemed she had made a second marriage, eventually settling in the Yorkshire city of Leeds.

And over the years I had put this information aside, even when the insidious whispering would return. But now the time had come to unearth more information about Mandy. I just couldn't leave it alone.

In the end it wasn't difficult at all to make contact. An Internet site—the kind that offers lists of people with whom you went to school or college—made it more than simple. I paid a small subscription to the Internet site and with trembling hands I typed out the message:

I need to talk with you.

There was no return message, and for three days I wrung my hands, wondering what I might do next. Then it came.

I don't think I want to.

So that was it. Except of course, it wasn't. I saved that email on my computer and looked at it every few minutes. There are spaces between words: loopholes, gaps, cracks, interstices through which anything can flow. She didn't *think* she wanted to talk to me. That meant she didn't know for certain. And of course the very fact that she replied to me at all meant that some small part of her did want the connection. She might have not replied at all. So in the ebbing tide I clung to the back of the little fish *think*.

I managed not to rush a reply. Finally I wrote:

All I ask is an hour, half an hour, to explain. Then I'll stay out of your life forever.

She wrote back almost immediately. Seconds after I'd sent the message.

That's a bit dramatic! Explain what?

Maybe I'd been driving myself mad by dwelling on something that for Mandy had long been consigned to the lumber-room of the past. Now this was much more tricky. Maybe I was filed in a dark corner of her memory along with a few one-night stands and foolish but laughable indiscretions. Everyone has a box of old photographs they never look at.

I'm not so egocentric as to think that I still had a central place in her thoughts or affections, or even that she ever thought about me. She'd had children of her own and the socks and underpants of at least two husbands to launder over the years. There was no reason to believe that she ever thought of me at all. Consciously.

But the past for me is an ever-present ghost. Time does not fade things for me. The chemicals on those old photographs we never look at become unstable. They unfix and yellow and fade. But experience—for me—does not. I can meet someone I haven't seen for fifteen years and my apprehension of them is as if it were yesterday. If they were kind to me fifteen years ago, I want to repay that kindness immediately. If they slighted me fifteen years ago, I hold a grudge right now. If I had an argument with them fifteen years ago I want to resolve it today. If we conflicted fifteen years ago, I'm still vibrating from the altercation.

This is how the world is for me. Perhaps I'm wrong in thinking it thus for everyone else.

Time does not heal. Time does not restore. The passage of many days does not smooth away pain, anguish, hurt, betrayal, grief; any more than it takes away the sights and smells and sounds of happy memories. Who first set loose the demon of that great lie? Was the liar who first said that trying to be kind? Trying to offer a salve?

I know how much I hurt Mandy and I have suffered for it ever since. She may have consigned that hurt to a place of forgetting. But you can't kill it off. All you can do is shut it in a cellar, turn a key and pretend not to hear the sound of its raging.

That's a bit dramatic! Explain what?

So perhaps I was mad. And perhaps I wasn't even on her radar. Until now.

I have a guilty conscience. I would appreciate the chance to explain why I left college so suddenly and without telling you.

Another two days went by before I got a response. The delay

didn't bother me in the slightest. After all, over twenty years had lapsed. What was the rush?

Oh that! Yes, it was rather sudden. I did wonder at the time! But don't worry, you're forgiven. We were just kids, after all. Xxx

No no no! I wasn't buying it. She was making out as if it counted for nothing in her world. She was faking it, like we all do. But I held a steady course. I manufactured a reason for being in Leeds the following day: a visit to some regional office of our organisation. I pressed for a meeting. A coffee. She resisted. I pressed again.

"Hello, stranger." It's what she always used to say. Sometimes she would say it if you'd seen her two days earlier.

I'd found my way to Whitelocks, a pub in an alley called Turk's Head Yard in the city centre for our midday appointment. She'd chosen the venue. Whitelocks? Turk's Head? Was she being funny? I had to do a paranoia check. But I recognised her instantly. She sat at a table near a window, slowly stirring her coffee with a teaspoon as I walked in. There were no other drinkers; it was perhaps too early. She looked up and she recognised me, too.

She was carrying extra weight, of course, and there was some kind of henna colour to her dark hair, maybe to disguise the grey. She had what some people call crow's feet but which I prefer to call laughter lines at the corners of her eyes. And she wore on her lips a half-smile utterly familiar to me. I remembered it from all those times when I might have done something she disapproved of. Whether it meant she was hostile or indulging me I didn't know back then, and I didn't know now.

I slumped into a chair and blinked at her.

"You mad bastard," she said. "What's this all about?"

"Hello, Mandy."

"God in heaven!"

"I need a drink."

"You always used to drink beer," she said when I came back from the bar. "You used to say wine was for poofs."

"Did I? Bless me for a fool."

She said the years had been kind to me and that I still had my good looks. I said the same for her, but in my case I meant it: I really did. "I've got an hour," she said. "Then I've got to be somewhere else."

I was disappointed to hear that, but not surprised. I said that I'd got a story to tell her, about why I'd suddenly left college. After a couple of false starts I finally pushed the boat out. I began by telling her about the occult book that I'd made but failed to finish—the one that Fraser adapted for his own schemes. But she interrupted me.

"Before you go on," she said, "can you explain why you suddenly felt the need to tell me all this?"

"There was nothing sudden about it. I've often felt I wanted to tell you. Over the years."

She put a hand on my wrist, very lightly. Her manicured fingernails were painted flamingo pink. I could smell her perfume. "William, we were just kids. This is like talking about something that happened at school, in the playground. Is it really that important?"

It was important enough to me. I'd taken a train a hundred and seventy miles to tell her about it. I'd also travelled over twenty years in order to be able to tell her. So she listened wide-eyed, but with her chin supported by her hand as I told her the lot. Rituals. Pentacles. Chaplains. Photographs. Demons. Girls dying. Girls not dying. Then I took a deep breath and explained that I'd made a pact with a demon to have her left alone. That I'd left in a hurry to protect her, to draw the demons with me. And that it was only years later that I'd learned—from Fraser—that I'd been misled about the fate of the girls in the photographs.

She blinked at me. "Bullshit," she said.

"No."

She laughed. "What have you been smoking? I always knew you were on another planet, but really." She turned her head away from me and ran a hand through her hair.

"I never tell anyone this," I said. "I never even told my ex-wife, who I lived with for twenty years. I never breathed a word of it."

"You're fucking serious, aren't you?"

"Those demons have never left me. They're here now. There is one sitting in that chair next to you."

She turned to look, quickly, but of course saw only an empty chair. She couldn't see what I could see. There was indeed a demon sitting in the chair. In fact there were five of them in that bar with us. They were utterly fascinated with where this discussion would lead. They were simply waiting, waiting patiently, for the outcome of this discussion."

She looked back at me. "This is nasty, William."

"I've learned to live with it. It's okay so long as I don't try to tell people. Not all the demons are bad."

"I don't mean that. I mean what you're doing to me. I mean, why are you telling me this stuff? Is it a game? Why have you come all this way? Just to upset me again?"

So there it was. I was right. The hurt hadn't gone away; it had just been hard-packed in ice. "Mandy, I promise you that hurting you again was the last thing on my mind. I just wanted you to know that I never rejected you. I was trying to save you."

"But why didn't you tell me any of this at the time?"

"What?"

"Why not tell me back then?"

"You don't believe me now; why would you have believed me then?"

"Oh no. That isn't the point at all. I'm asking you why you didn't even *attempt* to tell me."

"I was protecting you!"

"Nice try, William. But even if I were to buy this bloody story of yours, these pentacles and photos and what-have-you, I'd still say you were running away from me. The moment you decided to cut me out you were running away. You rejected me. So what? It's life. Happens all the time. We move on. I moved on. Why didn't you?"

"Wait, wait—"

"No, you wait, William. What did you expect by coming here today? Forgiveness? You have it. There you are. Understanding? I always understood you were a strange one. What did you want?"

I wasn't anticipating this. I don't know what I was expecting but it wasn't this burst of assertiveness. This dismissal. "I think I'm in hell, Mandy. I think I put myself there."

"Well, find a way out!"

"I think I have. But I need permission. From you."

She threw her head back and flared her eyes at the ceiling. But I knew that was just to stop me looking at her. "I haven't the faintest idea what you're talking about!"

"I need permission from you to fall in love with someone else."

Now she looked back at me. Her lips were compressed. She plucked at something in the corner of her eye. She said some words but seemed to address them to someone or something just over her shoulder. "I don't believe I've let you do this to me. I don't believe it. After all this time." Her eyes were filling up. "I really don't believe it."

I scrambled to my feet. "I'm sorry, Mandy. Sorry. Sorry."

I grabbed my coat and scarf and got out of there. I felt like a monster. I staggered out of the pub, blinking into the light of the alley. I leaned my back against the whitewashed wall of the pub for a single second before swinging off into the street.

A moment later I heard her calling my name. She caught up with me and linked her arm in mine. "Come on, we don't have to be like this with each other. You can at least walk up the street with me."

She was heading up to the Merrion Shopping Centre, where she'd arranged to meet her daughter. I was in a kind of daze, but I agreed to go with her. We talked a little more: catch-up stuff, summarising twenty-odd years of life without each other. It was a very slow walk.

We had to stand outside the entrance to the shopping centre for about ten minutes before her daughter appeared. During that time Mandy told me that Fraser had claimed to have been in touch with me for a year after I'd suddenly left college. I couldn't think why he would have said such a thing, and I told her so. "Were you and Fraser ever an item?" I asked her.

She pointed up the street. "Ah! Here's my daughter."

A girl of about nineteen was approaching. It was Mandy, when I first met her at college. For God's sake, even the fashions had come round again. She wore her long dark hair exactly the same way. I think I might have gasped.

"This is Natasha," she said.

We shook hands. Mandy introduced me as someone she went to college with. I couldn't help myself. "You're lovely," I said to her. "Your mum must be so proud of you!"

She blushed and mother and daughter exchanged a look containing infinite space. What I wanted to say to her was: *Can you believe it, Natasha? There are people in this world who actually think there are no demons, and no ghosts?*

But instead I declared my patent cheerful goodbyes and made my way to the station to take the train back to London.

Chapter 31

After my visit to Leeds I immediately went to see Fraser. I wanted to tell him that I forgave him. For ruining my life. For killing my relationship with Mandy. For lying all over the place. For stinking. For making me break his nose. For fucking Mandy after I was out of the way, which of course meant that he'd got what he wanted all along with his dirty rituals. I do wonder, however, if a demon told me I should, knowing perfectly well that Fraser wouldn't be able to take it. The trouble with forgiveness is that some people don't want to be forgiven.

He had a flat in Pimlico. I knew his address because he'd scribbled it on the back of that dead betting slip at his book-launch party. It was on the eleventh floor. I went up in the lift and rang a bell. A peephole-lens was countersunk in the door, and I put my hand over it. I didn't want him to pretend to be out or any of that nonsense.

My other hand was in my pocket, fingering Seamus Todd's exercise book. His Last Will and Testament. I had bought a brand new Arab headscarf in which to wrap it, so that it could be presented in exactly the way Seamus had given it to me. I was going to have to find a way of bequeathing it to Fraser. I thought it would be helpful to him, in the way it had been helpful to me. But I knew that it wasn't going to be easy to get him to accept it.

Fraser answered my ring and with a gruff greeting motioned

me to follow him down a narrow hall and into a living room. A glass door from the living room opened out onto a balcony, but it was closed. I sat myself down on a sofa without invitation.

Fraser sniffed suspiciously. "Have you come alone?" he said.

"I won't keep you long," I said, inspecting the room.

He'd made some progress from the odoriferous cave he'd originally maintained in the hall of residence. His contemporary pad was a scholarly sort of place, lined with groaning bookcases and crowded with overspilling stacks of yellowing magazines. I think he must have been a tea fanatic, because an entire bookcase was dedicated to the most obscure brands. Specially imported, no doubt. On his desk was a large black ledger-style notebook in which he'd been writing longhand. Perhaps it was his latest project.

I did wonder what he would write without me to make it all up for him. Perhaps he would publish Seamus's document. Whether he would or not, I felt very strongly that Fraser should read it. If I could find a way to slip it to him.

But Fraser was no fool. He would know perfectly well that anything I handed to him was likely contain a lot more than some words on a page. He protected himself too closely to allow casual contact with anything that might be living and breathing inside the exercise book. That's what all the amulets were about. I had to get him to willingly accept the thing. Or even to take it, in the same way that Seamus had managed with me.

I got up and went to the balcony window. "Lovely view!" I said.

And it was. I tried the door handle; the door swung open and I stepped out onto the balcony. The London evening was on fire. Pink and yellow clouds twisted and folded like angelic wings all on a darkening sky. I could see clear across the city: spires, towers, chimney pots, masts, thrusting modernist blocks, all in dramatic silhouette against a light that was almost polar-blue. Underneath it all was the hum that is the engine of London.

It also occurred to me that the city was like a vast unconscious mind. You could never know it. The act of cataloguing its chambers of history or its ever-changing geography or its migrations and its waterways and its rumours and its myths would drive you completely insane. All you could do was approach some of the dreams generated by this giant unconscious engine. Know it as Stinx might know it, through its art galleries and its drug dens; or as Jaz might know it, through its bathhouses and its fashion shoots; or as Antonia might know it, through its homeless thousands and its rough shelters; or as I might know it, through its bureaucracies or its pubs. Sometimes our dreams flow together, and touch, and cluster; and when that happens we console ourselves that we have found an island in the torrent of dreaming. A small land mass of consciousness. A mirage.

I looked out at the nightscape of old London and I felt liberated; I felt free. I don't know why, but it was all thanks to what was written in Seamus Todd's Last Will and Testament. The report of his experience had made it possible. For the first time in almost thirty years I was about to take my foot off the mine, and I knew there would be no bang. I felt absurdly light-headed. I felt as if I could float from Fraser's balcony and sail off across that polar-blue light above London.

I didn't do that. Instead I stepped back into the room. With Fraser eyeing me nervously I crossed over to his work-desk, where his ledger-notebook was spread out on the table. Fraser shuffled, fingering his collar.

"You published my stuff," I said. "Without my permission." I was of course referring to that farrago I'd written all those years ago that formed the basis of his recent book. "What is it called? *How to Make Friends with Demons?*"

He shifted his weight from one foot to the other. "You didn't seem to have any interest in it. You said before that you made it all up."

"It didn't seem to make any difference that I made it up, did it? Anyway, the point is that I'm not all that comfortable with it being *out there* as it were."

He sniffed at that. "You know perfectly well if you're not attuned or disposed to it already, it won't work. So where's the harm?"

"That may be so, Fraser. It doesn't matter. Even though you didn't ask me for my permission to reproduce my work I'm giving you my blessing. I'm moving on. I want to make way for something new to happen in my life."

I turned my back on him and quickly picked up his dark ledger, pretending to scan his notes. My other hand was still in my pocket, my fingers closed around Seamus's exercise book.

"What are you doing? That's private work."

"Come on, Fraser. You know I have an interest in these things."

He reached out to take the ledger from me, but I turned away from him, shielding it with the bulk of my body. As I did so I pulled Seamus's exercise book from my body and slipped it inside the ledger.

"Just put it down, will you."

I snapped the ledger shut. "Keep your shirt on!" I said genially. "Here. No harm done." I handed it back to him.

He snatched the ledger from me and made to return it to the table. But a frown crossed his face as he realised something was now compressed inside it. He opened the ledger and the scarf-wrapped exercise book fell to the floor. Immediately he saw what was done. You see, you have to *accept* a demon into your life. "What are you up to, you bastard?"

"You'll find it contains the demon of liberation. Make friends with it."

"What?"

"Just read it," I said. "Read it and weep."

He picked the exercise book up from the floor. "Take it away," he said. "Get it out of here."

"I've come to say you're forgiven, for everything."

"It's not staying here. You're taking it with you. And I don't want your forgiveness, thank you very much."

"I don't think you have much choice. That's the way forgiveness works."

"And you can take these two with you as well!"

A demon, probably the one who had found its way into Fraser's flat inside the pages of Seamus's exercise book, now stood behind me. A second demon, mine, but which I would leave behind, stood at the first demon's shoulder. They watched us closely.

Mostly they seemed interested in Fraser, though they appeared to be utterly fascinated by our exchange of words. I'd learned enough about demons by now to know they don't understand everything that is said; that their ability to understand is linked with their capacity to find a ride inside one of us; that once they get inside, then they can enjoy a psychic feed; and that once they have fed they leave a deposit behind them (analogous to shitting—you must understand I'm speaking by analogy here). This is why you don't want them. Even the demons of true love, with their eyes of blinding light and their arched golden backs and their tongues of flame—you don't want what they leave behind them.

But my own personal demon had already turned away from me, and had become more interested in Fraser. For me it was already fading. It knew, perhaps, that its time with me had ended. From what Fraser said, however, I knew he could see both demons with perfect clarity. Plus it was no good Fraser barking at me: he knew perfectly well that I had no control over the demons' presence in either of our lives.

As I crossed the room to leave, Fraser shouted, "Take them away with you, dammit!"

I shook my head. "I've no idea what you're talking about."

"Liar!" he shouted. "You liar! Take them with you! And take

this filthy book! You don't just dump them here!"

"Goodbye, Fraser."

I let myself out. He stalked after me, haranguing me, following me to the lift where I already had my finger on the call button. I was telling the truth. The demon that I had when I'd gone in hadn't walked out with me. There was nothing there over which I had any power. Or which had any power over me.

The lift doors closed on Fraser's angry face. Even as they did so he was screaming at me. "Liar! You can see them just as well as I can! Take them with you!" I heard him thump on the other side of the doors before the lift began to descend. "Get them out of here! Get them out!"

Chapter 32

I instantly sight my rifle on the Arab. He doesn't miss a stride, but he does raise the palms of his hands towards me, to show me he's unarmed. He certainly isn't dressed like a regular soldier. He wears a long flowing black *dishdasha* thing and he's barefoot. But I guess the Iraqis have auxiliary soldiers or a militia; whatever he is, I'm ready to drill him if he even looks at me wrong.

His red and white *shemagh* shrouds his face. He wears it over his head and high over his nose and mouth against the dust. All I can see are his eyes. Still showing me a clean pair of hands, he draws up about five or six yards away, not looking the least worried by my machine gun trained on him.

I say I can see his eyes: that is, he has one eye, of the most piercing blue I've ever seen. The other eye is stitched closed. The stitches are clumsy, angry black threads. His robe is dusty and his *shemagh* is smirched and dirty. He peers hard at me with that one blue eye. Then he looks around him.

The Arab seems confused. He puts a hand to his forehead, as if trying to remember something.

—On the floor! I bark this command, gesturing at the sand with my machine gun. —Get down.

He laughs. Just a little snigger, before peering hard at me again.

—Down! Now!

He shakes his head quizzically. Then he lowers himself to the sand. He takes a squatting position, clasping his hands in front of him. But I want him down on his arse and I bellow at him some more. —Down! Get down!

—If you wish, he says, as if this is a game.

—Speak English? You speak English?

He looks confused. Then he nods a yes, before looking round quickly to all points of the compass, as if expecting reinforcements or something.

—What's your unit?

—Unit?

—What's your company?

He shakes his head, making out he doesn't understand.

—Are you a soldier of Iraq?

He shakes his head, no.

—I'm holding you prisoner. You understand? Prisoner.

He is actually taken aback by my remark. I mean, he does that thing of jerking his head back in surprise at my words. He takes the *shemagh* scarf from his mouth and he smiles at me.

—Prisoner, I say again.

Again he looks puzzled. There is an expression on his face that makes me think of men I have seen who were concussed. I wonder if he's been wandering in this state. He certainly doesn't seem to know where he is, or what is at stake here. I think he might be retarded.

Finally he gestures at the mine beneath my boot. —You are in some difficulty.

His English is very good, though he speaks with a thick accent, like he has sand in his throat.

—You let me worry about that.

The Arab makes to stand up again.

—GET DOWN!

He sinks back down to the sand and spreads his arms wide. —I was trying to think how I might help you.

—Like I say, I'll worry about that. I've got people coming.

He laughs. Quite loud. —Who? Who is coming?

I flick on my radio and make the call. Still nothing but static. I give him a cold stare. —Where are you from?

Again he looks around him, all points of the compass. Though there is still nothing to see beyond the twenty-yard radius to the dust curtain. —I don't know.

—You don't know. Dark when you left, was it?

—Pardon?

—Never mind. Joke.

—Ah! Joking is good… in your predicament.

—Where did you learn to speak English?

He rubs his chin. —I can't remember.

—Funny fucker, incha?

—Inshallah.

I'm only asking questions to establish the upper hand, to show him that I'm in control. Given the situation, I don't feel in control and he seems to know that, too. —Name. What's your name?

He looks at the sky. —You couldn't pronounce it.

—Try me.

—It's many. And many don't like to repeat it.

He turns his one eye on me when he says this, and I don't know why but my skin flushes. I mean my skin ripples like the sand does when the wind moves it.

—Funny fucker, I say again.

We spend the next half an hour staring at each other in silence. My wristwatch tells me I've been there with my foot on the mine for seven hours. Soon it will be nightfall. The Arab makes no movement. But something about him has me scared. And I'm the one with the gun.

He breaks the silence. —Perhaps you should tell another joke.

—What?

—To improve your situation. Perhaps one of your jokes.

—Perhaps I should put a bullet through your head. That

would be a good joke.

—Then how could I help you? I'm thinking of how to help you, but this is all I have come up with so far. And you should not underestimate the power of levity. Your situation is grave. You must work against it.

—Excuse me, I don't know why but I don't feel like telling any jokes right now.

—The war you are in the middle of, the Arab states casually, —is only part of a larger war: which is the war declared by levity on gravity. Indeed gravity is what placed your foot in this difficult situation. Levity is what will raise you out of it.

I twist my lip into a sneer. —Are you taking the piss, you fucking rag-head?

He blinks at me with his one eye. —I don't understand this expression.

—No? Well, fuck off.

I try the radio again. I'm starting to suspect the batteries are failing. The useless static makes me want to toss my radio into the sand, but I keep my head, and I keep my gun trained on the mocking Arab. I'm thirsty. My throat is choked with dust, and I need a piss pretty bad.

My cramping leg by now is in a desperate state. I can't feel my foot at all and I'm afraid that the slightest gust of air will lift my foot off the mine and release the spring underneath it. Worse, a kind of involuntary tremor has set into my calf muscle. My shirt and my combat trousers are saturated with my own sweat. For the first time I actually begin to speculate how long I can hold this position. At some point I know I'm going to lose concentration and remove my foot. I keep my full weight on the mine, tapping the sand with my free left foot, bouncing lightly, just to work some feeling into my leg.

It's no good. I have to manipulate my cock out of my combat pants and take a piss on the sand. All while keeping the weight of one foot on the mine and levelling my machine gun at the

Arab. He watches this operation with great interest. My piss foams and sizzles on the sand. Finally I manage to put my tackle away. I'm exhausted.

—It's very difficult for you, he says. —Very difficult. I really think a joke would help.

I raise my machine gun and aim it right between his eyes. I'm very close to pulling the trigger. I want to. But it's against my principles, though he doesn't know that. He doesn't seem the slightest bit worried. He just keeps talking. —You know, God laughed this world into existence, my friend. He saw the night and he laughed. His very last snort of laughter created man. We were made from the snot in His nose, from His laughing too much. Do you know that the prophet said, *Keep your heart light at every moment, because when the heart is downcast the soul becomes blind.* Even now in your difficult situation, this is good advice.

—And you see, levity is the only thing we have in the face of the absurdity of death. Laughter is the cure for grief. But you know all this because you are a soldier and you have seen death. You have also killed. I know this. I can see into your heart.

He talks this way for an hour or more. I listen because it takes my mind off my situation. And after a while his voice becomes a kind of murmuring. I don't know how it happened, but without me seeing him get up he's on his feet and he's whispering these things in my ear. I must be tranced-out because I didn't see him get up—wouldn't allow him to get up. But there he is, an inch away, whispering, and I can feel his breath in my ear as he speaks. The sky has turned dark. Dusk is coming to the desert. I look at my watch. I've been standing on the mine for over ten hours.

—I've decided I'm going to help you, he says, —if you'll let me.

—Who are you?

He steps back, shakes his head. —I don't know. I've been trying to remember. All I can tell you is this: there was a white flash in the desert, an explosion and a terrible wind and there I was, wandering. And then I found you. I can give you a wish.

—Yeah, you're a fucking genie.

He claps his hands and jumps, laughing. The laughter takes over him for a moment. His black *dishdasha* flaps as he laughs and in a split-second of dizziness I hallucinate him as a black bird hovering near me.

—There, a joke! A good one! It will help. If I am a djinn I can summon up a wind. But if I help you, you will never be rid of me. You understand that?

—Get me out of here, I say.

This next part is the hardest part to write. The Arab is gone and in his place is the fluttering Red Admiral. The butterfly settles on the sand where the Arab has been, and within a second a black crow flies down from the sky and eats the Red Admiral, and I know it is the same crow that I hallucinated a moment ago, and the same crow that had come into my room that Christmas Day before I left for the Gulf. It eats the butterfly and it grows before my eyes, twelve foot, thirty foot in the air and I can smell the stink of its hot, black feathers and its birdshit and I see its yellow claws scrabbling the sand near my foot on the mine; I wants to shout: No! But already a screaming is coming across the sky.

— Incoming! I shout to no one. It's a mortar or a rocket and it lands maybe thirty feet away and the blast lifts me up high into the air and blows me clean across the desert. I'm already flying backwards when I hear the mine detonate safely, and then I'm dumped on the desert floor.

I don't know what happens next because I come round in a field hospital with about two hundred beds. I wake up and look around me and say —Where's my boys? Get my boots, I have to look after my boys.

Medic comes up to me and snatches a clipboard hanging on the end of my bed. —For you, Tommy, ze var is offer—

—Fuck off. Where's my boots?

—I'm serious, it's over. And not just for you.

He is serious, too. I've been unconscious for nearly three days and the fighting is done and dusted. I didn't know, but the Iraqis had retreated and we'd torched their entire fleeing army on the Road of Death. I've missed it all.

I get a visit from the brass and later that day Brewster comes by. —I'd heard you were awake.

—Brewster! Who brought me in?

—They said you'd stepped on a mine. The whole unit was out looking for you. We lost radio contact. The unit had to press on but the major left three of us behind to try to find you. Hours it was. Then some friendly fire came in. After that we found you.

—Friendly fire?

He smirked at me. —Yeh. It blew half your uniform off. We found you on your back giggling like a fucking drain, Colour.

—I don't fucking giggle.

—You was giggling like a fucking loony wiv no sister. There wasn't a scratch on ya but your tongue was 'anging out and you were giving it the big tee-hee-hee.

—Fuck off, Brewster.

—I'm tellin' you, Colour. And you had this rag on yer head.

He turns away and steps over to a cabinet at the end of the tent. Takes something out of the cabinet and brings it to the bed. It's a neatly folded, red-checked *shemagh*. I take it from his hand. —What happened to the Arab?

—Arab?

—The one who was wearing this? What happened to him?

—No, *you* was wearin' this.

I sink back into my pillow. The last thing I can remember is the Arab whispering in my ear, and then the blast of the incoming. That was it. Lights out.

Brewster is looking at me strange. —What happened? Where'd you get to?

—My fucking head is killin' me, Brewster.

—You want the medic, Colour?

—Nah, just a bit o' peace. All the boys sound?

—All present and correct. All relieved you're okay.

—Good boys, good boys.

We clasp hands and Brewster leaves the medic tent. Leaves me holding the scarf. I still have it. The scarf. The *shemagh*.

I didn't know it then but my army days were already numbered. It was true that the blast hadn't left a scratch on me—physically. But after what had happened I couldn't sleep properly and never have been able to since that day. I've taken all kinds of medication. Useless. And the lack of sleep led me to have headaches. I took even more medication for the headaches, and that led me to have bad dreams; so bad that I didn't even want to sleep.

My job relied on me being as fit as a flea. I couldn't ask any boy to do what I couldn't do. I hid it from myself for a while, but I suppose inside I knew it was all over. Then about a year after the Gulf War the colonel called me in one day and started to talk to me about career counselling and all the wonderful opportunities that can lie ahead of a man when he leaves the forces. There was counselling; there was retraining; there was a house-purchase scheme. This wasn't like the old days when you used to get dumped out of the army with nowhere to go, he told me. I remember listening to it all in stony silence. When he'd had his say I stood up, saluted him and marched out of his office.

I wasn't discharged or cashiered or anything like that. I retired with full honours and with an army pension. I got work. Mostly in security. I had a job with Group 4 Security for about three years. I was happy to take on night work since I couldn't sleep anyway.

I don't know how many times he visited me before I dropped to who he was. And anyway, that was his way: he would take over someone, maybe for just for a few hours, or maybe just for a minute or so. But he'd let me know. There would be something in what he said to me. Sometimes he would be quite open; sometimes he would give just a little hint, or a word or two to remind me of our moments together in the desert. Sometimes he would play games, you know, fuck with my head. He liked to wink. That would be like a reminder of his one eye, the wink. The trouble was of course that you do get people who like to wink at you in the middle of a conversation, and I would think: ah, he's here. But I might have got it wrong, and it was just someone winking. He knew that. He knew he was fucking with my head. It was his sense of humour. But for that reason I didn't like people winking at me, which I think is fair enough, given what I had to put up with. But other people just thought I was being cranky.

That day in the desert when I had my foot on the mine he'd told me that he'd always be with me. That was the price I paid.

I'd be in an interview for some shitty job as a night watchman for this or that corporation and the suit interviewing me would say I looked suitable or whatever and then he might wink. And I would have to look behind his eyes. But I'd have to make sure they couldn't see me staring.

It wasn't just winking. I'd go into a bar and there might be someone drinking alone there, you know, leaning against the bar, staring straight ahead, pint half-supped, fags and lighter lined up just so and he'd say, —Red Admiral.

Or something that hearkened back to our desert encounter. —What? I'd go. —*What?*

And the fucker would look at me and then look away. And I'd know it was *him*. See. But I couldn't challenge the drinker at the bar because it would be his way to leave immediately. Go from behind the eyes. Because they are in and out as fast as you like.

Sometimes he would stay long enough though to have a conversation. But I could never be sure. The thing I could never work out: was he riding these people, or was he riding me?

I went to a shrink. My headaches were getting worse, my sleep was a mess, I had pains in my liver and other problems. When I told my quack about the sleep disorders and the nightmares he arranged for me to see the shrink, but it didn't go well. The first thing I said to the shrink was, —Don't wink at me, I don't like being winked at.

—Why ever not?

—It don't matter why not, just don't wink at me and we'll be all right.

—I assure you, I'm not the winking kind of psychiatrist.

—Good. We'll get along fine. What are you writing down?

—Notes. We make notes, it's one of the things we do.

—Listen, I'm not an uneducated squaddie, right? I'm a colour sergeant. Was. So stop with the notes, because if I tell you what's on my mind I know exactly what you'll say, so there's no point to any of that, right?

—Oh? And what will I say?

—Don't fuck me around—you know, I know, we all know.

—Seamus, how can I help you?

—Just give me the medication. Just give it me.

I wasn't going to tell him. It's a short road from telling what happened to getting sectioned and put away. I'm not stupid. I never told him, never told the army doctors nor the quacks on civvy street. This here in writing is the first time I've mentioned it. There are some things you do not talk about.

My piss started to burn. Well, I hadn't had a girlfriend in a long time but I went down the GUM clinic anyway. Embarrassing thing was the doctor was a good-looking bird, sort of Arabic herself, I don't know. She shoved that metal cocktail umbrella down my pipe and I nearly hit the roof. She winced herself, closed one eye, and I thought: *Is it you?*

Nothing. Clean as a whistle. Just burning. Same with cum. I couldn't even have a J. Arthur Rank without my spunk burning.

There was something wrong me but they couldn't find out what it was.

I lost my job with Group 4. The lads called me "Winker" behind my back. I didn't mind that, but when one of them tried to take the piss out of me one day I broke his jaw. And his arm. And wrist. And I faced charges and I had to do a stretch. I was helped by an army lawyer and my previous clean record helped but I still had to do a stretch in Winson Green.

The Arab used to come to me in prison. Come as a guard, come as one of the other cons. There was another bloke in there from the Gulf, ex-Para, hard-case. Clever bloke. Good lad. In the nick the ex-army boys used to stick together. No one would fuck about with us. He used to talk a lot about the Gulf. Why we were there. Opened my eyes, it did. At first I used to want him to shut up, but he wouldn't let it go.

—It gets better.

This is how he used to talk. He'd always say *it gets better* when he was about to tell you something he thought you didn't know. We were in the exercise yard one day.

—It gets better. Wait till you hear this. So Saddam Hussein is the big Western ally, right? We've equipped him, sponsored him, trained him up, right? Fourth biggest army in the world. He thinks he'll steam into Kuwait no prob, right? No way his mates in the West are going to stop him. I mean, Kuwait—not even a fuckin' democracy, right? Just a fuckin' royal family, like ours, owning everything and running the show. And it turns out they've been stealing Iraq's oil.

—Give it a rest, Otto.

—The Kuwaitis, with Western investment, have been drilling for the oil *at a slant*, an angle, starting miles inside their own border but tapping the Iraqi oil reserves. Basic robbery.

—*I've heard of Arabs*, says Nobby, ex-Tank Battalion, biggest thief on the planet, inside for fraud —*who could steal the bedsheets from under your sleeping body...*

—Yeh, listen, Nobby, cos it gets better. So you all know about the PR firm who sold the war to the American senate? Hill and Knowlton, the biggest fuck-off PR and Marketing outfit in the fucking world, they're funded millions, and I mean millions, by the super-rich Kuwaitis and the oil fat-cats to persuade the American public and the Senate to go to war. They make news videos to make it look like reporting. They sell it like it's a bar of chocolate. They do everything. They even fake a story with a weeping fifteen-year-old girl who says she saw Iraqi soldiers dump three hundred and fourteen babies on the stone-cold floor to make off with the incubators.

—That's old stuff, I say, —we've heard all that.

—*What they do,* says Nobby, —*what they do is get a giant fevver, right, a fevver, and they tickle you while you're sleepin'…*

—Yeh, but what you haven't heard is this: that girl, that fifteen-year-old girl is a member of the royal family! Her dad is only the ambassador to the United fucking States!

—*They start on the right side of you wiv the fevver, and when you roll over they lift up the sheet on that side…*

—It gets better. The Senate was persuaded by just five votes, right? That means that if three senators had voted differently, there would have been no Desert Storm and none of us would have gone to war. Now then—

—*Then they nip round the other side of the bed with the fevver and they start working on you from that side…*

—Forget about all those senators who are invested in the oil business, here's three Democrats for you: one's a Bible Belt Christian and they've got him stitched up with a beautiful Kuwaiti boy; another is having a long-term affair with a Kuwaiti princess, not the one who sobbed about the fake incubators, another one…

—*So then you roll away from the sheet that side…*

—And your third senator (this is all true, I'm not making this up, no fuckin' need) admits he voted the wrong way because he had a terrible headache that day.

—*And that's it, they fuck off, you wake up hours later with no sheet underneath you. Fucking brilliant, it is...*

—So that's it then: Yanks go, Brits follow, baaaaaa baaaaa and we're out in the desert heavy breathing depleted uranium.

—What's that then, Otto? I says.

—*One fevver. Brilliant, it is...*

—What? Depleted uranium? That's another story, mate. But you see what I'm saying? One PR job, two fucks and a headache. So who is the cunts? Eh? Eh? Who?

And when he says this Otto doesn't wink, no, but he pulls one eyelid down with his forefinger and looks at me with one blue eye, and I know who is talking to me. I don't know how long he's been there, sort of inside Otto, but it's him all right. I turn away.

—You all right, Seamus?

—I'm all right, Otto. Catch you later, son.

Otto has a way of trying to look after me. I don't need looking after, but he keeps checking up, see if I'm okay, all that. He tells me about depleted uranium. Tells me what it is. I didn't even know we were using it. Explains the flashes in the desert and the way those Iraqi corpses were all shrunk but their boots weren't burned. That had been bothering me for a long time. But with Otto there's always more. He reckons it can explain the illnesses I've been having these last few years. He reckons there's a lot of American soldiers been making legal claims, but their government isn't wearing it. Same as ours isn't wearing it.

I don't know. I just don't know.

Otto gets out of nick before me. I miss him. He's a good lad. He comes back and visits me once a week. He's got ideas about us starting our own security business after I get out.

But the migraines get worse, the internal pains get worse. When I do finally get paroled out, Otto is there to collect me. Takes me off to a pub called the Sandboy—yeh—for a slap-up lunch and a few pints, so we can talk about this security firm. We're going to call it AV Security to suggest "armoured vehicle" without saying it. We both know it's bollocks—ain't gonna happen. But we get pissed and talk about the nick and pretend like it is.

Out of the blue and after seven pints of flat Courage bitter Otto goes, —Believe in evil, do you, Seamus? Do ya?

—Eh? I notice he can't keep his foot still.

—We got mugged in this last lot, mate. Turned over. Done up the arse.

—Leave it out, Otto.

—Look Seamus, my nerves are shot. Your health is fucked. What for? Makes no sense we were even there.

—Strewth. Supposed to be having a good time, ain't we?

Otto's hands are shaking. He taps the table with his box of ciggies. —Sorry, mate. Drink up. One for the road, eh?

We never talk any more about AV Security. Otto gets a payout for his arthritis. He tries to help me with all the forms and paperwork and so on but the doctors seem to think all my complaints are in my head, so I get nothing. Anyway, Otto sinks his money into a toyshop. He says he wants to see happy faces. He offers me a job "dealing with stock." I took one look at his "stock" and realise he's just being kind. Plus I don't see myself lining up boxes of moulded plastic soldiers on a shelf.

After that I slipped. I lived in some odd places. Hostels. Squats. Derelict buildings. Stone me, I even washed up at the Sally Army more than once. And the Arab showed up in these places more than ever before. He told me it was easier in these places for him to get inside someone for a minute or two. I always knew when he was about to take someone over, maybe a fellow inmate at the hostel, maybe the Salvation Army hostel director, maybe some tattooed psycho sharing the squat. A fuzzy grey shadow would appear, like soot everywhere, there's no other way to describe it. Then their faces would go luminous for a moment, just for a passing moment. And the Arab would be there, maybe dropping me the wink, just talking, always talking, like he was trying to teach me things. Tried to teach me Arabic, he did, and older languages. Mathematics. Loads of stuff. I was no good at it. The migraines. Plus there was a particular thing he used to say, every time, every encounter, just to wind me up. I'm sure it was just to wind me up. Taunt me.

The terrible thing is that as I look back over the last few years, I don't know how I've lived. I can't remember most of it. It's a half-life. Sometimes I do wonder if I died that day in the desert. Took my foot off the mine and died, and this is me dragging on my way over. I've no markers, you see. No coordinates. I'm adrift.

I see Otto sometimes. I go to his toyshop and he hands me a few quid, to help me get by. But I wonder if he's dead, too? Died in Desert Storm like I did. It would add up. This is limbo. I don't know. A beer doesn't taste the same. A cigarette doesn't taste the same.

I don't know.

I was a soldier of the Queen. I am a soldier of the Queen. I have wept for myself in the dark.

Strange things happen. You might be standing in the doorway trying to hustle for a drink. I says—I'm trying to get a cup o' tea—and there's this dapper gent, reckons he knows me. Of course he knows me. His face lights and it's the Arab. Puts me in a cab, pays the driver. Takes me to GoPoint. What a place. It's crawling with ones just like the Arab. And there's this lovely girl. Antonia. She gets me writing. She gave me this exercise book to write in. Therapy. But I don't let anyone see what I've written here. Noone gets to see it. There's a good reason. Antonia asks to see it but I say, —No, my darlin'. No.

I keep the exercise book wrapped inside the Arab's red and white *shemagh*.

Yes, sometimes I wonder if I am dead, and sometimes I wonder if I'm still in the desert with my toe on the mine. It could happen. I'm well trained. Maybe I've just been there for like twenty-four hours and I'm still waiting for my boys to find me. Like I'm tranced-out but I'm still covering that mine, muscles locked into position, holding down that spring. It could be. It really could be. I'm well-drilled enough to make that happen. And maybe all these things that have gone on since Desert Storm are just things swimming inside my head. It would explain a lot.

So either I'm still alive somewhere with my foot on a mine; or I'm dead and for some reason I can't go over; or a third possibility is that it did all happen and what I'm left with is worse than the other two alternatives.

I think the Queen can answer my question. I think she is probably the only person on Earth who can. If I could find a way to talk to her she would make it all make sense. I'm going down to Buckingham Palace. They can change the guards all they like. I'm going to chain myself to the railings and I'm going to ask the Queen to come down and have a chat.

I want to take my foot off the mine.

It's been too long. I'm tired, even with all my training, I'm tired.

I'm not writing any more. This is the end of my will and testament. I said I keep this wrapped in the *shemagh*. This is not to keep other people out but to keep the Arab in. If anyone ever reads this, the Arab will pass over to them. The Arab told me that.

Not that you can trust the Arab. There's that other thing he's always telling me, though I know he's a liar. He's just out to get a rise from me. Every time. I don't take the bait. Every time I see the Arab I know that at some point he's going to reach with his forefinger to pull the loose flap of skin under his one good eye, and he's going to say:

—Seamus, there was no mine.

He's a liar. That Arab is a liar.

Chapter 33

You have to take your foot off the mine at some point.
I chose the cellar bar of the Coal Hole near Waterloo
Bridge, between the Thames and Strand. I liked this place, if
only because William Blake lived and died above it; though in
dreadful poverty. I liked William Blake because he saw angels
and demons everywhere, too. Some of them were the same ones
that I was seeing.

I also liked this pub because the cellar was the nineteenth-
century meeting place of the Wolf Club, an actors' den of drunks,
orgies and loose women. I don't know why, but I thought it
would make a good venue to tell Yasmin the truth. All of it; all
the stuff that had been holding me back from her.

Spill the beans, lift the skirt, open the box, shave the cat.

I asked her to wear her black and red cheongsam dress, the
one she wore on the night when she wanted me to go back to
her place but I ran screaming from the taxi. I thought if I lost
her after telling her everything, then I could at least remember
her in that dress. I knew I might easily lose her. It had occurred
to me that when she became apprised of what a necromancer/
nutter/functioning schizophrenic/whatever she'd been playing
with she might want to leave in a hurry and without paying the
bill. But then again I knew I could lose her any time after that,
too. I was committed, come what may.

When we were settled into this old fornicator's den, its cellar creaking, she said, "You seem to have something on your mind tonight."

"Yes, I'm in a strange mood. Drink your wine. I'm going to tell you some stuff about me."

She put her hand on my wrist. "Listen: you don't have to. You don't have to tell me the slightest thing about yourself. No one comes without history. Least of all me."

It was an unexpected tenderness. She was trying to protect me. But I wanted her to know it all, so I began to tell her. I continued to tell her over drinks, and right through dinner. I lifted the stone from above each and every demon. I told her that I'd done things in my youth that had placed me beyond the comfort and shelter of love, and so I had conducted my life in retreat. That my neat suburban existence had been a refuge and my bureaucratic work a hideaway. But I also told her that I have paid a higher price than anyone to know what lies beneath the manicured suburban lawn, and to see what tormenting ghosts are at play behind the commuter's daily newspaper.

"None of this would matter," she said, "if you would just let yourself go with someone."

I answered that by saying that love is a fraudster. A demon with sweet breath. It tricks you into thinking you are unique; that you are the first lovers in the garden. She then said that my trouble is that I think everything is a fraud; that I think life is a con-artist; that I reckon the universe is out to get us.

She didn't agree with much of what I had to say that night. She claimed that love is Nature's way of showing you the very best of yourself; and that your best is different from everyone else's best. That it's Nature's way of scraping back the surface of a dirty world, so that everything can be seen again, cleansed, shining, luminous.

Oh, that Yasmin! I told her that her way of thinking was dangerous. And she said, "Yes, love is dangerous. It is supposed to be dangerous. It should be like rage. It should consume us, until the next time, and consume us again."

And I said that's dramatic, and she said yes, love is dramatic.

And then she said, "I love you. I always have. Right from that day you walked into GoPoint and I said, *You don't look like an angel,* and you said, *Let's sit down.*"

And my dessert froze in my mouth, and I went, "*What?*" and some of it sprayed across the table.

It was like one of those moments when the band stops playing and you hear yourself shouting too loud, and everyone in the restaurant looks round at you. Except there was no band.

"What?" I repeated. "What did you say?"

"If this is an evening of confessions," she said, "it's my turn. Remember how I told you I used to work at GoPoint? With Antonia?"

"Yes."

"Well, it was only partially true. I did work there in a sense: Antonia asked me to organize a library out of all the books that were donated. So that was one of my jobs. I was actually an inmate. Rather than someone who worked there. What Antonia always generously refers to as someone *in recovery*. Do you still want to come back to my place?"

"Yes, if you'll pay the bill," I said. "Another thing I have to tell you is that I am completely broke."

We took a cab. Naturally I asked her to elaborate on what she'd said in the restaurant, but she refused to say any more until we were back at her place. She asked why I had no money. I explained that I'd given the whole lot—and some I didn't have—to Antonia at GoPoint. It made her scream. She found this funny. I didn't know why.

There was a cold, shared hall with paint peeling everywhere, and some long-dead post and junk mail littering the space inside the door. A flight of echoing, dusty stairs took us up to her room, which was neat and tidy enough but it was like a room someone is just about to move into or out of. There was a large bed with a white duvet and fluffy pillows almost fresh from the factory packaging. A hanging rail with a few dresses. An ancient central-heating radiator under the window kept the place warm.

The first thing she did was to pull down the blind and switch on the bedside light.

I said, "Do you have any wine?"

"Wine, no. Coffee we have." Still in her coat she went out to the kitchen to make the coffee. I took the opportunity to cast about the room looking for all the detritus of living that would yield up some more information about her, but there was precious little. Finally—and since there was nowhere else to sit—I perched on the edge of the bed, and waited.

When she came back, she handed me both mugs of coffee to hold so that she could take off her coat. When she'd done that she kicked off her shoes, kneeled on the bed and took back her coffee, never seeming to take her eyes from me. We drank the coffee in silence. I watched her lips on the rim of the mug every time she took a sip.

"Good coffee," I said after I'd finished mine. She found that funny, too. Again, I don't know why. I was proving to be pretty hilarious all round. "Do you know what this place reminds me of? It reminds me of a student room. You know, minimal."

"It's been a good while since you've done something like this," she suggested. "Hasn't it?"

"A bloody long while. I'm quietly freaking out here."

"It all makes sense to me now. You think you did something very bad when you were young; and now you think you're cursed and not entitled to anything good. You think you're not entitled to love anyone. You also think you have to do good deeds to atone. Hence everything you do for GoPoint."

"Well, that's overstating it all a little."

"Is it?"

I'm sure I sighed heavily and ran my fingers through my hair. "I'm sorry. I've forgotten all the dance moves."

"Dance moves?"

"What to say. What to do with my hands. Starting with what to do with my coffee cup."

She drained her own coffee cup and threw it over her shoulder and across the floor. It bumped on the bare board, but didn't break. She took mine from my hand and did the same with that one. It bumped into the corner of the room, also without breaking. It was a pleasing sound. It was a sound that said maybe we'd gone past the point of no return. It was a sound that said just surrender to the demon.

She shimmied closer to me, her nylons swishing on the white cotton duvet cover as she drew near. Close enough for me to tell the difference between her perfume and her natural body scent. Then she kissed me, and the kiss drew all the tension out of me and at that moment it was like something else came into the room, riding on smoke. Some dark enfolding power, black like sleep, red like embers, white with snowy wings. She held my face between her hands and gently pressed her tongue into my mouth. I felt myself going under; I wanted to swoon away, like a girl.

Perhaps because of that I put my hand on her breast. She moved it away. "No. Not until I've said what I have to tell you. I'm going to take off my dress but I just want you to hold me. Is that okay?"

I didn't know what was going on, but I said yes, it was okay. I watched her unbutton the cheongsam dress and take it off. I was hypnotised. She was like the snake-charmer. A slight shimmy or movement to the side had me almost swaying.

She made me lie back on the bed and took off my shoes before stretching out next to me, her head on my chest. "Listen to me," she said. "I'm going to tell you some stuff about me and you may not like me so much when I'm finished."

I lay there holding her, partly relieved that I wasn't expected to fling myself on her and rut like a porn star, partly disappointed that I couldn't.

"As I told you, I was actually an inmate at GoPoint. I was adrift. I was coming off a lot of drink and drugs at that time. Perilously close to a life of whoring. It's a greyer area than you think, especially if you can move in wealthy circles and your options for work are limited. A man buys you a bracelet, an expensive Blackberry device, a pair of Jimmy Choo shoes. But he doesn't want to see you at the weekends."

"Ah! There's a name for a demon of that grey area."

"Benefactor. You realise what you've become and you hate yourself. You do it, but you can't get rid of your own conscience hovering at your shoulder, watching you, watching you."

Oh yes, I thought. Seen that.

"So you do more drugs, all so you don't even have to see that thing watching you. And you step out all sexy in your designer shoes. But you pull back from the good-time-girl thing, just at the brink. Where are you going to go? You live with a boyfriend; boyfriend gives way to a friend; friend gives way to an acquaintance; acquaintance gives way to a squat. Down the spiral. More drugs. William, I'm giving you the shorthand, right?

"I played in a band, been there, done that—I can sing, you know? I'll sing for you one day. More drink. And you gig, and you live rough and fast. You split from that scene and the drink is a need by now, not a choice, and that thing, that ape, that shape at your shoulder is following you everywhere; and then comes a night when you realise you have no resources, and no friends who will take you in, and I mean no one. And someone gives you a card with the words GoPoint on it and they say, *here, it's pretty desperate but it will keep you warm for a few nights.*

"And there's this extraordinary woman: Antonia, who is like a lantern in the storm and who asks no questions and who makes no judgement, but slowly she helps you start to make a fist of yourself again. And then one day she's running around trying to straighten the place up because, she says, our *angel* is coming.

"And of course she means *benefactor,* but we all get into scrubbing down the doss-house so as not to scare this angel away. And when this angel comes, I do wonder what sort of man just hands out his cash to a lot of deadbeats, so I approach him. Of course I'm not a pretty sight: my lips are blistered with cold sores, my hair has been hacked back and I'm wearing shades because the light gives me migraines, and I say, *You don't look like an angel.*"

Those last few words went right through me. "That was *you?*"

"And you said, 'Let's sit down.'"

"Yes," I said.

"I remember you sweeping some muck off a plastic chair—for me—and you sit down in your fancy coat and I sit down in my filthy jeans and you take out a packet of cigarettes and offer me one but you don't take one for yourself, and you say, 'Do you know what an angel looks like?' 'Sure,' I say. 'No you wouldn't,' you say. And you proceed to tell me your philosophy of demons.

"I think: he's cracked, completely cracked. But it's amusing. You're funny. And clever. Then you tell me I have one right alongside me, a demon. You are so convincing that I actually look round. You say it's listening with interest to our conversation, attending on the outcome, waiting to see if the exchange will make a difference to me. Suddenly that isn't funny. It creeps me out. I ask you how they work, these demons, and you tell me that mostly they just wait.

"Of course I ask you: Wait for what? And you say you don't know, but that it seems like they are waiting for some kind of opportunity. You say we should spend our lives keeping them out, except for the good ones, which we should let in; and you say that these are called angels but that they amount to the same thing. And if I remember right I say: I want some of what you've been smoking. But you ignore that remark as if I haven't even said it.

"I say, 'Here's a reality check for you: you can't change the world.' And as you stand up to leave, you say, 'Ah, but you can change one person's world.' And then you go off to say your goodbyes to Antonia, and the strangest feeling passes through me. Like a beam of light. Not literally, of course, but that's how it feels. And with it is the feeling that I want to go with you, right then. But I know of course that I can't.

"After you've gone, I ask Antonia about you. 'That's William Heaney,' she says. 'He keeps this place open.' 'Is he rich?' I say. 'No,' she says, 'not in terms of money.'

"Your words stay with me long after you've gone. I dwell on what you'd said about changing one person's world. I even have dreams about you. You see, William, that tiny interaction, that little sit-down chat, plants something inside me, and it's growing and has been growing ever since. There's a chain reaction going off inside me.

"After three days of thinking about it, I ask Antonia to help me clean up. Seriously. I tell her I want a job, any job. We talk about things. Languages have always come very easily to me—I'd picked up some French and German from touring with the band—so she thinks I could train for secretarial work. She fixes up the training and pays for it all with GoPoint funds. Your money? I dunno.

"Even while I'm training it's easy to find temporary work. Big corporations, they don't know or care who you are, where you've been. Someone always wants a pile of photocopying doing. Antonia pays for a suit of clothes for me and she arranges for better accommodation. I practice hard at my skills and I soon get better work. If you have the knack of anticipating what your boss needs you can become indispensable.

"In one year I transform myself from dosser to serious PA. I admit that some mornings I look in the mirror and I see the doss-girl standing just behind the smart PA, like a bad photocopy, like a ghost, but I do the work. I network. I let people know what I've got. I blag work sometimes, then I dig in to make up for anything I lack. I get international work. I get special assignments. I move so far away from the person I was at GoPoint that I change my name."

"What was your name then?" William asks.

"Anna."

"I knew! I knew it! I've no idea why I knew."

"I introduced myself and shook your hand. Maybe you remember it from when you met me? I like the idea that you remembered somewhere. It means a bit of me stayed with you. Anyway, the next six years take me to some interesting places. (I was a lap-dancer for a while, how do you like that?) But that life takes me a little too near what I've escaped from. It's all another story. The thing is, over those years, I often think of you. You had come into my life and turned it around. I never forget that. So I finally decide to find you again.

"It's ridiculously easy. You still look after GoPoint and you still work for that odd organisation. If you want to know why I chase you, it's because I need to repay you somehow. To give something of myself. Naturally I have no way of knowing whether or not you would want me, or anything from me. But when I find you I'm elated to see that you have so much need. I know I could be here for you at a time when you need it. Just like you were there for me. You still listening? You haven't gone to sleep?"

"Oh, I'm listening," I told her. "I'm listening."

"I'm telling you all this because you have to know that I didn't meet you by accident."

"But that day when I met you, you were with Ellis."

"No. We weren't ever lovers. I just used him to get close to you. But I wanted it to look like we'd met by accident. I followed you into a poetry reading. I waited to get my book of poems signed by him and heard you both arrange to meet. It was easy to get close to Ellis after that."

"You stalked me."

For the first time in her story she lifted her head from my chest and looked me in the eye. "Yes, William, I stalked you. I targeted you. I decided I would make a demon of myself and wait, wait for an opportunity to slip into your world. And here I am. A piece of karma in a pretty dress. But before you dismiss me, let me tell you that you can do what you want with me. If you want me to I'll leave you alone. It's not my plan to hang round your neck. I don't ask anything from you except what you want to give."

I was stunned. I didn't know whether to feel amazed, angry or perplexed.

"I think it's pretty funny that now you're the one who is broke. Aren't you going to say something?"

All I could think of saying was, "Why?"

"You were my angel. Now I'm yours."

Chapter 34

We both got up the next morning like an ordinary couple and made ready for work. In her bathroom I inspected the tip of my penis, sore from an entire night of fucking. And my balls ached. I was a bit shocked to be reminded of the honeycomb where uninhibited sex can take you. I did hope my blood pressure was up to it.

We left her small flat together like Mr. and Mrs. Workaday, taking the Tube together, her to her office, me to mine. Before parting company we arranged to meet up for lunch, in the Jugged Hare on Victoria Bridge Road, an elegant pub of marble and of dark wood, with fluted pilasters and a giant chandelier.

The walls of the pub were full of prints. We sat under one grand painting depicting old-timers slouched in that very alehouse a hundred years ago. The pub was in every sense a fine old historical London alehouse. Except that it wasn't; it was a fake old pub, like so many of them. It was a bank that had recently been converted to a pub. The old-timers loafing in the picture were fakers.

I ordered a bottle of Marqués de Griñón Reserva and poured Anna—yes *Anna*—a glass. As she lifted the glass to her lips I stopped her. I had something for her—a perfectly ordinary dull yellow-gold Yale key—and I placed it on the table with a delicate click.

"What's this?"

"I want you to come home after work. I think my house is more comfortable."

The key glittered faintly on the table, reflecting that dull yellow light from the overhead chandelier. She looked down at it. "Too soon," she told me. "Slow down."

"Why not? You know you want to."

"Yes, I do, but I can't take it yet. Because I'm not sure if I've tricked you. Deceived you in some way. I'm not sure if I'm that homeless girl; or that smart girl who works in an office; or that hippie-chick; or that lap-dancer; or so many others, really."

"Oh," I said, clinking glasses and taking a sip of wine. "I was on to you right from the beginning."

"How?"

"Your demon told me."

"My demon?"

"Oh yes. He was there right from the beginning. Or rather, *she* was. At least, I think it's a she." I squinted at the chair next to her. "You can't always tell. She's sitting there now. At this very moment. Right next to you."

And she couldn't help herself. She couldn't help turning her head a fraction, just to check out the adjacent chair, just to see for herself.

"Just kidding," I said.

These really were Antonia's last days. She'd finally surrendered to her doctor's request and was taken into hospital. Anna—I had to get used to calling her Anna now—and I went in to see her. Anna wanted to tell her story, and I wanted Antonia to hear it, so I left them alone for a while. I wanted Antonia to die in no doubt that *Some Good* could be done in this world. I do believe in the possibility of *Some Good*. Truth was, Antonia didn't need telling that. She was beyond the argument. Perhaps I was still trying to persuade myself.

I don't know: I almost expected her bed to be surrounded by

angels and golden light. It wasn't. It was an ordinary hospital bed in a shared ward that badly needed a lick of paint. A screen of curtains on wheels had been pulled around the bed. The odour of chrysanthemums streamed from a vase on the bedside table, skirmishing with the smell of hospital antiseptic.

Antonia was half-propped on a pile of pillows. I kissed her on the cheek. My nerves ached for her. My love for her was a decayed, unconsummated love; a withered-chrysanthemum love.

We'd brought our own flowers. Trumpet lilies. But there was no vase to put them in, and because I knew Anna had some things to tell Antonia I said I'd find one. I wandered the wards trying to locate a receptacle for them. Eventually I unearthed a wine carafe, of all things, and I filled it with water.

When I returned behind the screen, the two women were talking in low voices. I put the carafe on the side table. The lilies were really too big for the carafe. There was a second chair on the other side of the bed so I sat in it, and, without breaking her conversation with Anna, Antonia reached out to hold my hand.

"I'm sorry I didn't recognise you at first when you came to see me," she was telling Anna. "Then again, I'm not sorry. It shows what a long way you've come."

"How could you be expected to remember everyone? There must have been hundreds."

Antonia laughed, a tiny laugh; but it made her cough. "Over a thousand. I keep count. But not everyone is a success story, like you."

"You rescued me."

"No, you rescued yourself. Has William told you about his demons?"

"Oh yes."

"And do you see them, too?"

"No. At least not quite in the same way that he does."

"No? Well, I do. But I never admitted it to him. I didn't want to encourage him. William, do you see any here now?"

"No," I said. "They don't seem to like you, Antonia. I've told you that before."

"Anna," said Antonia, "I'm going to tell you what it is he sees."

"What does he see?" Anna said.

"Suffering," Antonia said. "He sees other people's suffering. And his own. He sees it as demons. Real demons."

"But I don't see yours, Antonia," I said.

"No. That's because I trick them. You know you once asked me what it is they seem to be waiting for. Always waiting. You know what it is they wait for? Permission to leave." She shook her head at me. "I love you, William, because for you life has never stopped taking your breath away. Because you are generous to all its creatures. You give them a home. But sometimes they don't want one. I'm dying, William—I had to say this to you."

"Antonia," I said. "Antonia."

"Shhh! Listen to this," she said. "Anna is going to take over the running of GoPoint."

"What?" I said. I looked at Anna, who nodded back at me. "When was this decided?"

"Just now. While you were looking for a vase," Anna said.

After leaving the hospital I desperately needed a drink. I couldn't face the braying, cigar-smoking demons of Chelsea so we headed up to the Embankment, to the more civilised caves of Gordon's Wine Bar, where they play no music and serve only wine.

In Gordon's low-cellar bar you need to stoop to get to a table. The light from the candles doesn't even penetrate to the dark corners and everyone in the place seems to be engaged in either a tryst or a conspiracy. Samuel Pepys lived in the building in the seventeenth century; Rudyard Kipling wrote *The Light That*

Failed in the parlour above the bar. It's one of my favourite bars in all of London, but it didn't do much to lift my spirits.

"She's only got weeks," I said. "Maybe only days. You're full of surprises, you know that?"

"That's me," Anna said.

"The funding is a constant nightmare."

"You'll help us." She knew all about the antiquarian-books racket, because I'd told her.

"I'm having trouble funding myself just now. You'll be exhausted. It will drain all your energy."

"I'll have you to comfort me."

"It would be easier just to pass on the assets to one of the neighbouring agencies. St. Martin-in-the-Fields. They do good work."

"What's easiest is not always what I want."

"You'll be broke all of the time."

"Yeh. Could be."

I looked around the cellar bar, casting an eye over the gloomy corners and the huddled couples, as if a spy or an enemy might be in the bar, listening to us. But everyone had their own private conspiracy to worry about. I thought Anna's idea to keep GoPoint open was crazy, even though I would support her if I possibly could. All this made it more crucial than ever for me to get hold of Stinx, to find a new buyer to step in for Ellis. The truth was I didn't know where to begin.

I didn't have to ask her why she wanted to do it. Because while the world is filled with people who just need to let their demon go, there is another group who need to find themselves one.

Chapter 35

Just three days before Christmas, Antonia died.

When someone dies—someone whom you love—the world is a changed place. A distinctive light has gone out of the world. Nothing puts the world back as it was. I've said before that these lies are told as a kindness and a sedative, but they don't help. They are demonic, actually. They cheat our humanity. They take our attention away from the true value of the fleeting moment. It's a value only people like Antonia ever learn: the briefer the life, the more precious; the more certain we are that life is a sealed unit in time, the more we should celebrate its infinite space; the more dark and absurd, the harder we should strain our eyes to peer into the miracle of it.

I didn't cry when I heard about her death. There was no need to. She'd led an impeccable life. I would more likely cry for myself, for my stupidities, vanities and wasted time.

But even though I didn't shed a tear I did feel adrift. I desperately wanted to have people around me, and I suggested to Anna that we get a big silly dinner going for Christmas Day: invite everybody and half of hell. She was all for that.

I knew that Fay would want Sarah at home with her for Christmas dinner and that Lucien would want to blowtorch a live goose or whatever was fashionable. However, I had no objection to the kiddiewinks staying with me and Anna. Neither of us were great cooks but we could probably stick a feather in a dish of pâté and call it Norwegian Woodcock, à la Lucien.

Sarah was passionately against catering Chez Lucien. There was a third option of their spending Christmas with Mo's mother and father. In response to this suggestion, Mo said nothing, but looked like he'd rather scalp himself with a chainsaw.

So it seemed to me that Sarah and Mo would be there, and Jaz didn't have any better invitations. "As a Sikh I'd be very glad to join in with your Middle Eastern shepherd-cult-of-death festival. By the way, I've got some news about Ellis. He told me he still wants the book. But he's refusing to deal with 'that loony.' I think he means you."

"Oh," I said. "Yes, I was a bit brusque with him."

Jaz also revealed that Stinx had once given him a key to his studio apartment. I was pretty tied up with work, what with all the administrative oversee of the GoPoint, not to mention chairing the first meeting of the government's useless Youth Homelessness Initiative, but I did manage to go round there one evening.

I didn't find Stinx, but under the workbench I saw a rat the size of a small dog gamely chewing on a green loaf of bread. I had to throw a toaster at the rat to chase it away. I saw not a trace of the work I'd hoped was nearing completion. Nothing. I washed up some dishes before leaving, and left a note pleading with Stinx to get in touch.

Christmas Eve fell on a Saturday and Anna and Sarah together came to the startling realisation that we hadn't got a tree. They determined to fix that, and out they went to kidnap one from somewhere. While they were out I received an unexpected visitor.

"Robbie! Come in, come in! What a surprise!"

He was wearing this long, black trench coat, like one of these schoolkids hell bent on peer-assassination. He looked over my shoulder. "Is Sarah here?"

"Cool coat! She's out looking for a Christmas tree."

"Is Mo here?"

"He's out with her. Are you stopping?"

"What about your new girlfriend? Is she here?"

"Anna, she's with them. They seem to have formed a posse."

"We don't say posse any more, Dad. Or cool."

"No, of course you don't. Come on, let me help you off with that lovely coat."

We went through to the lounge and sat down. I offered him a beer—I know I was trying too hard. He opted instead for a glass of pop. I found some age-old stuff but he complained that all the fizz had gone out of it. I asked him how his mum was, and how Lucien was and how Claire was, and he answered me rather formally. He kept rubbing the sides of his shoes together. Despite the fact that I work for a youth organisation I'm not great at talking with teenagers, even my own. In fact, I'm useless at it: there, let it be said. They hit thirteen and they are swallowed up by the Valley of Demons for seven years. I do know that some people don't emerge until they are thirty-three-and-a-third, but most come out from the undergrowth clutching, by the time they are twenty, a shiny nugget of reasonableness.

Then Robbie astonished me by blurting out, "Can I stay here over Christmas?"

"Here? You want to stay here?"

"Yes."

"Of course you can, Robbie. Of course. You're very welcome, you should know that. What's gone off at home?"

"Nothing. But last year was a nightmare, right? Lucien and all his cooking, right? He gets all worked up for three days. He's started already. You can only eat what he says when he says. Even if you want cornflakes, right? Everything has to be a perfect Christmas and he gets me to video it all? I don't want a perfect Christmas. I want to be somewhere where it won't be. Won't have to be perfect."

"Well, you've come to the right place."

"I don't mean that. I just mean, right, that like, it's a nightmare, right?"

I heard the door open. The tree-hunters had returned with an enormous blue-green Serbian Spruce. There was some excitement as to how we were going to get it in the house and when we did it was of course too tall for the room.

"Anna, this is my son Robbie. Did you have to get such a big one?"

Anna kissed Robbie on the cheek and wished him a Happy Christmas. He couldn't take his eyes off her. "It was that one or a real scrawny, tiny, tired-looking thing, wasn't it, Sarah?"

I was sent to get a saw so we could hack a foot off the bottom of the tree. While I was working away at the trunk, I told Anna that Robbie wanted to stay.

"Good!" she said. "But have you told him what we're doing tomorrow?"

I hadn't had a chance. Anna and I, along with Sarah and Mo, had promised to go down to GoPoint to help organise a Christmas party for the homeless people there. Not everyone's cup of cold custard is it? But that was what we were doing.

"I'll tell him," said Anna.

I continued to saw at the trunk as Anna steered Robbie away. I pretended to be engrossed in the task as she put her hand on his shoulder, told him what we were going to do in the morning and asked him if he'd like to come along.

"What, with like, like, dossers?"

"Yes," she said. I didn't have to look. I knew she would be giving him the big-eye. "It'll be great. You wanna come with us?"

"What, Christmas with the tramps, like?"

"Yeh! Pretty wild, hey?"

He said nothing. He didn't look like he thought it was pretty wild at all. I carried on sawing. A tiny snowstorm of sweet pine dust scented the air.

There were some minor domestic complications. If Robbie had now joined his sister Sarah in deserting the home front, that would leave my other daughter Claire gamely trying to shore things up, even though of all three she would be the one who would rather be here with me the most. But there you are: she was also the unselfish type who would put her own comfort second. The thought of Lucien in his holly-decked designer kitchen, stuffing his sausage and spinning his pastry for a deserted dining room, was too much even for me.

I called a counsel of peace and asked what could be done to save everyone's Christmas. I asked the kids to think about Claire. "Come on," I said, "it's Christmas Eve. Think." As if brain-power was in greater supply during the festive season, like dates and walnuts.

"You could," Mo offered, "invite all of them round here for Christmas dinner."

"No," three voices snapped back at him. One of them was mine.

We found a solution. Instead of deserting Claire, it was decided that Robbie, Sarah and Mo would have the big Christmas lunch with Fay and Lucien after spending the morning at GoPoint. Then in the evening all four of them would come over and join us for a second Christmas dinner. I would have to square it with Fay, of course, but at least no one need feel neglected or trapped. I celebrated this small victory for common sense by opening a bottle of a very special Châteauneuf-du-Pape while the kids decorated the tree with thrilling sparkly crap they'd bought in a last-minute sale.

I think it's good to leave things until the last minute. I sipped at my wine watching my children in the act of decorating the tree, holding aloft glass decorations of green and gold, baubles of silver and red.

On Christmas Eve every year one of the old twilight demons

comes down the chimney, and we all take part in a conspiracy not to believe in him. But we actually have faith in him so much that we would never let go of the bizarre rituals associated with this particular demon.

There are other things that happen, too, and I wanted to stay awake until midnight to see them.

But before that could happen we had more visitors. Jaz and Stinx turned up together. They'd bought with them not only an unplucked orange-beaked goose that someone was going to have to de-feather and gut but also their respective partners. Tagging along behind Jaz was a handsome Australian rugby player; and stepping in Stinx's wake came the ethereal Lucy.

"We finally get to meet!" I said to her, pumping her hand. I was surprised. This heartbreaker, this temptress, *this demon*—I mean Stinx's other demon, besides the booze 'n' drugs—turned out to be a jolly but rather plump and matronly middle-aged woman. Maybe I'd been expecting Mata Hari. I think I looked at her with rather too much intensity, trawling for something fiendish behind the eyes, because she looked away from me rather nervously.

"He's been hiding from us," Jaz said.

"It's true," Stinx said. "Come with me, William. Got a Christmas present for you."

He beckoned me out of the kitchen and into the front room. I switched on the standard lamp and there was his folder. He hadn't wanted the kids to see it. Stinx quietly closed the door behind us, shutting out the buzz of conversation emanating from the kitchen. In the quiet of the room he laid his folder on the table and unzipped it.

I wanted to grab at the results immediately but I knew I had to let Stinx unwrap, because even his wrappings are works of art. It's part of the persuasion. We're in the business of preciousness. The jewel is served up inside the Fabergé egg, and the egg comes on a velvet cushion.

I mean his packaging was itself gorgeous vellum. Stinx makes patterned, stitched wraparound covers so beautiful they distract the eye from the object—the forgery. Even though the forgery will fool or at least confound the most trained eye, the cover, the special wraparound, is somehow the clincher. Stinx gets the calfskin himself, soaks, limes, de-hairs, scrapes, dries, cuts, sews and embosses it. To hell with the forgery, this man is a consummate artist. The customer is so enthralled that he always has to ask if the vellum cover comes with the price. No, it's not for sale. It's a presentation jacket, protective and beautiful, to enhance the rare object within.

Then we relent. At a high price.

There were two copies as promised, three volumes apiece bound in morocco green leather. The bindings were lightly scuffed in different places and on one copy the binding threads were fraying badly in the middle of one of the signatures. The broken leather grain of one cover was scourged with red-rot and the other had "fallen victim" to some advanced photochemical degradation caused by sunlight. The joints in both books were starting to give. I hardly wanted to touch them: the samples were durable enough and yet promised—pleasingly—to fall apart with extreme age at the touch of careless fingers. Inside, even the paper mottling varied between the two copies. I held one of the copies up to my nose and sniffed. Stinx blinked at me as I inhaled two centuries of mildew, gas-lamp pollution, sunlight in a study, and finally the varnished oak of a bookcase upright against which the book had rested this last century or so.

The copy in my hand was miraculous. It was a work of genius: perfectly flawed.

"All right?" said Stinx.

"All right."

"Didn't let you down, did I?"

"Stinx," I said. "Stinx. Let me open a bottle of something very, very special for you."

"I'm sorry, William, I've got to tell you this. I've been drying out. That's where I've been these past few days. Lucy said the only way she'd come back to me is if I give up the drink. And everything else. William, I'm having to resign from the Candlelight Club. Forthwith, sort of thing. Official."

I carefully set down the beautiful forgery. "Heck, Stinx. That's serious news. I mean, we have a right to celebrate. We have a book and we have a buyer."

"I can have a lemonade with you," Stinx said.

"Coming right up. Let's join the others."

No one seemed to want to go anywhere and by eleven o'clock everyone except Stinx but including Lucy was pretty sloshed. But high on the early onset of temperance he was in great humour. He tried to talk me into joining him; then he gave up and instead he outlined his ideas. "Installation art," he pronounced. "That's our next racket. I'll churn it out. Jaz will proclaim in the papers that he's turned his back on poetry and is going into Art."

"Or," I said, warming to our enterprise, "we can do collectible wines. All you'll have to do is forge the labels."

"Or," said Jaz...

I was happy with these ridiculous plans. Everyone was animated, talking, wine-glow and candle-light shimmering in their eyes. Even Robbie was laughing and joking with Anna. I thought that on the morrow he might even come to GoPoint with Anna, Sarah, Mo and myself, to help the staff make a bit of a party for the inmates. Who knew whether he would or he wouldn't? He might, and that was enough. And if he did it would probably be to follow Anna around like a puppy. My son is smitten with my girlfriend. I know a demon approaching the landing strip when I see one.

With everyone talking and rather too full of Christmas cheer I looked at Anna, and I thought: I can be allowed to love this woman, even if she won't take my key. I looked from her to the boisterous scene in my kitchen. Well, it wasn't a family exactly:

but it contained enough trouble to be as good as one.

I managed to peel away from the group and stepped outside into the backyard behind my house. There is an event that takes place every Christmas Eve at midnight and I didn't want to miss it. I don't know why or how it happens, but it does and always on the stroke of midnight. I call it the Ascent of Demons.

I folded my arms, stepped back and craned my neck to get a good view of the skyline. They had already started, dozens of them, quickly turning into hundreds. Yes, hundreds of demons, slowly ascending into the night sky over London. Up they went, perfectly still, like floating statues, each with its own clear space, rising like helium-filled balloons, but much more slowly. The ascending demons had taken on a uniform hue of resplendent, golden-brown. Up they went, leaving the Earth. I have no idea why. I knew they would be back, but right now they were leaving.

Someone burst out of the back door, looking for me.

"Here," shouted Stinx, "what you looking at?"

"London,' I said. "What a place."

He was quickly joined by all the others. They were all craning their necks now, trying to see what had so commanded my attention. But it was pointless trying to tell them. Pointless. You might as well try explaining it to the police. You might as well try telling your mother, or your child. If they can't see it, they can't see it.

The sky was filled with ascending demons now, all rising softly and slowly, many of them become only pinpricks of light, disappearing.

I looked from the sky to Anna, and from her to the rest of them. Unable to see anything in the sky, they had re-fixed their gazes upon me. Anna smiling, Stinx with one eyebrow raised, Sarah and Mo looking puzzled and indulgent, Robbie slightly disgusted, Jaz looking like he wanted to laugh. What an odd group. I loved them all. I fancied that I could see myself in the shining brilliance of their eyes. They reflected back at me, which was appropriate, because the biggest demon I faced was the one I saw in the mirror. Because he was the master of all the others. What should I say? I had lived in the shadow of a wrong I didn't commit and in doing so made a counterfeit of my own life. Faked my own death, in a way.

I knew it didn't matter what happened with Anna. Though I needed her more than ever to help me through, I was prepared for her to love me or leave me, to destroy me on the wheel of sex, to crush my heart to dust: I no longer felt I could control it, or her, or even that I should. We can't live with our foot over the mine. We can't. For the first time since my youth I was unshackled. I had love, even though it scorched me.

You let go. It's as simple and as complicated as Antonia had told me. You cry. You come. You sing. You laugh. You scream. You let go. No one needs to hang on to a first edition. Whoever wrote it; even if it was Moses.

I looked back up at the sky, blinking at the lustrous beauty of the ascending and departing demons. They formed an alphabet I was beginning to learn to read. They were fire in the sky.